Raising Warrior Queens

Teresa C. Smith

iUniverse, Inc.

New York   Bloomington

Raising Warrior Queens

This is a work of fiction. All of the characters, names, incidents, organizations, and dialogue in this novel are either the products of the author's imagination or are used fictitiously.

iUniverse books may be ordered through booksellers or by contacting:

iUniverse
1663 Liberty Drive
Bloomington, IN 47403
www.iuniverse.com
1-800-Authors (1-800-288-4677)

Because of the dynamic nature of the Internet, any Web addresses or links contained in this book may have changed since publication and may no longer be valid. The views expressed in this work are solely those of the author and do not necessarily reflect the views of the publisher, and the publisher hereby disclaims any responsibility for them.

ISBN: 978-0-595-52420-4 (pbk)
ISBN: 978-1-4401-0365-0 (cloth)
ISBN: 978-0-595-62474-4 (ebk)

Printed in the United States of America

iUniverse Rev. 10/23/08

To my two beautiful warrior queens

Mandy, my daughter/sister/friend, my life started when you drew your first breath. I did not exist before you came into the world.

Annalisa, forever my baby, you have taught me how to let go and have shown me that the tiniest person can be a force to be reckoned with.

I dedicate this book to you both and pray that you might understand even a fraction of the depth of my love for you.

To Dr. David Williams

Without your undying faith in my ability and your constant encouragement as a mentor, I would have never put pen to paper or had the courage to
call myself a writer. You have my eternal gratitude and respect as an outstanding teacher, artist and all around renaissance kind of guy.
Thank you.

Mazzy

Mazzy stared at her ringing land line. Everyone she knew called her on her cell with the exception of bill collectors, salespeople, and occasionally her grandmother. Either way, the prospects were grim so she let the answering machine pick up.

"Hi! I'm either A) feeding the homeless or carrying out other charitable deeds, B) at a fabulous party that you obviously weren't invited to, or C) screening my calls to see if I want to talk to you. So leave a message and I'll get back to you when I can." BEEEEP!

"Mazzy? Are you there? Young lady, that is a horrible message! You better not be sitting on that couch listening to me right now and not picking up the phone. Mazzy? This is your Gramma. Are you there? Hello?"

Jesus, she'll blow up the machine if I don't answer. "Hi, Gram! I'm here."

"There you are. You should change that answering machine, missy. How rude! Were you sitting there listening to me?"

"No, Gram. I was in the bathroom." *Lie.*

"And when is the last time you fed the homeless besides making dinner for that no-account boyfriend of yours? Charity indeed."

Deep breath, Mazzy. Breathe. Now change the subject. "When did you get back from your trip, Gram?"

"Yesterday afternoon. I had a lovely visit with your cousin Jack while I was up in Victorville. You know, he got his two front teeth replaced, and they look as good as new. His boss at Jiffy Lube is letting him do oil changes now instead of just clean-up. Isn't that something? The counselor from the developmental center said he was ready to live on his own now, so your Great Aunt Shelly and Uncle Ronnie let him move into their little back house."

"That's great, Gram. How are Great Aunt Shelly and Uncle Ronnie?"

"They're fine. Ronnie doesn't know what to do with himself since he retired. Follows Aunt Shelly all over the place like a lost child. I told him to take up a hobby like painting or model cars, but you know how he is. I caught him looking kind of interested when I was working on a sketch of their dog, Daisy, but he'd never admit it. Men are all the same, I tell you. Aunt Shelly just tries to find errands to send him out on to get him out of her hair. Anyway, I took a whole roll of film while I was there and already had the pictures developed. Sav-On has one-hour processing, and you get your second prints free. You can look at them tonight when you come over for supper." *Oh God. Oh God, no.*

"Tonight? I kinda already have plans, Gram."

"Oh, I see. What kind of plans?"

Root canal, rectal exam, anything but okra and Kodak moments of Victorsmell. Mazzy grabbed her Zippo and lit up a smoke.

"What's that noise? Was that a lighter? Are you still smoking? You should really think about quitting. You know it causes cancer, not to mention yellow teeth. Oh, and the smell! Lord almighty, it's enough to knock a bull over."

Here we go. "Gram, smoking is my only mortal flaw. If I up and quit I'll be a flawless, hence perfect, human being. Since no one is supposed to be perfect, I would literally upset the balance of nature, causing chaos and inevitable anarchy. I don't think either one of us wants that on our hands, do we?"

"Young lady, I did not raise you to sass me."

Uh oh. Mazzy knew when Gramma Lucy used outdated Southern slang that she'd gone too far. "Uh, I'm sorry, Gram. Um, I'm just tired and I don't want to argue."

"I didn't realize that my caring for your well-being was grounds for an argument," she countered in a wounded voice.

Damn, the old woman is good. Very good. "It's not, Gram! I'm sorry." *Come on, Mazzy. You know what you have to do.* "Why don't you come over on Sunday? I'll make dinner and we can play cards. I'll even make pecan pie."

"Well... all right. I'll bring the pictures. And none of those dead fish rolls."

"It's called sushi, Gram."

"I'll see you at four. Bye dear." *Atonement through crazy eights and a taco casserole.*

Mazzy grabbed her pink fuzzy pen and her notepad and started writing a to-do list -- buy anti-tobacco candles and Nicorette gum, dispose of all smoking paraphernalia, and tell Alan to stay far away on Sunday.

Knock, knock. *Speak of the no-account devil.*

"Come in! It's unlocked!"

Alan, in all of his lanky glory, came strolling in dragging a three-foot-tall Christmas tree behind him. Mazzy's little one-bedroom So Cal apartment really didn't have room for it, but Alan had insisted. He had taken all of her knickknacks off of her trunk by the window and now set the spindly little tree on top.

"Did Charlie Brown forget to pick up his tree this year?" Mazzy asked teasingly. She knew he would get a tree like this. If there were a dying plant or a ragged-looking gold fish at the fair that no one would ever choose after winning the ring toss, Alan would pick it. Perhaps it was his being adopted after his teenage mother gave him away that was the source of his perpetual advocacy for all things unloved. Like this tree.

"I'll have you know we just saved this little sapling from becoming mulch. And," he opened his backpack to reveal an array of tiny silver balls and red velvet bows, "when we get her dolled up with her accessories here, she will be stunning." He knelt down and planted a soft kiss on Mazzy's nose.

"Oh, it's a she is it? And how did you come to that conclusion? Maybe it's a he, and now he will have some kind of gender identity crisis because you insinuated he was a female."

She reached into his backpack and pulled out a bow. A tiny red bow. She wasn't a "bow" type of gal as a child. Not exactly a tomboy, but certainly not a bow-sporting girlie girl either. She hated bow-sporting girlie girls. She tossed it back into the bag and opted for a ball instead, hanging it carefully on the very end of a slender branch.

"I know because I asked the sales guy at the tree lot. He is a professional, you know." Alan was arranging the ornaments so that each one was spaced equally apart, taking his time and putting full consideration into the effort for a pleasing visual effect.

Mazzy caught her reflection in one of the silver balls, distorting her face and making the big zit on her chin look like Mount Fuji. "You're a college-educated man; you should know. Isn't it against some law of physics to have wrinkles and acne simultaneously?"

"I don't think so. Although I might have missed that chapter last semester when I was out with the flu." He put the last bow on the tree and pulled out an ornament from his jacket, a silver star with gaudy glitter he placed on the very top. It was probably the last item in a 50%-off bin he figured no one would want to buy. "There, our little girl is beautiful."

"Well it should be." Mazzy sulked off to the kitchen to get a brownie.

"Should be beautiful?" he asked as he plopped down on the brown futon that they had bought for Mazzy at the flea market for $20 from a Hispanic couple that looked like they were trying to pawn everything they owned.

"No. Should be against the law of physics. My wrinkles? This zit?"

"You don't have wrinkles."

"Look! When I smile," she twisted her face up in an exaggerated grin, "crow's feet."

"I don't know about crow's feet, but if you kept your face like that, you'd be a dead ringer for the Joker. Jack Nicholson needed a team of make-up artists to achieve that look."

"Smart ass," she said with a mouth full of brownie.

"Come on, Mazzy, you're gorgeous. Most women would kill for your curls and mocha skin. Girls at school pay lots of money to try and tan to that color and spend hours curling their hair, but still don't come close to you."

"You think Kate Moss is gorgeous, so it's hard to take your opinion as a compliment."

"Ah, Kate," Alan stretched, laid his head back and closed his eyes dreamily. "Hundreds of photographers can't be wrong."

"She reminds me of a hammer-head shark." Mazzy was now powering down milk, straight from the carton.

"You're so critical."

"Seriously. You can't tell if she's looking at you or for you," Mazzy countered as she reached for another brownie.

"She has an exotic look that can only be appreciated by those with exquisite taste. Now toss me a brownie."

"You live on pizza and listen to emo music. I would hardly define your taste as exquisite." She tossed him a brownie which accidentally/purposely hit him in the ear.

"Oops. My bad. Sorry."

"Let's see, my opinion is worthless, and my taste sucks. Want to critique my choice of friends next, Dad?" Alan huffed.

"Jesus, Alan, I'm sorry. Am I being that bad?" Mazzy walked over to the couch and sat down at his feet, resting her head on his corduroyed knee.

"Yeah, you are. Now what gives?" He begrudgingly stroked her thick, curly hair, and she sighed. She loved having her hair stroked.

"I'm late."

"Late for what?"

"My period." His hand stopped in mid-stroke but remained on her head.

"Define late," he said slowly.

"A week. Eight days to be exact." She looked up at him. "I'm never late, Alan."

"Yeah, I know. Wow. Okay. Well, why didn't you tell me sooner?" His hand left her head altogether.

"Does it matter?"

"No, I guess not. Have you taken a test yet? I mean, do you know for sure?"

He gently nudged past her and stood up. Running his hands through his hair, he started to pace slowly around her tiny living area looking, in her mind, like a caged animal in search of an escape route.

"No. I've been too scared. I'm scared, Alan." Her voice hitched and she slumped on the floor, huge tears threatening to brim over her long lashes.

"Oh, hey. It's okay. Don't worry. Everything will be fine." He bent down and gathered her in his arms. "We'll figure this out, babe." She nuzzled his neck as he resumed stroking her hair again.

"My Gramma called," Mazzy sniffled.

"That's enough to make anyone cry. What did old rent-a-smile want anyway?"

"Be nice," she scolded. "She's coming over for dinner Sunday, so you need to be scarce. I don't need the added grief right now."

"All right." He tilted her face up to his. "But don't change the subject. Let's go get a pregnancy test, so we know what we're facing here. We could be stressing for nothing." He stood up and pulled her to her feet. At six-foot-one, he was a good six inches taller than her. She had to crane her neck back to look into his intent green eyes which were demanding her attention.

"We'll get through this, okay? Besides," he said, encircling her waist with his arms, "we said we wanted a puppy, didn't we? This would be like having a hairless Chihuahua in diapers."

"Diapers?" *He wants to keep it! He wants to keep it?* "Whoa there. I didn't …"

Alan cut her off mid sentence. "Yeah, you know. Those white things you stick on their butts? You're too funny. Come on, grab your coat. Let's head down to the pharmacy."

Mazzy didn't budge. She was a tree. She was now a tree that had grown roots through her feet into the floor, and to try and move would be impossible. Alan already had his coat on and his hand on the front door before he noticed that she wasn't right behind him. She stood motionless in the middle of the room. Mazzy, the mighty elm.

"Are you coming? Mazzy?" he asked. Still no sign of life. "Mazzy...?"

Jeez, woman, snap the hell out of it! "I have one. A test, that is. I bought it a few days ago, but..." *Atta girl, just relax until you know for sure, then you can tell him he's nuts if he thinks you are having a...*

"Great! Why didn't you tell me before? Saves us a trip out. You... uh....want to go take it?" He hung his coat up and flopped back down on the couch.

"Yeah. I'll be right back." *As soon as I can move my feet and place one in front of the other until I reach the bathroom.* Alan stared at her with an apprehensive look that asked: You aren't waiting for me to offer you help, are you? *Maybe he just grew roots from his butt into the couch?* The visual made Mazzy smile and got her feet moving.

"I'll be right back."

She didn't need to read the directions. She had them memorized. Instead of watching American Idol or reading People magazine, she had spent the past two evenings reading and re-reading the instructions. When she had felt that pressing urge in her bladder, she would think, should I? Shouldn't I? But in the end she just went back to reading the instructions or checking the expiration date and wondering what there was to expire.

She peed on the test end of the wand for the required 10 seconds, wiped, flushed, washed her hands and reentered the living room. Alan was watching a basketball game on TV when she sat next to him on the couch.

"How long before we know?"

"The instructions said up to five minutes before the test strip changes color."

Or sooner. Gone was the little white window with its blissful ignorance, forever to be replaced by a knowing pink symbol. They both stared at the urine-drenched wand with stupid fascination, like the screaming pink plus sign was a mystical omen sent from an omnipotent being, instead of what it really was -- a home pregnancy test asking the cruel question, *Condoms don't sound so inconvenient right now, do they dumb ass?*

Mazzy picked up the directions and re-read them for the hundredth time, hoping she had skipped over some fine print stating that if you do not wish to be pregnant at this point in your life, click your heels three times and say, "There's nothing like abstinence! There's nothing like abstinence!" But alas, no such luck.

"Doesn't get much pinker than that, does it?" Alan said, his typically baritone voice having taken on a noticeable soprano quality.

He grabbed Mazzy's hand and held it tightly. She couldn't tell if he was trying to comfort her or calm his own trembling fingers. Either way, his knuckles were turning as white as his face while she was losing all sensation in her left hand.

She gently pulled away from him and started pacing around her living room, picking up clean clothes from yesterday's trip to Laun-do-rama, and throwing away diet soda cans over flowing with Capri Menthol cigarette butts. *Even if your life is a mess, your house doesn't have to be.* Gramma Lucy's voice, advocating for a compulsion toward cleaning in the face of adversity, still found a way of whispering unsolicited advice into Mazzy's subconscious. She put on yellow rubber gloves, lit a cigarette and started scrubbing the grout on her kitchen counter.

"Do you really think you should be smoking right now since...?" Alan began.

"Oh, don't even start that shit with me, pal! Do I really think? You know what I really think? I think..." her voice broke as she started to sob.

Alan put his arm around her shoulder and said, "Shhhh. Honey, it will be okay."

She was furiously scrubbing with one hand while sucking the life out of her Capri with the other. *God, why do I want to impale him with an ice pick right now? How can he be so damn calm? This must be some kind of demented hormonal surge.*

"Mazzy, do you want me to..."

She couldn't take the calm in his voice. The sweet loving calm voice that sounded nervous yet a little excited at the same time. She flung his arm off her shoulder and started shouting.

"I WANT YOU TO BE AN ASSHOLE, SO I CAN HATE YOU! I really need you to be a big asshole so I can blame...it...on...you..."

With Ajax all over her GAP T-shirt and mascara trickling down to mix with the snot dripping out of her nose, she stood bawling in the kitchen.

Alan stared at her. "You know, you're dead sexy for a chick with snot dripping down her face."

Mazzy started laughing, which made matters worse because when she laughed she snorted, making the nasal mucus problem even more prominent. Alan handed her a Kleenex. As she cleaned herself up, he found an extra scrub brush and silently set to work on her grout. He stayed there with her, scrubbing side-by-side until her kitchen was spotless.

Mazzy stared at the ceiling, amazed at Alan's ability to find REM sleep in a span of thirty seconds. She closed her eyes and tried deep breathing for several minutes while focusing on a tranquil stream. The stream was nestled in rolling green hills with purple wild flowers at the water's edge. She breathed deeply and looked up at the puffy white clouds lazily floating through the bright blue sky. Mazzy was analyzing an intricate cloud that was shaped like the Eiffel Tower when a voice behind her startled her.

"I like Magenta better than Blue. She's pretty. Who do you like, Mommy?"

The baby was sitting in the red Thinking Chair with her Handy Dandy Notebook. She looked less than a year old and was wearing a diaper and pink booties. She had chipmunk cheeks and a small tuft of soft brown hair on the top of her head. Her eyes were hazel and framed by long eyelashes. There was something obscene about watching her, with her small mouth and two bottom teeth barely poking through, talking so clearly.

"I... I don't know. I've only seen it a few times."

"Oh. It's my favorite. I liked Steve. I think he is gay." She took out a Kool and lit it.

"Let's play Blue's Clues, Mommy. I'll show you three clues out of my Handy Dandy Notebook, and you guess what I'm trying to say." She sucked on her cigarette like it was a pacifier.

"Here is clue number one." She showed Mazzy a picture of a syringe. It was drawn in black Crayola on a yellow page. "Can you guess what's going to happen?"

"I don't know." Mazzy's voice was trembling.

"Well then, let's look at clue number two. It comes after clue number one."

She flipped the page to show a picture of an arm. A hot ash fell from the tip of her Kool and landed on the soft flesh of her leg. She sucked in her breath for what seemed like a full minute, as only a baby can do, and let out a blood-curdling cry. Her face turned red as her bottom lip started to quiver.

"Fuck! That hurts, Mommy!"

Mazzy reached out to hold her, but she jerked away from her.

"No, Mommy, look at clue number three!"

She flipped over the page to show the last picture, but this one wasn't in crayon. It looked like a graphic color picture from a medical journal. It showed a tiny fetus on a metal table. You could see it was missing an arm, and its tiny spine was mangled.

"DID YOU SOLVE BLUE'S CLUES, MOMMY?! THIS IS ME! THIS IS ME!" She tumbled out of her big red Thinking Chair and crawled into Mazzy's lap. She bunched up her angry little fists and started beating them against Mazzy's chest.

Mazzy started to scream. "Oh, God, I'm sorry! I'm sorry! I'm so sorry..."

"Jesus, Mazzy, wake up, honey. Wake up, baby."

She opened her eyes to see Alan above her, brows twisted up in knots of concern. He was stroking her hair, drenched in sweat and tangled from thrashing in her sleep. "It's OK baby, I'm right here."

Mazzy's Hawaiian print comforter was kicked off the end of the bed. She wanted to reach down and pull it up over her head but was afraid to move, afraid to look down. She was convinced if she did the baby would be there. She would see that soft angry face and immediately have a heart attack. She could still feel her heart pounding in her chest.

"It was terrible." Her voice came out strangled and panicked.

"Sweetheart, what were you dreaming? You were putting your hands in front of your face and kept saying you were sorry and crying."

Mazzy looked at him and was struck with the thought of how vulnerable she was during sleep. To take your most inner fears, childhood traumas, and human dysfunction and twist them into some Quentin Tarantino-directed dream for your own torture was bad enough, but to act them out involuntarily in front of another person, naked and unedited... that was too much. Too much raw exposure, too little control.

Mazzy sat up silently and reached for her smokes on the dresser but instead knocked over a glass of water in the dark. She didn't even bother an attempt to clean up the spill, but instead headed to the kitchen while telling her self that it was just a dream and there was no baby crawling behind her with a Kool dangling out of its mouth.

She flicked on the dim light over the stove and searched for her cigarettes in the junk drawers, shoving aside pizza coupons and old paycheck stubs. She could have sworn she had a spare pack of Capris in there somewhere. Maybe her purse?

She rummaged through her Louis Vittan-knock off in vain and was about to have a nicotine hissy fit when Alan walked in behind her in his baggy red boxer shorts and handed her a pack he had found next to the bed. She knew he hated the fact she smoked.

"Thanks." She lit one off the gas stove, savoring the minty burn in her chest. She could literally feel the nicotine pour into her. She knew it was a horrible habit, an addiction, but she loved it and didn't want to stop. It was always there for her, it was comforting and relaxing. And besides, it wasn't illegal. If it did kill you, it did it slowly when you were older and your kids were already grown. You couldn't overdose on it like an asshole and leave your kid abandoned to be raised by her grandmother.

She hopped up on the counter and dangled her feet, watching her toes wriggle. Mazzy had always taken a childish delight in the rebellious act of sitting on counters, floors or desk tops...any place that her butt was not supposed to be.

"You gonna tell me?" Alan tentatively asked.

"Tell you what?"

"What the hell you were dreaming. I've never seen you that upset and scared when you were awake or asleep."

"I don't know. I don't remember exactly." She took another drag off her Capri as she contemplated how to mix enough truth with the lie to placate him. "Just a feeling of remorse. Like one of those dreams that wasn't really about me but I was in it. I don't know. It's fuzzy now, slipping from me."

"But this just happened two minutes ago! How can you forget that quickly?"

"What the hell is this? The Spanish Inquisition? Get out of my butt already!" She angrily flicked her cigarette in the sink.

"I'm sorry. I was just concerned. I'll leave you alone." Wounded, Alan turned around and went back to bed.

She wished he would just go home so she could be alone. She didn't want to share this. She wanted to crack open a beer and blast her old Pearl Jam CD while she sang along with Eddie Vedder. She was barely dealing with her own feelings and couldn't handle dealing with his. A part of her wanted to go after him and apologize and give him strokes for being the kindhearted boyfriend that he was, but the much larger part of her just wanted him to be sleeping at his own place, so she could just BE and not feel like a mean bitch.

She grabbed her smokes, lighter, candle, CD head phones, Corona, Mazzy Star from the used CD store and an ashtray, and then headed for the bathroom.

Alan heard the click of the door lock and knew she would be in there sitting on the blue tile floor chain smoking and listening to the same CD over and over again, only to emerge hours later exhausted and silent, completely spent from her own personal exorcism. An altogether different form of purging at the foot of the porcelain alter. He didn't understand it. He ached for her to talk to him instead, but he knew better.

Out of love and respect, Alan turned off the kitchen light, left Mazzy sobbing quietly in the bathroom and climbed back into bed.

Gramma Lucy didn't care for photo albums. She kept the vast majority of her pictures loose in several boxes: dark stained wood boxes with bronzed leafing, lavender cardboard boxes with daisy print, felt-covered boxes with purple-jeweled knobs. She had a dozen of them throughout her two-bedroom house and Mazzy loved to look through them when she was a child. On rainy days, she would pretend they were buried treasure chests and she, captain Mazzy of the pirate ship Sparkle (otherwise known as her bed), would haul them up one at a time and spend hours appraising the riches within.

She had every picture cataloged to memory and could even tell which box to find it in. The picture of Cousin Jack's sixth birthday party -- red satin-covered hat box in the living room next to the fireplace. Gramma Lucy's high-school graduation picture -- plain oak box next to her dresser. Her favorite box, painted gold with pink stars traced on the lid, contained pictures of Mazzy with her mother Kennedy.

Mazzy had no memory of her mother but through hours of treasure gazing knew every contour of her face. Her full lips, dark caramel skin, high cheekbones, slightly broad nose with tiny nostrils and intense hazel eyes that bore into you from beneath abnormally long black lashes haunted Mazzy even in her day dreams.

On a particularly hot day during the summer before seventh grade, when Mazzy was home alone and Gramma Lucy was at work, a severe case of boredom found Mazzy in Lucy's huge mirrored closet trying on her heels and long white spaghetti-strap slip. She looked in the full length mirror critically, assessing her potential. Her skin was a lighter shade than her mother's and, while she was blessed with her long lashes, she had not inherited her light hazel eyes, but instead had plain brown eyes, something she planned to correct later in life with colored lenses. Her hair was a wild tangle of frizzy curls she had yet to tame and was a focal point of ridicule with her whiter peers at junior high. She longed to be beautiful. Not the exotic beauty Gramma Lucy claimed her to be, but the kind of beauty that the boys at school would stare at shamelessly, like Amber Brown with her huge boobs and straight blonde hair that she would play with incessantly. Mazzy closed her eyes and imagined herself a supermodel. Long legs, flowing hair and natural grace. As she practiced sauntering down an imaginary catwalk in Paris, her heel caught in the slip and sent her flying forward into a face plant on the floor by the foot of the bed. Her head exploded in pain and she saw stars.

As the throbbing subsided, she noticed a box she had never seen before under the bed. Feeling less like a supermodel and more like a marauding pirate, she reached in and pulled it out. She couldn't remember the last time there was a new box to discover! She trembled with excitement as she kicked off her heels and trotted back to her own bed with the booty in hand.

It was an old box, wide and shallow, with mismatched brush strokes of oil paint all over it – a splash of alizarin crimson here, a glob of cobalt blue there -- as if the owner had used it not only to hold his oil colors, but also as a pallet. She lifted the lid and found an array of aging photos and papers.

The first photo was of a teenage girl with long brown hair wearing a black turtleneck and matching barrette with a cigarette dangling out of her pouty lips. On the back was written, "Lucy, all my love, Shel." The next picture was a black-and-white group shot of people cheering. Mazzy spotted a handsome black man with one arm up in the air flipping the peace sign and the other arm around the shoulders of what looked like a very young and beautiful Gramma Lucy, who was laughing and clapping.

Mazzy took a closer look. Was it really her? Her nose was straighter and the huge scar on her right eye wasn't there, but yes, it was her. Mazzy had asked before where the scar had come from, but Gramma had only replied, "war wound", and left it at that.

Next in the box was a piece of lemon-colored paper with a poem written in simple black type:

> Yellow wings, gilded cage
> Admired bird when contained
> Send me down through the hole
> All around me darkened coal
> They wait above to hear me sing
> For then they'll know that they can breathe
> I want to soar, just to be free
> Motherfuckers won't let me be
> For blue above and leaves below
> I swear to God I'd sell my soul
> But here I am locked in my cage
> Another song, another wage

Mazzy was used to Gramma Lucy's artistic side, but this was far outside her usual repertoire of haiku and watercolor abstracts. She had barely digested the last anger-packed verse when the phone rang, startling her into a shocked yelp. Her heart was thumping in her throat as she ran to answer.

"Mazzy? Are you all right? You sound strange," Gramma Lucy said.

"You always think I'm strange, Gram. I'm fine. What's up?" Mazzy was proud at how off-handed and casual she sounded when she thought she might have actually wet herself.

"I'm at the market. Do we need anything?"

"Um, I don't know. Pop maybe?"

"I am not buying you more pop so you can rot your teeth out. Drink some water for a change. Anything else? Oh, check how much dish soap we have left." Mazzy could hear a car honking its horn in the background at the Alpha Beta parking lot two blocks from the house. She would be home in ten minutes, fifteen max.

"A half an inch in the bottle."

"Okay. I'll pick some up. Be home soon… you sure you're all right?"

"Yep. I'm sure."

"Hmm. See you soon."

Mazzy walked back to her room and gathered the poem and pictures off of her bed. She took one last glance at the contents of the box, and a picture caught her eye. She knew she was pressed for time but picked it up. She was in her mother's arms, a tiny baby wrapped in a yellow knitted blanket. Her mother was sitting on a man's lap in a wheelchair. Why was this picture in here instead of the other box with the pink stars?

She examined the picture of the man more closely. He had dark brown hair that barely brushed his shoulders. His brow was prominent, framing deep brown eyes, and his nose had exaggerated nostrils like that bad kid in The Breakfast Club.

Mazzy was shaking. Could this be her father? Gramma had said she had never met the boyfriend that knocked up her mother and then abandoned them. Is that why she was hiding this picture? She couldn't bring herself to put it back in the box. Instead, she shoved it into her diary, replaced the other items, and then ran back to her Gramma's room.

As she pushed the box back under the bed, she heard a car door slam. How could Gramma Lucy have gotten home so quickly?!

Mazzy raced out of the room, slamming the door behind her. The front door opened.

"Mazzy?" Gramma Lucy called from the front hall. "Why don't you come with me, and we'll go to the discount market?"

Mazzy waltzed in from the hall way flushed and looking guilty as hell.

"Hi, Gram. How was the market?"

"Young lady, what the hell do you think you are doing in my good slip?" Oops. Mazzy had forgotten all about it in her haste to get rid of the box.

"Um, I was just, uh, trying it on."

"Since when are you allowed to go pilfering through my things? Put that back right now, and if I ever catch you going through my things again, I'm going to tan your hide. Got it?"

"Yes, ma'am." She scurried back to her room to change into her own clothes.

A week later, when she went in search of the box during Gramma Lucy's weekly gin game at Lydia's, it was gone. She never found it again.

Mazzy could still feel the ghost of Alan's whispery goodbye kisses on her forehead when her swollen eyes finally opened around ten. He had slipped out an hour earlier to go to work and had left her to sleep. She found a note next to her pillow.

Maz, I get off work around 5. Let's go to dinner and talk after. Love - A

She would have just enough time to meet with him before heading to work at six. Morning sickness was just starting to creep in, and she dreaded the thought of handling raw fish tonight at Wasabi Tsunami's, even though the upbeat atmosphere would probably do her good. She loved being the first Mulatto female sushi chef in the South Bay area.

She went to the bathroom and checked out the damage in the mirror, hating the aftermath of a good cry session. No time for cold tea bags if she was going to make her eleven o'clock yoga class at the rec center. She brushed her teeth, pulled her hair back in a tight bun and jumped into her workout clothes. One power bar and a bottled water and she was out the door, opting to walk the half-mile to class to help wake her up, clear her foggy mind.

She loved to walk. It was her favorite form of exercise. She loved losing herself in a disassociative state behind the anonymity of dark sunglasses while mindlessly covering miles of pavement.

Which would explain why yoga was so difficult for her. It took a disciplined, focused mind, and Mazzy was finding her short attention span and the physical need to just pound pavement were hindering her progress.

Her friend Abby had suggested they sign up for the class a month ago, and it just sounded so cool. She envisioned herself being that serene self-actualized woman who drinks soy milk and could stay in Lion's Pose without busting her ass laughing. She even went out and bought a book on Ayerveda at her instructor's suggestion and was planning on reading it, soon.

"Hey, Maz! Over here!" She spotted Abby on the corner in front of Starbucks sporting her tattered blue hoodie and black yoga pants. She joined her friend and stole a drink of her mocha.

"Jeez, Abb, when are you going to shoot that thing and put it out of its misery?" Mazzy teased, pulling on the bottom of Abby's beloved sweatshirt.

"As soon as you start wearing underwear. Hey, what the hell happened to your eyes? Alan finally get sick of your mouth and smack you around last night or what?"

"No. Steel Magnolias was on TBS again and I'm PMS-ing, so I had a good cry fest." Mazzy downed the rest of the mocha, almost gagging on the chocolate syrup coagulating at the bottom of the cup.

"Hmm. Yeah, okay. Let's get in there and grab a spot in the back." Abby replied, knowing full well that Mazzy was full of shit.

After signing in at the front desk they followed the gray carpeted hallway past the weight room to the aerobics room and unrolled their purple mats on the hardwood floor. The two positioned themselves behind Todd the aging hippie and a very pregnant woman they had never seen before. Todd had introduced himself to them, and to everyone else in the class upon his arrival two weeks ago, and had given them his entire unsolicited bio including his newly divorced status. Mazzy and Abby had an hour-long discussion afterward about his comb-over/pony tail combo and why aging men did this to themselves.

As the class started off with the standard Mountain Pose, Mazzy tried to empty her head and focus on her breathing. *I am a mountain. I am a mountain. Eight months from now, I will be a very pregnant mountain like that woman up there. About to pop. Yes, I will be a very pregnant mountain. I'm pregnant. Fuck, I am pregnant. What the hell…no, no. Clear my head.* (Deep breathe) *I am a mountain. I am…*

"All right class let's move onto the next pose." *Damn it.*

Thirty minutes and a pulled groin muscle later, she couldn't take it anymore. She tried to discretely roll up her mat and head to the door quietly while the class had their eyes closed, sitting Indian style.

"Where are you going?" hissed Abby loudly enough to attract a few students' attention away from their ohms. Mazzy didn't look back and kept moving straight towards the door.

Ah, freedom! She went to Starbucks and ordered a triple-shot soy grande mocha then headed out to the patio area to light up a smoke. As she tried to get comfortable on her black iron chair, she looked up and saw Abby stomping toward her in a huff.

"There you are! You bailed on me and left me to fend for myself with comb-over boy and the ticking time bomb ready to break her water in front of us."

"Fuck inner peace. Let's chain smoke and scarf coffee beans till we start tweaking."

"I knew it. Steel Magnolias my ass. What gives?" Abby sat down at the table and chugged on her water bottle.

"I'm pregnant," Mazzy stated bluntly. Abby choked on her drink until her eyes were watering.

"Shut the hell up," she croaked after she regained her composure. "Are you sure?"

"Sure as a heart attack. Did the pee test last night."

"Maybe it was a false positive," Abby said hopefully.

"Nope. I'm very late and very sure. Besides, I think you can only get false negatives, not false positives. Or is it two negatives make a positive?"

"How can you joke? I would be freaking out right now." Abby shook her head in amazement.

"Oh, I'm freaking out. Make no mistake. I think I'm still in shock." She took out another cigarette and sparked it up. Abby looked at it and raised an eyebrow.

"Don't do it," Mazzy warned slowly.

"I'm not! I'm not. Wow. What did Alan say? Does he know?"

"Yeah, he was there when I took the test." Mazzy noticed the other tree huggers emerging from the rec center, with Todd leading the pack in the after-class pilgrimage to worship the caffeine gods. "Shit, here comes the single hippie. Let's roll."

They took off walking together in the opposite direction.

"So what did he say?" Abby asked.

"At first he was stunned. Then he said something about diapers. I think he wants it, Abby. Compared it to having a hairless Chihuahua." They made a right turn and started to circle back around towards Mazzy's apartment.

"Well, that makes the whole thing sound appealing doesn't it? Compare it to a yippy territorial rat with a Napoleon complex that most people want to drop kick. What did you say?" Abby was only five feet-tall and was having a hard time keeping up with Mazzy's long legs and fast pace.

"I didn't really say anything. Kinda freaked out and started crying, but didn't say much." Mazzy was starting to pick up the pace, forcing Abby to jog. "I don't want a hairless Chihuahua! I mean, think about it. I know enough about myself to realize I'm too self-involved to have a baby. Remember that summer trip to the river? I was actually pissed at the thought of having to look for someone to water my plants. I couldn't find anyone and knew they would die. I didn't want to have to deal with their dead carcasses when I got home so I gave them away to that weird lady next door."

"The Christian sniper?" Abby was puffing now.

"Yeah, her. I would rather give them away than try and be bothered with them, and Alan wants me to have a baby?!" Mazzy was power walking at this point.

"God damn it, will you slow down?" Abby stopped in her tracks with a stitch in her side.

"Oh, sorry. I'm just worked up."

"I know you are. I would be too. Listen, don't you think the plant comparison is just a little extreme? It's not like you would even be taking a trip to the river if you had a kid," Abby teased.

"Exactly!"

"Oh, I was just kidding, Maz." They resumed walking at a leisurely pace.

"No, no. That's exactly it! I would have no life, no freedom. I can't even handle a plant tying me down. I sure as hell don't want a baby tying me down. And I am just not one of those cooing oh-look-at-the-cute-babykins type. I don't even really like kids, to tell you the truth. I mean, I don't want to run one over with my car, but I don't want one up my butt 24/7 either. I went to Donna's little girl's birthday party at Chuck E Cheese and had to listen to those screaming yard apes for an hour. If they didn't serve beer there, I would have blown my fucking head off."

"Okay, so we have it well established you aren't the maternal type. Sounds like you've already made up your mind."

"Pretty much, yes. I just don't know how to tell Alan." They arrived at Mazzy's white stucco apartment and sat on the front steps. "I better figure it out quick, though. He wants to meet after work and talk about it. Any ideas?"

"Singing telegram? Oh, wait, I know! Send him fresh-baked bread you made yourself with a note that says, 'This is the only bun you're getting out of my oven, pal. Love, Maz'." Abby started laughing heartily.

"You really amuse the hell out of yourself, don't you?" Mazzy poked her in her ribs.

"Ouch. Yeah, I do." Abby wiped a tear from her eye and continued. "But seriously Maz, just be straight with him, minus the crass references to screaming yard apes and eating the end of a shotgun."

Mazzy took a shower and spent the rest of the afternoon cleaning her apartment and reorganizing her walk-in closet while she rehearsed what she would say to Alan.

After she had her speech down to a non-negotiable presentation that even he would be able to see the logic in, she decided to write down several iron-clad reasons why they could not have a baby. She figured a written list might help him since he was a male and all men were supposed to be more visually oriented than women.

1. We are too young. Why help perpetuate the 'Babies Raising Babies' phenomenon?

2. I am not the maternal type, and I will never buy a mini-van.

3. We can't afford it, and I refuse to be a part of the welfare system.

4. I have no medical insurance (see #3).

5. I am not getting fat and scarring myself with stretch marks.

6. The world is already grossly overpopulated.

7. How well do we *really* know each other? We've been together less than a year.

8. I don't envision ever referring to you as "my baby daddy."

Alan called Mazzy after work and they agreed to meet at Shooter's. When Mazzy arrived with her list folded in her purse, Alan was already in a booth ordering a batch of hot wings and looking positively giddy.

The neon beer signs and loud happy-hour patrons over stimulated Mazzy and made her anxious the minute she walked in the door. She took a deep breath and marched to him, ready to stand her ground. When he saw her, he jumped up to hug her. A look of mild confusion crossed his face when she didn't respond and instead stood stiffly clutching her handbag with a death grip.

"Hello, beautiful." He stroked her hair and kissed her forehead. Mazzy looked into his eyes -- his deep, tender, excited eyes -- and wanted to cry. He would be the doting soccer dad who would get up for 3 a.m. diaper changes and then bring her coffee in bed. He would be the office dork who taped shaky stick-figure drawings from day care up in his cubicle and would proudly drink from his coffee mug that had #1 DAD written all over it. She knew she was not worthy of this pure unadulterated love, and that, even though she loved him so much it was physically painful, she would crush him.

"Hey, it's okay. Sit down. Do you feel all right?"

She lowered herself into the booth and he cozied up next to her, taking her hands in his. She'd always loved his hands. They were masculine, but not overpowering. She hated big meaty paws with hairy knuckles and loathed long skinny fingers on a man. His were the perfect size.

"I feel fine," she said forcing a smile. "How was work?"

"Same old, same old. I started looking into my insurance, though, and I think there is a chance I can get you and the baby on there!"

Shit, scratch number four from the list. "Alan..." Mazzy tried to interrupt.

"I mean, I know it's an HMO and all, but it's better than nothing."

"Alan, I..." Mazzy tried more forcefully, taking her hands out of his.

"Suzy said the OB/GYN she found through them was great and..." He was on a roll.

"Suzy?! You told your supervisor?" Mazzy shouted, drawing a few inquisitive looks from other patrons.

"Yes," Alan admitted sheepishly. "She won't tell anyone else until I do Maz, I promise."

"Alan, you shouldn't have done that." Mazzy moaned and put her head in her hands.

"What's wrong?" Alan asked, truly befuddled by her reaction.

"We need to talk."

"I know. There are so many plans to make."

"No! No, there aren't. There is only one plan to make." She lifted her head and turned her teary eyes to him. "I am not having this baby, Alan."

"You can't mean that." He looked thunderstruck. "You... you can't mean that."

Her mind went blank. She struggled to remember her speech, her well-rehearsed and thought-out speech that would show him that she was right, but she came up with nothing.

Panicking, she reached into her purse, pulled out the list and thrust it at him. He looked at her like she was crazy and slowly scanned the list.

"Tell me you're not serious. Is this a joke?" he asked incredulously, anger starting to seep into his voice.

"No. I'm not joking."

He scanned the list again. "You don't want to call me your 'baby daddy?' What the fuck are you talking about Mazzy? Is that some kind of race comment? Do you think I care my baby will be part black?"

"What? No! That's not what I mean." She was confused. The list seemed like such a good idea at the time.

"Then what exactly do you mean?" he demanded.

"I don't want a baby, Alan. I don't want children, ever."

"Are you saying you want an abortion?" His voice was growing louder. "And you made this decision before even talking it over with me?"

"Shh! Keep your voice down!" Mazzy could feel nosy ears perking up around them. "And where do you get off? You were picking out my fucking insurance and doctor without discussing it with me!"

"This is my baby, too! You can't compare making the decision to take its life with looking into medical coverage, God damn it!" he hissed through clenched teeth.

The waitress approached them apprehensively with their order of hot wings. "Uh, are you ready for your food now?" she asked in an embarrassed tone.

"Yes. Thank you," Alan responded in a tight voice.

The waitress set the plate down and hurried back to the kitchen. Mazzy's stomach was in knots. This was not how she had wanted this to go.

"Let's slow it down and actually talk about this, Mazzy. What are you afraid of?"

"Why does it have to be fear-based? What if I just don't want children?" She stuck her chin out defiantly.

"How can you not want children?" Alan asked in disbelief.

"Where is this unwritten law that states if you own a vagina you HAVE to want a baby? Am I less of a woman because I don't feel the need to reproduce in order to make my life complete?"

"Is it that you don't want children, or you just don't want children with me?" he asked in a wounded tone.

"That's not it. If I wanted children, I couldn't think of a better father than you," she said honestly.

Alan was relieved until the reality of the statement hit home. "So you really just don't want kids then. Ever?"

"No, I don't. Never have." Mazzy hated people's reaction to that revelation. Most were more open-minded and receptive to hearing that you were a member of a satanic cult than hearing that you had no desire to have children.

"I had no idea you felt that way."

"Obviously." They both sat quietly trying to digest the conversation while letting the chicken wings go cold.

Alan eventually cleared his throat and took on a matter-of-fact expression before addressing her again. "This is my baby too, Mazzy, and I DO want children. I'll raise it."

"I'm not going through with it, Alan."

"Have the baby. I'll take it. Maybe you'll change your mind. If not, I will raise it myself, but please, *please* don't do this. Don't kill my baby," he pleaded, making her feel like a cold-hearted murderer.

"Don't ask me to do this, Alan," she sobbed.

"It's only nine months," he coaxed.

"That's easy for you to say! You won't be the one pregnant with stretch marks, going through the pain of delivery!"

"God damn it, Mazzy, could you stop thinking about yourself for one fucking minute?! Do you even hear how selfish you sound? You would rather commit murder than go through a few months of discomfort?!"

"A few months of... you fucking bastard!" she cried as she bolted from the booth, nearly knocking their table over and sending the chicken wings flying. She fled the bar in tears while Alan was left, mouth agape, splattered in buffalo sauce.

Mazzy sat on the beach taking deep breaths and letting the wind caress her skin, cleanse her mind and calm her shaky nerves. She tried to empty her mind. No need to think about it now. *Plenty of time after work to chain-smoke and recount how badly that had gone.*

She dusted the sand off her behind and made her way towards the stone steps leading to the pier. The sunbathers and mothers looking for free entertainment for their children had dispersed for the day, and all that remained were couples indulging in pre-dinner strolls and dog owners taking their pets out for a crap on the beach after being locked out on their million-dollar town home balconies all day.

She climbed the stairs slowly, taking in the last clean breeze from the ocean before walking down the pier, weaving her way through souvenir shops, the open fish market and hot dog stands. The combined smell of suntan lotion, raw fish and corn dogs was doing a number on her stomach. She reached in her purse and pulled out a saltine cracker she had stashed for emergency purposes.

She heard Wasabi Tsunami's before she saw it. Bob Marley greeted her ears as she rounded the last trinket shop and came to the end of the pier where the restaurant was located. The building looked like a huge Hawaiian hut and had a green neon sign that pulsated to the music drifting out of the windows. Initially deemed an eyesore and an insult to Japanese tradition by old school critics, Wasabi Tsunami's was embraced by the local college crowd and bored thirty-something's thirsting for anything new and cool. Begrudgingly written food reviews attesting to the talent of the chefs and freshness of the menu, mixed with raves by word of mouth, cemented the loyal following of patrons.

"And here comes my favorite sushi diva!" exclaimed Mazzy's flamboyantly gay boss Rex. He was holding court on the front patio with his adoring minions, fake martini in hand.

Rex had been sober and in recovery for five years, but instead of boasting his achievement, he chose to walk around with a martini glass containing nothing more than water with a splash of lemon. He refused to be one of those cliché twelve steppers who pounded coffee and preached abstinence, preferring instead to give the illusion of a sexy-martini-drinking-cosmopolitan homosexual. When Mazzy had asked him why, he had replied, "Darling, martini glasses are just so sexy! Who in the world would get turned on by a coffee mug with brown stains on the rim?"

"Hey, boss. Did Queer Eye for the Straight Guy come by and do an impromptu group make over?" Mazzy said teasingly while gesturing to the huddle of metro-sexuals seated at his table. Their young female dates laughed heartily, but the men didn't quite take to her humor.

"Oh, don't mind her boys. She's a naughty bitch but the best sushi chef in the South Bay.

"Darling, what in the world is wrong with your eyes? You look like hell. Did that adorable boyfriend of yours keep you up all night?" Rex gave her a knowing wink then turned to his patrons. "You should see him. Looks like a younger version of Ty Pennington."

"Something like that. Let me get cleaned up and get to work." Mazzy scurried into the restaurant before Rex could inquire any further.

The interior décor was truly something to behold. Strings of Christmas lights adorned the walls as did reggae posters, anime drawings and voodoo dolls straight from New Orleans. It looked like a Cajun pot-smoking elf from Japan had gone berserk.

She made a beeline for the bathroom and splashed cold water on her face. After downing another saltine, she doused her eyes with Visine, touched up her makeup and psyched herself up for show time. It wasn't enough to be a great chef here. She also had to be charming and entertaining. *I can do this. Five hours of schmoozing and nausea won't kill me.*

When she finally left to go home, Mazzy was proud of herself. Two hundred dollars in tips and she had to excuse her self only once to go hurl in the bathroom. (It was watching a grandmother celebrating her eightieth birthday slurp a quail egg through her dentures that put her over the edge.)

She passed on Rex's offer to go out for drinks with the rest of the staff and drove directly home, fell into bed and slept for ten hours. She dreamt all of her teeth fell out and Rex fashioned them into a bracelet for Ariel, The Little Mermaid.

The next morning she awoke feeling oddly rested and able to wrap her head around the thought of eating a normal meal. She scrambled an egg with parsley and ate it with a sourdough muffin and a cup of tea while surfing the Internet on her second-hand laptop.

She Googled "morning sickness remedies" but came up with nothing better than her saltine fix. *Might as well sift through the junk email while I'm at it.* Thirty-seven emails, ranging from mortgage ads to stupid forwarded jokes from Abby about why women are superior to men, were waiting for her. FXZY9783 wanted to tell her how she could shed that unwanted extra ten pounds. *Delete.* Ralphie0078 wanted to know if she remembered him from last weekend. *Delete.*

Kelly12 again? She knew she had seen that address before. *There has to be a way I can block these people.* At the same precise moment she hit the delete button, the subject line registered in her stunned mind – I KNEW

YOUR MOTHER, KENNEDY. She froze. *Oh shit. Oh shit oh shiiiiit!* Mazzy grabbed her cell and speed dialed Abby.

"Hello?"

"How can you retrieve deleted mail? Tell me it's possible, Abby!"

"You know, proper etiquette requires you to say 'hello' before you jump down my throat with a question."

"Abby! Please!" Mazzy pleaded.

"God, okay. Easy Beavis. There's an icon at the bottom of your mail page that says 'Recently Deleted Mail.' Click on that to recall it. What the hell did you delete, anyway?"

"I'm not sure. I'll call you back." She disconnected before Abby could reply.

Mazzy found the icon. Willing to take the risk of a virus that could possibly eat all of her iPod downloads, she opened the email.

Dear Mazzy – First of all, let me say that if this is not the Mazzy Dawson I think it is, my apologies for bothering you. But the odds are, if you are indeed reading this instead of sending it to deletion heaven, I caught your attention with the subject heading and you must be the Mazzy I am looking for. As I said, I knew your mother, Kennedy. I also knew you when you were a baby until your grandmother Lucy moved you away. I have wondered all these years how you were doing… what you were like… if you were happy. I would also like to tell you about your mother, at least what I knew of her. I think she would want that. I know this is bizarre and you are wondering who the hell I am. If you would like to talk, we can communicate by email. If you don't, I will understand. Kelly Judd

Before she could pull her jaw up off of the floor, Mazzy's cell phone rang. She answered it dazedly.

"Yeah?"

"Young lady, that is no way to answer the phone," Lucy scolded. "What has gotten into you lately?"

"Gram, who is Kelly Judd?" she asked flatly.

Silence. No hemming or hawing, just total silence.

"Who is she?" Mazzy demanded.

"Who is she? I don't know. I can honestly say I don't know any woman named Kelly Judd," Lucy responded with an odd undertone of relief in her voice. "Why do you ask?"

"Are you sure?"

"Are you insinuating that I am lying?" Mazzy knew Gramma Lucy abhorred liars. And yet something wasn't right.

"No, Gram. Look, my cell phone is about to die. I'll have to call you later."

"Wait one minute. I wanted to ask you what kind of side dish you want me to bring this afternoon."

"Oh, yeah, about that. I was asked to put in an extra shift at work, and they really need me. We'll have to do it another time, Gram. Shoot! My battery is going."

Mazzy pressed "End" and shut her phone off. She was going to get to the bottom of this and wasn't going to let Gramma Lucy barrage her with a bunch of questions until she did.

Dear Kelly (if that is your real name) – If you are some twisted piece of work looking to get their kicks by screwing with my head, I swear I will hunt you down and destroy you for the evil bitch that you are. With that said, I want some info about you before I give any about me. Who are you, and how did you know my mother exactly? How did you find me, and why do you care how I am? Mazzy

A bit brutal, a tad defensive and paranoid perhaps, but direct. She pressed send before she could change her mind. Then she waited. And waited. And then waited a bit more, staring at the screen until her eyes started to cross. *I'm being stupid. She needs time to write back.*

Mazzy took a long shower and shaved her legs. No reply. She made her bed, did the dishes and vacuumed. Still no reply. She wrote Christmas cards and licked stamps and envelopes till her tongue was thick with glue. And yet still, no reply.

God, I am being ridiculous! What if she only checks her email once a day? I've got to get out of here or else I will go insane.

She hopped into her car and drove aimlessly, not knowing what to do with herself. Strip malls turned to freeway then to houses as she wondered who Kelly was. Was she one of her mom's drug buddies? Was she an old college or high-school friend? How could she know Gramma Lucy if Gram said she didn't know her?

Mazzy found herself in San Pedro at the Friendship Bell on top of the cliffs. The wind up there was strong, and even though southern California remained fairly warm by national standards all year long, there was still a chill in the air, so she pulled a sweater out of her trunk. She sat on the grass and watched the late morning fog burn off as awkward tourists took pictures of one another in front of the bell. The seventeen-ton, twelve-foot-tall-bell was housed in an ornate pagoda-like stone structure that had taken ten months to construct. It was a sight to behold.

Gramma Lucy had brought Mazzy here years ago for Sunday afternoon picnics. Angels Gate Park was home to not only the Korean Friendship Bell but also Ft. MacArthur Military Museum and the Marine Mammal Care Center. After lunch they would wander through the underground passageways of the bunkers and then climb to the top and marvel at the spectacular view of Catalina Island. Gramma Lucy would then take Mazzy to the open Mammal Care Center where they could watch volunteers feed the wounded sea lions. Mazzy thought they were so adorable with their big brown eyes and wanted one for a pet until she witnessed a few of them try to attack the volunteers. Barking loudly and baring their teeth, they'd attempt to take a plug out of their unsuspecting victims.

Mazzy was asked by a young Hispanic couple to take their picture in front of the bell, and she obliged. The two huddled on the pavilion steps in a loving embrace and thanked her afterward.

Mazzy remembered doing the very same thing with Alan almost one year ago. The picture was framed and on her bookshelf to commemorate their first date. After going out to lunch at the marina, Mazzy had brought Alan up to Angels Gate to give him the tour. He had been amazed that he had lived in Southern California his entire life without ever knowing the place existed. They had shared their first kiss in front of the bell as the sun was setting on the ocean in a blaze of orange and pink.

Mazzy pushed the memory out of her mind and walked slowly toward the Mammal Reserve. She passed the visitors' center and rounded the corner to the fenced-off section where the animals were kept. It was a large square area with multiple pools separated by chain-link fence. Visitors could walk the perimeter in hopes of catching a glimpse of a baby seal at play.

Mazzy walked to the far side of the reserve and sat on a bench away from the spectators. She watched an old man with a boy who appeared to be his grandson, ask a volunteer what had caused the long scars on one small pup's back. "Boat propeller," she replied.

He shook his head in disgust. Mazzy could almost hear his inner dialogue. *See, I knew these new-fangled inventions would lead to no good. Row boats! That's what we used in my day!*

A young couple strolled by leisurely with their toddler girl nestled in the father's arms. "Look, Ashley! See the seals?" the mother exclaimed while pointing toward the pools.

The little girl, face full of expectant wonder, spotted the pup not ten feet away from her and smiled broadly, stretched out her chubby little hands to the fence and exclaimed "Baby! Baby!"

The pup woke with a start and barked loudly in protest, scaring the little girl half to death and sending her into inconsolable shrieks of terror. The young couple scurried away, their first educational trip with baby to the reserve shot to hell, and Mazzy was left in a fit of uncontrollable giggles.

Oh shit, that was priceless. Mazzy wished Abby were there with her. She would have appreciated Mazzy's twisted sense of humor; whereas, Alan would have chided her for her insensitivity. Her first good laugh of the day, and she was again sorely reminded of their differences.

She checked her watch and decided to head home to get ready for work. As she drove back to her apartment, she called Abby on her cell to bring her up to speed and apologize for hanging up on her. After giving her the rundown, Abby didn't know where to begin.

"Holy crap. Wow. Well… who do you think this Kelly is?"

"Hell if I know. And Gramma acted weird when I asked if she knew her."

"Mrs. Tell-the-truth-the-whole-truth-and-nothing-but-the-truth? You think she's lying?" Abby asked in disbelief.

"No. Not really. But something was wrong." Mazzy slowed down as she spotted a cop car coming up behind her on the freeway off ramp. The last thing she needed was a ticket today. She breathed a sigh of relief as he sped past her, sirens blasting, and pulled over the poor bastard two cars in front of her.

"You getting arrested over there or what?"

"No, the guy in front of me got pulled over." Mazzy could see the *well fuck me* look on the man's face. "Better him than me… especially since my freaking insurance lapsed last week, and I haven't gotten around to renewing it."

"And Alan. What a prick. Expecting you to give birth just because he wants to play daddy."

"I don't know that he exactly wants to *play* daddy…" Mazzy countered.

"Oh, don't start making excuses for him, Mazzy. He was a total dick… calling you selfish! Where does he get off? Men are such assholes," Abby said with venom. Mazzy had always marveled at Abby's ability to be a staunch member of the We Are Women Hear Us Roar Men-Haters Club and yet still manage to fall head over heels for every unattainable narcissist in Los Angeles County.

"Well, it didn't go well, that's for sure. I'm so jacked up right now, Abby. I just don't know what to think."

"Are you saying you've changed your mind?"

"No, no. I know I don't want kids." Mazzy flashed back to the scene at the Mammal Reserve and smirked. "I know I'm not cut out for motherhood. I'm sticking with my decision. It's just… a lot of shit has gone down the past couple of days. It's thrown me for a loop. And I know you don't want to hear this, but I already miss Alan. I do love him, Abby, and I can't believe that one day we are this great couple and the next… we're just over."

Mazzy had arrived home and pulled into her carport. She closed her eyes and leaned her head back as a tiny wave of nausea served as an unwanted reminder of exactly why things were over.

"I'm sorry, Maz. I wish I could think of something to say to make you feel better," Abby said, softening. She hated to hear her friend in pain. "I tell you what, out of respect for your feelings, I'll pull the needles out of my Alan voodoo doll and put it back away in its box."

"Thanks. I appreciate it."

"Are you working tonight?"

"Unfortunately, yes. I have to go get ready now."

"Me, too. Call me later, okay?"

"Okay. Bye."

Mazzy stashed her phone in her purse and walked to her apartment. She took one last hopeful look at her email before getting dressed, only to be rewarded with a glaring zero in her mailbox status.

After a slow, uneventful night at work, she returned home and this time found an ad for Victoria's Secrets and an email from Aunt Shelly asking her if she was coming to Victorville for Christmas Eve. Disappointed, she went to sleep and resigned herself to the fact that it could be days or even weeks before the mysterious Kelly wrote back.

The next day, she took her iPod to the beach and pounded miles of sand, losing herself in the rhythm of her steps as she made her way to the Venice boardwalk. She knew her mother had spent her summers in Venice when Aunt Shelly and Uncle Ronnie lived there many years ago. Cousin Jack had told Mazzy with longing in his childlike voice about his and Kennedy's many days spent body surfing and eating ice cream.

Feeling mildly lightheaded, Mazzy took a seat under the shade of a palm tree and watched the basketball players hammer the hell out of each other, jockeying for respect while their girlfriends sat on the sidelines, straight-faced and oozing attitude. It was a different culture on the Venice courts. Go to any college or high school and the girls would be clapping or cheering their men on. Come down here and a woman better know her place, which, it appeared to Mazzy, was to guard his belongings and give quiet nods of approval at a score while their single friends stood next to them, posturing and running their mouths off, trying to catch the attention of the players in between games.

Mazzy left the courts and walked the boardwalk, taking in the sights and smells. She passed the psychic palm reader who had abandoned her post and left a sign that read, "Your future will be back in thirty minutes," and The Body Art Shop where she had come very close to having a pierced nose one summer day after splitting a case of Corona with two of her girlfriends from work.

A pale, sweaty man wearing torn jeans and a gray hoodie came up behind her and asked Mazzy if she knew where he could score. She shook her head and kept walking, avoiding eye contact. He moved on to the anti-war demonstrators who held posters decrying the war in Iraq and demanding that George W. bring our boys back home.

She refilled her water bottle and headed back down the beach toward home, wondering what Venice had been like in the seventies, back when her mother and cousin Jack used to spend carefree summers exploring the boardwalk.

Mazzy took a short nap after arriving home and managed, with a moderate amount of pride, to avoid going near her computer before leaving for work.

The restaurant was packed for most of the evening. With her nausea temporarily in remission, Mazzy was able to focus on her work, enjoying the fluidity of her own movements and engaging the patrons in her customary repartee. By the end of the evening she had received a round of applause from a dinner party, multiple compliments from her regulars and enough in tips to make her car payment.

"California roll and some eel ought to do it," said Abby, appearing out of nowhere at the sushi bar.

"Hey, girl. What are you doing here?"

"I had the day from hell. I forgot to cancel one of Dr. Lee's appointments this afternoon, this crusty old woman who's a total bitch to begin with. Let's just say when she showed up after taking the afternoon off from her job, she was a bit salty with me. I got a parking ticket from the Hermosa sphincter police on Adams Avenue, and then had a fender bender in the Seven Eleven parking lot with an INS fugitive that of course had no freaking car insurance."

"Damn. That *was* a rough day. How's your car?"

"Minor dent and a few scratches. I can't afford an increase in premiums and the fugitive couldn't afford to have the police checking his immigration status. He was begging with me in Spanglish, something about five kids and deportation. He gave me a twenty, and we called it a day. Fuck it.

My car's a piece of shit anyway." Abby pulled out a twenty-dollar bill and laid it on the counter. "I say we take my car settlement and go to $1 ladies night at the Sand Pit. When are you done here?"

"About half an hour, but I don't know, Abb." While the nausea gods had been good to her over the evening, she wasn't sure if she wanted to tempt their wrath with alcohol.

"Oh, come on, Mazzy. You need to get out, too. At least come and hang out for a while and have a Coke. Please?" Abby gave her puppy dog eyes and pouted.

"All right, all right. Put the lip away. I'll come but I want to go home and change into something that doesn't smell like fish."

"Yay!" Abby clapped her hands in glee. Mazzy slid a bowl of rice to her on the sly, raw fish wasn't really Abby's food of choice, and finished up her orders. Rex kindly let her skip out a few minutes early and, after a quick change and cleanup at her apartment, they arrived at the Sand Pit ready to blow Abby's enormous car settlement.

They sat outside at the patio bar next to the volleyball pit, enjoying the lazy breeze as it caressed the flames of the decorative tiki torches. Mazzy watched a group of sweaty college boys in the middle of an intense match while Abby chatted up the bar tender Clark. Abby had long since developed a not-so-secret crush on the dark, brooding Clark and had made more than one reference to wanting to play Lois Lane to his superhero alter ego.

The college frat boys eventually finished their game to the death ending with a spectacular shouting match. The self-declared champions retired inside to celebrate their victory while the other team sulked in the corner and grumbled about bad calls, poor sportsmanship and the other team's being all-around pricks.

When the excitement quieted down and the losers left to go salvage their pride through engaging young coeds, Mazzy stared up at the night sky and zoned out in her own thoughts. She was still on her first tentative beer by the time Abby was hitting her fourth drink and feeling no pain from her rotten day.

"He is so godly," Abby swooned when Clark walked in the back to clock out of his shift.

"Mmm hmm," Mazzy replied absentmindedly.

"Hey, earth to Maz. Where are you right now? You look a million miles away."

"Just thinking."

"About Alan?"

"No, actually, about my mom."

Abby laughed bitterly. "Well that's the last place I ever let my mind roam."

Mazzy knew very little about Abby's family except that she loathed them and had severed all ties with her parents. Mazzy couldn't imagine having parents and not talking to them. She would have given anything just to have met her parents.

"What's the deal with that anyway? How horrible is your mom? I mean, does she have no redeeming qualities whatsoever?" Mazzy asked with genuine curiosity. Abby downed her drink and pondered for a moment.

"One thing that could be said about my mother is that she stood by her man. The one quote from her that I think epitomizes this undying loyalty came when I was in high school. Dad grounded me over something I didn't even do and my mother knew it. When I confronted her, she said, 'Abby, long after you and your sister are gone, it will just be me and your dad. I'm not going against him.' I think that sums up my mother's involvement with her children perfectly; that comment followed her and bit her in the ass in years to come I might add," Abby said with a wry smile but without elaboration.

She lit one of Mazzy's smokes and made sad attempts at blowing smoke rings. Mazzy had a sinking feeling she had tapped into an inner well of pain in her friend that she hadn't meant to.

"She did, however, have enough maternal instinct to not allow him to kill us. I remember one occasion when we were all in the car driving somewhere, and Dad was trying to beat the shit out of my older sister Marie. Mom said, 'Good God, if you're going to do that, at least pull the car over before you kill us all.' Which he did, then proceeded to knock Marie into next week. Or maybe that was just self-preservation on Mom's part? Who knows?"

"Wow, your dad would beat you guys, and your mom would let him?" Mazzy said in astonishment.

"She would sit in silence and watch with a disapproving look on her face while he gave me or my sister a fat lip then tell us later, 'Well it's your fault for...' Abby held up her fingers in air quotes, "Insert assorted heinous childhood crimes here." Abby pounded the business end of the cigarette into the ashtray.

"God Abby, I never knew. I'm so sorry." Mazzy wanted to cry over the thought of little Abby being physically hurt by anyone, let alone her own father. Gone was the happy, love struck look in her eyes from flirting with Clark mere minutes earlier, only to be replaced with bitter sadness. "I'm sorry I even brought it up."

"It's all right, Maz. Now you know why I stopped talking to them years ago. I'm not a strong supporter of the 'blood is thicker than water' bullshit. I mean, yeah, you should tolerate more crap with your family than you do with others, but at some point you have to draw the line," she said resolutely.

"Do you still talk to your sister?"

"Marie? No. She definitely suffered from the ass-kissing-overachieving-oldest-child syndrome. Marie, her husband and their five yard apes live within ten minutes of Mom and Dad up in Sacramento. Dad found God and a self-righteous position as elder in his church, and mom remains his faithful disciple. I'm sure they all spend Sunday dinners together patting themselves on the backs for being the good little hypocritical Christians that they are and praying for my sinning ass."

"Have you ever tried confronting them about it? Make them take responsibility for what they did?" Mazzy finished the last of her beer and signaled for another from the new bartender. Abby nodded in his direction for another, much to Mazzy's dismay. Her blue eyes were starting to look glassy, and her lips were having trouble wrapping themselves around her words.

"Of course, but Mom is a devoted rewriter of history. I don't mean fudging a few of the details here and there out of embarrassment. Oh no. I mean rewrites on the scale of 1984. Big Brother would have hired her as his right-hand man, and Winston would have been answering to her for his lack of creativity. Dad, of course, doesn't mind because it makes him look good, and Marie would rather live in denial and have their approval than rock the boat."

Mazzy's face must have shown the blatant pity she felt for her friend, for Abby snapped out of her PTSD-ridden stroll down memory lane posthaste. She picked up her newly delivered drink and raised it to Mazzy in a toast.

"To the families we choose... our friends!" she said loudly.

"To friends!" Mazzy chimed and tipped her glass in agreement.

"Now where the hell did my Superman go? I'm gonna go look for him. Be right back." Abby hopped off of her bar stool and swayed ever so slightly. Mazzy gave her a questioning look but Abby held up her hand.

"I'm fine, I'm fine. Not to worry. I'll be right back," she said, sashaying into the main bar.

Mazzy was left on the patio with her own troubled thoughts. Abby's revelations about her abusive childhood stunned her. While she struggled between guilt and self assuredness in regard to her own lack of maternal instincts, she could not fathom the thought of bashing the head of a child, especially one's own, into a wall. How a woman could allow someone else to do so, be it the father or not, was beyond her.

Could her own mother have been physically abusive? Was that why Gramma Lucy never talked about her without having her arm twisted? Sure, she told Mazzy that her mother had loved her and she had been a good person, but if that were true, then why would Lucy never offer any details? And why did she tense up whenever Mazzy started asking questions?

Mazzy noticed the door to the main bar swing open and expected to see Abby dragging the resistive Clark along behind her. To her happy surprise, she saw Alan, momentarily taken aback at the unexpected sight of her. She immediately wanted to leap recklessly off of her stool and throw her arms around him, nuzzling his chest while he stroked her hair reassuringly. But wounded pride kept desire in check and she smiled instead. He managed an awkward wave and walked tentatively to an empty seat next to her.

"Hi."

"Hi yourself," she said with false congeniality, her response sounding more casual than both of them knew it to be.

"Mind if I sit?" he queried.

"No problem," she said as she motioned for him to sit. "What brings you here?"

"Meeting a group of people here to discuss a class project for psychology. And you?"

"Spending every last dime of Abby's colossal cash settlement from a near fatal car accident."

Mazzy gave a summarized version of the day's events to Alan, and he asked the bartender for his standard Miller Light. Mazzy caught the momentary eyebrow lifted at her own drink.

"So, you see, I'm just supporting my friend after a long, hard day," she ended lamely as an explanation for the half-empty beer in front of her, immediately kicking herself for feeling the need to defend her own actions.

"Yeah, I thought I spotted her inside drooling on the bartender," said Alan, a tad too judgmentally for Mazzy's liking.

"I highly doubt she was drooling."

"Might as well have been."

"What is your problem with her?" Mazzy demanded.

"She... nothing. I don't have a problem with her." Alan took a deep breath and turned to face Mazzy. "I don't want to talk about her. I'm just happy to see you. I've missed you the past few days." Alan's sincerity took the angry wind out of her sails.

"I know. I've missed you, too."

"How... how are you feeling?" he asked, taking her hand in his.

"Fine. Well, kind of queasy actually, but I'm okay." She let the warmth of his comforting hand fill her from her fingertips down to her toes.

"I wanted to call you. I must have started to dial your number a hundred times, but I was afraid you would just hang up on me." His pleading eyes bore into her, blasting his way past her shaky defenses.

A ruckus at the door tore their attentions away from each other. Abby was laughing vivaciously and hanging on Clark's arm, surrounded by some of the regulars. She spotted Alan huddled up with Mazzy, and her laughter died instantly. Clark was too busy admiring her ample cleavage to notice her change in mood.

"We're all going to the Hop, Maz. Wanna come?" Abby insisted more than asked.

"Um, no, Abb. I'm good. You go have fun."

"Okay. If you're sure," Abby replied slowly, eyeing Alan suspiciously as she left.

Mazzy heard the familiar ring tone emanating from Alan's pocket. He checked the caller ID then answered his phone.

"Yeah? Oh, hey man, what's up… that sucks… well, good luck with that and give me a call tomorrow. Bye."

"Everything alright?" Mazzy asked.

"Bart's car broke down and he's stuck up in the valley. We'll have to reschedule our meeting for another night," he looked into Mazzy's eyes. "Looks like both of our plans have changed."

He touched her lips with the tips of his fingers. "Mazzy, I have missed you so much. I went up to Fort MacArthur the other day and just sat in front of the bell, thinking about us, about our first date."

"So did I," she said quietly. His fingers burned on her lips. She wanted so much to love him, and to be loved. They leaned and kissed each other softly. That was all it took.

Without another word they left and sped back to Mazzy's apartment. A desperate urgency weighed on the silence between them, both afraid to speak for fear of prematurely derailing the inevitable train wreck that lie ahead. They struggled franticly with stubborn buttons and zippers before Mazzy could fumble her way through unlocking the door, hungry for the warmth of vulnerable skin, rabid with the desire to fill and be filled.

They tripped over clothes and furniture till blindly finding the bed where they tumbled into the sheets in a tangle of naked limbs and probing mouths, determined to reach the place they had been brutally torn from only days before. They loved deeply, with tear rendering desperation until neither had anything left to give, then slipped into peaceful sleep in each other's arms as the sparrows outside stretched their wings to greet the promise of a new dawn.

Mazzy woke to the smell of herbal tea and cinnamon rolls baking from the kitchen. She remained in bed, burying her face in the pillow, savoring Alan's musky scent on her sheets and the lingering feel of his roaming hands all over her body. A demanding pressure on her bladder slowly prodded her to reluctantly leave their love nest.

When she sat up and reached for her robe next to the bed, the first blast of nausea hit. Nausea turned rapidly to retching as she scrambled for the bathroom, barely making it in time to save herself from a carpet cleaning bill.

Alan heard her gagging into the toilet and came charging into the bathroom wearing nothing but her work apron and a look of frightened concern on his face.

"Oh, honey! You poor thing," he soothed as he held back her hair. When she had nothing left to purge, he handed her a cool washcloth and retrieved her robe from the bedroom. With his arm around her waist, he gingerly led her to the couch and brought her a glass of water.

"Thanks," she said weakly before cautiously sipping, afraid she would not be able to keep the fluid down.

"You're welcome. How do you feel now?" he asked while taking the rolls out of the oven.

"Better. A little woozy." Her stomach was beginning to settle. Dehydration was overcoming her fear of throwing up again, so she chanced retribution and downed half of the glass.

"You shouldn't have drunk alcohol last night. Didn't seem like you had much though, so everything should be okay." Mazzy looked at him questioningly as he stood in her kitchen naked, frosting the rolls.

"What do you mean, everything should be okay?"

"Well, I don't think a couple of beers would do any real damage." He brought over a plate of rolls and sat down on the couch next to her.

"Damage?"

"Yeah, to the baby."

"What are you talking about, Alan?" Mazzy could feel the remaining warmth from last night begin to drain from her body.

"Well, I just thought... since we... last night..." he hemmed and hawed.

"You thought what exactly?"

"I thought you had come around. I assumed since you brought me home that you realized you had made a mistake."

"So the only reason you came home with me... the only reason you loved me last night was because you thought I had changed my mind about getting an abortion?"

"Well..." he paused.

"I understand. I'm not worthy of love unless I give you a child," she said, her voice beginning to crack.

"That's not what I mean, Mazzy. I..."

"Get out."

"Mazzy, please! Damn it, don't I have a say in this?" he demanded.

"GET OUT NOW!" she yelled, jumping off the couch. The sudden movement sent her head spinning and she almost stumbled over the coffee table. Alan grabbed her arm to support her and she slapped his hand away.

"No! Don't touch me! Get your shit and get out!" she cried before fleeing to the bedroom. She tossed his clothes into the hallway and slammed the door shut.

Alan quietly got dressed and left while Mazzy sat slumped on the floor and wept.

After crying the last remaining fluid out of her dehydrated body, Mazzy forced herself to drink a glass of water and eat a few crackers. With a renewed sense of purpose, determined to put all weak emotions behind her and forge ahead, she cleaned the toilet, took a shower and sat down with the phone book. After finding the number, she screwed up her courage and dialed.

"West Side Physicians. How may I help you?"

"Um, hello. I need an appointment." Mazzy was chewing on a piece of Dentyne, taking out her anxiety on the gum and smacking in the receptionist's ear. *Why didn't I go buy a pack of smokes?*

"Okay. Have you been seen here before?"

"No." Smack.

"And what will you be seen for?"

"Um, I need an abortion." Pop.

"All right," the receptionist replied, unfazed. "We have an opening this Friday at eleven a.m." Mazzy accidentally swallowed her gum and started gagging.

"Are you all right, miss?" the receptionist asked.

"Yeah, sorry. I'm fine now," she replied. "Wow. That's quick."

"Does that day not work for you?"

"No, no. It's just so quick. I wasn't expecting it to be so quick." *What do I need more time for? I'm being stupid… the quicker the better.*

"Please arrive fifteen minutes early to fill out paperwork. The fee is $375. Cash or credit card only. Can I have your name please?"

Should I give an alias? Will this go on my permanent record somewhere?

"Hello?"

"Yes?"

"I need a name dear," the receptionist coaxed.

"Yes, Mazzy Dawson." *Shit! Shit! She knows my name. I should have used Abby's.*

"Mazzy, you will need to have someone drive you. You will be sedated after the procedure."

"Okay. What's the address?" Mazzy took out a pen.

"You can call the morning of the appointment for the address. We open at nine."

"The morning of? That's weird. Why?" Mazzy imagined a dark alley somewhere in Compton where a medical school dropout waited with a rusty hanger and a blood-smeared fold out table.

"Safety precautions for the physicians."

"I don't understand."

"This is a family practice and not everyone supports our physician's rights to perform abortions. If this is a problem for you, there are other clinics," the receptionist countered curtly.

"No! No, that's fine. I'll call Friday morning. Thank you." Mazzy hung up before the receptionist could tell her to take her business elsewhere. She dialed Abby's cell.

"Whu?" she muttered incoherently.

"I did it."

"Who is this?"

"It's Mazzy."

"Oh, hey. What did you do?" Abby whispered. Mazzy thought she heard the rumbling of a man snoring in the background.

"I made the appointment... for the abortion."

"Yeah? When do you go?"

"This Friday."

"As in the day after tomorrow Friday?" Abby said alertly and with more volume. "Wow, that's quick."

"I thought the same thing! I mean, doesn't that sound too quick? And it was weird. She told me I couldn't get the address until Friday morning because of precautions for the doctors. Isn't that creepy?"

"Probably afraid you could be some whack-job protester or something."

"I guess. Hey Abb, can you take me?"

"Absolutely. I take it you and Alan didn't make up last night," said Abby. Mazzy started sobbing all over again, unable to believe she had the capacity to produce more tears. She told Abby what happened in between hiccups and blowing her nose.

"That fucking bastard!" roared Abby. The snoring in the background ceased abruptly and a disgruntled voice mumbled something Mazzy couldn't quite make out.

"He thinks I'm Medea now."

"Me-who?"

"Greek mythology? Never mind. Let's just say I don't think he wants to ever talk to me again," Mazzy said sadly, but images of the night before passed quickly to Alan demanding his rights this morning. "And quite frankly, now that I think about it, I don't want to talk to him either."

"Good for you. Hold onto that thought. And the next time I see you with him, don't hold it against me if I walk up and bitch-slap you."

"I'll hold it against you if you *don't*."

"Good. You want me to come over? We could rent a movie or something?" Mazzy could here the chainsaw resuming in the background.

"Where are you anyway?" she asked.

"Hold on a sec. I'm walking to the bathroom," Mazzy heard a door close before Abby began to speak again. "I'm at Leo's place."

"Leo? What happened to Clark?" While Mazzy was glad Abby wasn't at Clark's house, she thought their mutual friend Leo was an odd substitute. Leo was a thirty-year-old virgin who suffered from a mild case of OCD. Nice guy, but not exactly romance potential.

"We all went to the Hop last night, and not fifteen minutes after arriving, Clark picked up some little twit that I'm sure got in with a fake ID. They were practically fucking on the dance floor. Perfect end to my perfect day."

"How did you end up at Leo's?"

"I was so wasted. There was no way I was driving home, especially after Leo took my keys away from me. I think I remember yelling something to the effect of 'fuck undocumented immigrants and all superheroes!' when he took them away and insisted I crash at his place. He's such a nice guy. Too bad he's pushing a deuce and a half."

"Yeah, he is a nice guy. I'm glad you're not road kill somewhere on PCH." Mazzy remembered doing battle with Abby on a few occasions in the past for her keys and didn't envy Leo one bit.

"So, do you want me to come over then? It would be a good excuse for me to exit stage left before he wakes up and discovers I puked on his sweatshirt."

"Ah jeez, Abby! You didn't!" Mazzy could picture Leo hyperventilating at the sight of someone else's vomit.

"I know. Nice repayment, huh? I want to sneak out of here and take it home with me to wash before he wakes up. I definitely owe him lunch."

"If you don't have your car, how are you going to get here?"

"Duh, that's right! God, my head hurts so freaking bad. I can hardly think straight." Mazzy could relate to that. She still felt a dull throbbing in the back of her head. She would hate to be stranded, hung over and needing a shower.

"I'll come rescue you then."

"Cool beans! How soon can you be here?"

"Give me twenty minutes. He's at Vista View apartments still, right?" Mazzy had been to Leo's once before for a Super Bowl party two years ago. She had never seen a grown man that worshipped Clorox Wipes and had Prell hand sanitizer stationed every ten feet.

"Yup. Just pull up to the security gate. I'll be waiting."

"Make sure you wrap that sweatshirt in a bag or something."

"Will do. I'll even pour some Fabreeze on it. See you soon, and thanks, Maz."

Five minutes later, Mazzy pulled her Neon out of the carport and cringed as the brakes squealed, an obnoxious flaw in her otherwise perfect car. She had taken her blue baby back to the dealership after discovering the defect and had been told, "Most Neon's just do that." Two subsequent trips to different auto mechanics had confirmed this, although no one could offer a satisfactory reason as to why. Even with new brake pads it would scream as if grinding rotors, much to the chagrin of her neighbors, every morning after it had set outside for more than a few hours.

But she loved her car. After running her rusted out Civic into the ground, this little economy car was like a luxury sedan. It was like breaking up with a loser boyfriend to marry the man of your dreams, only to find out he had Tourette's.

By the time she arrived at Leo's apartment complex, the squealing had subsided and she was saved from Abby's usual commentary. Abby met her at the security gate and they went back to Mazzy's house to commiserate and drown their sorrows in jelly-filled donuts and an afternoon marathon of "Lost" on DVD. At the end of the day, they both agreed – nothing cured a hangover like greasy sweets. And who needed boyfriends when they could drool over Sawyer, sexy beast that he was?

The next day Mazzy busied herself with mindless errands -- a trip to the post office to mail her Christmas cards, haggling on the phone with her car insurance agent, cleaning her apartment, washing her car inside and out, filling out her new address book. She was able to keep her mind blissfully preoccupied until early in the evening when the phone rang and she answered without checking the caller ID.

"Hello?"

"Mazzy? Hey, it's me. I didn't think you would even answer the phone," Alan said.

His voice unraveled the curtains she had struggled so hard to keep over her mind's eye, reminding her of what tomorrow held.

"What do you want, Alan?" she asked briskly.

"I want to talk, Mazzy."

"Well, I don't."

"We can't act like nothing is going on here, Mazzy."

"I'm not acting like anything, Alan. I'm taking care of it."

"What does that mean?"

"I'm getting the abortion tomorrow."

"Mazzy, please. You can't do this..." he said forcefully.

"Good-bye, Alan."

She pressed End and turned her cell off. Knowing she had no chance of falling asleep on her own, and not wanting to spend the night crying into her already tear stained pillow, she popped a Vicodin left over from last year's wisdom tooth extraction and chased it with a beer. Within ten minutes, she was in slumber's sweet oblivion.

Mazzy checked in with the receptionist and was handed a medical history questionnaire. Her hand was shaking so badly that Abby had to ask her the questions and fill in the answers for her. She handed it back to the receptionist along with the cash then sat down again.

How appropriate that The First Noel is playing on the office intercom. It wasn't bad enough that she hated Christmas with all of its yuletide joy; now she would also have the memory of killing her unborn child associated with this holiday tune. Merry fucking Christmas.

And how the staff here loved the holidays! Someone worked extra overtime decorating a six-foot tree with angels and crystal ornaments. Over the receptionist's desk, a dozen stockings hung with the employee's names embroidered in gold thread. Multicolored lights lined the doorway and a five-foot-high cardboard Santa proclaimed "Ho! Ho! Ho!" on the far wall.

To make matters worse, when the receptionist told her this was a family practice, she wasn't kidding. It was also an OB/GYN practice and there were hugely pregnant women waiting for their turns while reading the latest edition of Parenting magazine, cooing over bootee ads and comparing trendy names like Piper and Scout. There was something obscene about the thought of getting an abortion while in the next room someone else was shedding tears of joy over hearing her baby's heartbeat for the first time. She felt like a Nazi spy in a synagogue.

"Miss Dawson? You can come in now." The nurse beckoned her with professional sincerity. Mazzy was sure she was secretly thinking, *come right in you baby hater, and don't forget your $375.*

Mazzy looked desperately at her friend, a part of her wishing Abby would jump out of her seat and drag her down to the parking lot out of this medical office with its cardboard Santa and blinking lights on the walls. Instead, she patted her hand and smiled.

"Do you want me to come with you?"

"No. That's okay… well… yes, please." She could barely talk through the tears that were threatening to burst her dam of resolve and flood the waiting room. Abby put her arm around her shoulder and stood up.

"I'm sorry, miss. You'll have to wait here," the nurse said matter-of-factly.

"Oh, come on! Can't you just…" Abby began to protest, but the nurse cut her off.

"I'm sorry, you have to wait here. You can come back when she is done. No exceptions."

Abby was about to launch into attack mode, but Mazzy grabbed her hand. As much as she wanted her friend's support, she didn't want a scene either.

"It's all right, Abbs. I'll see you in a little bit."

Abby gave her a tight hug then whispered into her ear, "Find out what her name is. I'll put a turd in her stocking."

Mazzy managed a weak smile and followed the nurse into the doctor's office. The nurse showed her into an exam room and gave her a waiver to sign.

"You need to read this through and sign at the bottom. There is a one in two hundred chance of complication. In some cases, hemorrhaging may occur due to…"

Mazzy didn't hear a word she said. Silent Night had entered the intercom's musical medley, and the song's sweet tribute to mother and child tortured her. She looked at the waiver but the words were swimming before her eyes. After rereading the first line for the fourth time, she gave up and signed on the dotted line. Twenty minutes later, she was on her back in a hospital gown staring at the ceiling.

"Hello, Miss Dawson. I'm Dr. Carter. Do you have any questions?"

The doctor had walked in with a nurse and was reviewing her medical information. He reminded her of Alan's barber. Alan insisted that he would never go to a salon and had been going to the same barber, Harold, since he was a boy. Harold had watched Alan grow up and became somewhat of a grandfather figure to him. Alan had insisted on Mazzy's escorting him to one of his appointments so she could experience the charm of the place firsthand, but it was lost on her.

Mazzy envisioned Harold in a doctor's coat coming toward her carrying long scissors asking, "Do you have any questions?" The thought of it made her knees slam shut.

"Miss Dawson? Any questions?" he repeated.

"What's going to happen?" she asked apprehensively.

"We're going to give you some Demerol so you won't remember much. Then we will dilate your cervix and scrape your uterus. You will experience some cramping. It won't take long at all." He had not even finished speaking before the nurse was injecting Mazzy with the Demerol.

"Wait, what?" her voice trailed off into a sigh. Within seconds the drug took hold. Not the high that she had heard people rave about, but a dead, apathetic feeling. *This is what it feels like to be dead.*

She was separate from herself, looking down and observing the doctor walk towards her with the longest needle she had ever seen, advancing between her legs. He injected it into her cervix not once, but multiple times. Then time passed… seconds, hours? She didn't know. *Maybe I am dead.*

She heard voices, then some type of machine, suctioning. Her stomach cramped sharply and she moaned.

"There, there. Almost done. You're doing great."

More noises, someone said she was done, then a new voice. A familiar voice. She heard something about antibiotics and rest, and then Abby appeared by her side.

"Hey, Maz," she said softly.

"Hey," Mazzy managed faintly. The fog was already beginning to lift.

Abby helped her into her clothes and walked arm-in-arm with her out of the office, past the nurses excitedly discussing their upcoming office party, past the stockings with the gold trim, past the joyful expectant mother sharing her sonogram picture of her baby boy in the waiting room and down to the parking lot where, unbeknownst to her, Alan sat in his car across the street watching her departure, sobbing and banging his head against the steering wheel for not dragging her down to the parking lot earlier, out of that medical office with its cardboard Santa and blinking lights on the walls.

Mazzy had no idea her friend knew how to make casseroles, but there they were, lining her freezer and cooking in her microwave -- a tuna casserole and an attempt at a turkey potpie that turned into a casserole. Abby apparently thought Mazzy was going to starve to death.

"I didn't think you would feel like going out to get anything, and I knew better than to think you would cook," Abby said as she dished up a plate of heated nacho surprise.

Mazzy was bundled up on her couch with her lavender fuzzy blanket getting ready to start their movie favorite's marathon. The Demerol had completely worn off, but she wasn't in any real pain. All she wanted to do was crawl into bed and go to sleep, but Abby refused to leave and Mazzy refused to be an ingrate.

"Thanks, Abb. Movie is ready to go." They watched Uma Thurman overdose through their dinner, John Travolta save the day in Greased Lightning over Ben and Jerry's Chunky Monkey and Riff Randal swoon over Joey Ramone while finishing their second Coronas. They switched over to cable just in time for a laxative commercial, a pink pill especially designed for women.

"Have you ever noticed that laxative commercials are geared toward women? There is always a feminine slant to them. Do men never get constipated?" Abby asked philosophically.

"Hmm. I don't know." Mazzy's eyelids were getting heavy and her bed was calling her name.

"And now that I think about it, don't men love to take shits? I mean, most guys go multiple times a day, make a leisurely trip out of it with some form of reading material and then announce the outcome and quality of the experience when they're done. Women don't do that! If they can't go privately with no one else knowing, they'll hold it till they explode. No wonder we get more constipated."

"You are so random." Mazzy giggled tiredly. She downed the last of her Corona.

"Is it okay for you to drink those?"

"Frankly, Scarlet, I don't give a damn."

"Atta girl." Abby looked at Mazzy thoughtfully. "You really feeling okay?"

"Yeah, I'm fine." Mazzy switched off the TV and closed her eyes.

"You want to talk about it? I mean, what happened?" Abby asked tentatively. "No. Not yet. Not now," Mazzy replied slowly.

"I'm sorry, Maz. I don't mean to pry," Abby said quickly, kicking her self for being so insensitive.

Mazzy dragged herself off the couch and went to her friend. "Abby, it's okay. Thanks for being there and for going on a Martha Stewart binge with the food."

Abby laughed, and Mazzy hugged her gratefully. "No problem. I only wish you could have gotten that nurse's name for me."

"You're evil. I like it. Now go home so I can sleep."

Abby looked at her doubtfully. "I mean it, Martha, get on out of here. I'll be fine," Mazzy ordered with mock force while shoving her towards the door.

"Okay. You promise to call me if you need anything?"

"Promise."

"And you promise to take that antibiotic before you go to bed?"

"Abby!"

"All right! All right. Bye."

Mazzy locked the door behind her, went directly to bed and slept for twelve hours straight without moving an inch. When Mazzy awoke, it was to Gramma Lucy's voice booming from her answering machine. She scrambled for the phone, still thick and blurry from oversleeping.

"What?" she asked groggily.

"What? Is that any way to answer your phone?"

"Who? Oh, Gramma, hi. What time is it?" Mazzy looked around for her clock.

"It's nine in the morning. We're going to breakfast, and I won't take no for an answer." *What is it with everyone wanting to feed me?*

"But Gram, I'm not even up," Mazzy protested, but Gramma Lucy wasn't having it.

"You already canceled on me last weekend, Mazzy. Something is wrong with you. I know it. I'll be there in thirty minutes." She hung up before Mazzy could reply.

True to her word, there was a sharp rapping on the front door exactly one half hour later. Mazzy barely had time to take a quick shower and straighten up the living room just in case Lucy barreled past her to perform her usual visual inspection. It drove Mazzy crazy to watch her survey the place, taking a mental inventory of her belongings and lack of cleaning skills.

Mazzy opened the door and stepped swiftly into the hall before Lucy could make her move.

"Hi, Gram." She had the door locked and was proceeding down the hall before Lucy could respond.

"Where's the fire?" Lucy was still standing in front of the door. "Don't you want to finish getting ready? I can wait."

"I am ready, Gram." *Hey, if my velour sweats and wet ponytail isn't enough for the old woman on thirty minutes' notice, she can bite me.*

"Hmm. Okay. If you say so," she said skeptically. She cast a suspicious eye toward the door before following Mazzy down the stairs.

"Where to?" Mazzy followed Gram to her VW Beetle knowing full well that she would sooner walk than get into Mazzy's blue Neon.

Lucy did not trust anyone but herself behind the wheel of an automobile. If it were up to her, Mazzy would have never received her driver's license. And boy had that been a battle. Mazzy was the only person she knew who had to wait until she was eighteen to get one. From the time she turned sixteen, she nagged, whined, reasoned and cajoled Lucy to no avail. It wasn't until she solicited the help of Aunt Shelly that Lucy finally acquiesced, giving in after two bottles of wine and an entire evening of arguing behind closed doors. Mazzy had pledged her eternal love to her aunt that night.

"How about that new place by Parkside Center? I'm told they have great omelets. Funny name, though... what was it again?" Lucy pondered as she put on her seat belt.

"Oh, yeah. Humpty Dumpty's. That sounds fine, Gram." She was still full from last night and couldn't care less where they went. It had taken all of her strength to crawl out of bed to put her self together, and now she was starting to drag. She felt blunted, hollow, but was almost glad for the distraction. She was afraid to let herself think about yesterday.

They arrived and were seated immediately. The morning rush didn't usually start until after ten, so they were graced with a good table next to the window. Mazzy's head spun with all of the exotic options on the menu. She opted for a no-nonsense cheese omelet while Lucy ordered the daily special, kiwi and mango waffles.

After critiquing the wait staff – *Seems like a nice girl, but she should smile more* – and the décor - *The quaint feel is inviting, but the animated egg decorations are a little over the top* – Lucy proceeded to describe in painstaking detail the latest multimedia art piece she was inspired to create after seeing the Vagina Monologues -- an anatomical creation made with an assortment of dried fruit and oil paints.

Mazzy would normally be amused and fascinated with her grandmother's latest art project, but she could barely muster a polite *uh-huh* in response to her enthusiastic descriptions. As they fell back into silence and sipped their coffees, Lucy eyed Mazzy suspiciously.

"What? Why are you looking at me like you're sizing up a criminal?"

"Why? Feeling guilty about something?" Lucy countered slyly.

"No, as a matter of fact, I am not," Mazzy snapped.

"What has gotten into you lately, young lady? You have been avoiding me, answering your phone like you were raised with no manners, and now you are biting my head off."

"I have a lot on my mind, Gram. I don't mean to take it out on you," Mazzy said tiredly.

"Well, that's exactly what you're doing. What's going on that has you so cranky and preoccupied? What's on your mind?"

"I don't want to talk about it."

"Why not? Was it that boyfriend of yours? Alan?" Mazzy couldn't shield the pained look on her face from the mere mention of his name. "It *is* him! I knew it! What did that bastard do to you?"

"He didn't do anything, and I am not talking about it," Mazzy replied matter-of-factly.

"We used to be so open with each other. You used to talk to me," Lucy said sadly.

"WE used to be so open? WE? No, I was open with you while YOU remained fairly closed, to my recollection." Mazzy could feel her hackles rising.

"I… I have not been closed with you!" Lucy replied with blatant surprise.

The waitress delivered their food and they ate quietly, absorbed in their own thoughts. Mazzy made a half-hearted attempt at her omelet while Lucy slowly ate her waffle. Not wanting to venture where she suspected Mazzy might be going, but not being able to tolerate the silence, Lucy finally pushed on.

"How many grandparents, or even parents for that matter, talk with their children openly about sex? How many discuss politics and arts and world news with their kids and treat them like they have minds of their own?"

"Not many," Mazzy acquiesced as the waitress brought them the check. She left a twenty and made her way toward the door with Lucy following in apprehensive bewilderment.

The morning rush had started and people were packed in the waiting area making navigation difficult. By the time Lucy walked outside, Mazzy was already standing by the car, leaning on the door with her forehead resting on the roof.

"Then how could you say that to me?" Lucy said in exasperation as she was struggling to find her keys. Mazzy lifted her head and met Lucy's eyes.

"Tell me about my mother." Mazzy could see her grandmother physically tense.

"What is this about?" she replied impatiently.

"Tell me about my mother," Mazzy said with slow deliberation.

"Oh, for heaven's sake. You act as if I have never talked about your mother before."

Lucy finally got her door unlocked, hopped into the car and unlocked the passenger side. She started the car and had her seat belt on, but Mazzy was still leaning on the outside of the door, not budging. Lucy banged the wheel in anger and got out of the car.

"Are you coming or not?" She was becoming unnerved by Mazzy's unrelenting stare.

"Tell me about my mother."

"God damn it, Mazzy! What do you want to know? Huh? What do you want from me?"

"I want answers," she said more forcefully. "How did she die? How *exactly* did she die? And don't tell me 'from a drug overdose.' I want details. Was she high all the time? Did she do drugs in front of me?"

"Shh! Get in the car right now, Mazzy! I am not discussing this in a parking lot." Lucy hissed, looking over her shoulder to see if anyone was around.

"No! Did she love my father, and who the hell was he? I mean, am I the product of some drugged-out one night stand, or did she love him? And don't tell me you don't know anything about him!"

Mazzy was on a roll. All of the questions she knew her gramma would have never answered, all of the bitterness that had slowly brewed inside over the years from being kept in the dark came pouring out of her like a stream of projectile vomit aimed directly at Lucy.

"And while we are on the topic of fathers that bastardize, who the hell was her father, my grandfather? Don't I have a right to know where the hell I came from? Why is everything in this fucking family such a deep, dark secret?!"

That was the straw, the two-ton straw that broke Lucy's back. Without a word she slammed into the car and screeched out of the parking lot, leaving Mazzy standing alone in a worked-up frenzy.

After almost taking out a pedestrian and running two stop signs, Lucy pulled the car over and shut the engine off. Her entire body shook. She sobbed violently into the steering wheel for fifteen minutes before she could still her trembling hands and catch her ragged breathe. When she could finally see straight again and breath at a normal rate, she started her car and headed directly to Victorville.

Mazzy walked the two miles to her apartment. Uncorked rage fueled the first mile speed-walk, but depression and exhaustion kicked in by the halfway point leaving her to crawl the last block.

She stumbled in her door and collapsed on the couch, sleeping for nearly two hours before the morning's coffee kicked in and forced her up to go to the bathroom. As she passed her computer on the way back to the couch to fetch her cigarettes, she noticed the You've Got Mail icon blinking at her. She lit a Capri and dragged deeply, then clicked on her email. She nearly choked when she saw it. *She wrote back!*

Mazzy,

Sorry I didn't write back sooner, but I was out of town for the last week. Let me first say that your blunt style and take-no-shit attitude had me laughing and crying simultaneously. It sounded like something your mom would have said.

I don't know what you do or don't know about your mother's past, so forgive me if this winds up being too much information at once. I have thought of you often over the years and have practiced what I would say to you in my mind over and over again. Now that I have the chance, I find myself staring at the keyboard.

I met your mother at a detox unit when we were both first kicking heroin. She was pregnant with you, and I was paralyzed and in a wheelchair. After getting off to a rocky start – to say your mother loathed me would be putting it mildly – we slowly became allies. That stay on the detox unit was like doing a tour of Nam, and we eventually wound up war buddies. After detox, she supported me during physical therapy and learning to walk again, and I supported her while she was going to college and raising you. We weren't a couple, but we were way more than friends. Hell, I don't know what you would have called us.

You were the one and only reason she stopped doing drugs and finished college.

I can honestly say that I have never seen a mother more in love with her child than Kennedy was with you. In her eyes, the sun rose and set on you.

She remained sober for almost three years when what should have been a one-time stupid relapse, a bump in her recovery, took her young life away.

There is so much to tell you, but I have no idea if you want to hear what I have to say. In case you decide to tell me to go to hell entirely, I want to make sure to share this last thing with you.

Your mother knew she was having a girl before you were born. No sonograms... she just knew. One day soon after we met, we were discussing girl's names and I told her about a comic book character named Mazzy. She was a sidekick who could travel forward in time. Your mother said to me, "Mazzy... my little sidekick. Just me and my little girl against the world. I like it." She even dressed you up in a little superhero costume for your first Halloween. You were the cutest thing I had ever seen in baby spandex.

I hope to hear from you soon. Something other than a death threat would be wonderful. Kelly

It's a guy! *The guy in the wheelchair!* Mazzy ran to her room and frantically searched for the picture. She found it in her top drawer and examined it for the millionth time with new vigor -- the long brown hair, bulging arms and exaggerated nostrils. He was telling the truth. He had known her as a baby!

Then it hit her, so hard that she sank to the edge of her bed. If he had met her mother when she was already pregnant with Mazzy, there was no way he could be her father. The Judd Nelson look-alike that Mazzy had secretly hoped might have been her father all these years was just a friend of her mother's. Gramma Lucy must have been telling the truth about her father after all.

Her mother had loved her! Her mother really had wanted her after all. She had gotten clean just for Mazzy. This new mental picture of a loving, nurturing mother who had just screwed up collided with the deeply ingrained image of a woman who was forced into motherhood against her will and took the easy way out.

And this photograph... Gramma Lucy had to have known Kelly and she said she didn't! She said... *Hang on a second. She's a he. Kelly is a HE, not a SHE!*

It all made sense to her now. Lucy had said she knew no WOMAN named Kelly Judd. *That tricky old bitch! She fucking KNEW who I was talking about and used a God damned loop hole to lie about it! That's why she sounded relieved!*

Nothing was what she thought it was. She buried her head in a pillow and screamed.

"Lou! What brings you here and without so much as a phone call?" Shelly asked in surprise.

Lucy's turning up on her doorstep without at least a week's notice on a Saturday afternoon was not a usual occurrence. Upon close inspection, Shelly saw that Lucy's eyes were swollen and bloodshot and her nose was Rudolph red.

"Good Lord, Lou, what's wrong?"

"Are you going to invite me in or just stand here playing Twenty Questions? Because if I'm not welcome, I can always turn around and go back home."

"Don't be pissy with me. Come in, have some iced tea and tell me what's got your panties in a bunch."

Shelly showed Lucy to the enclosed backyard patio and brought out raspberry iced teas on a tray with home-baked lemon bars. The white wicker furniture and yellow cushions were all immaculate, and there was not one trace of dust on the glass plant stand.

Lucy was impressed with how Shelly always seemed ready to entertain on a moment's notice, while Lucy needed a few days bare minimum to prepare for a casual coffee. *The roll reversals between us. Who would have thought?*

"So why do you look like you were just informed that Michael's Arts and Crafts went out of business?" Shelly inquired.

"Shell, I don't know what I'm doing anymore. I'm losing her. It's like I'm losing Kennedy all over again."

Lucy stared out the patio window into the back lot at Shelly's guesthouse. She could hear Jack humming from within, busying himself with his weekly laundry. She envied the arrangement -- having your child in your back yard, a stone's throw away, to watch over and protect.

"Oh, god. What's wrong with Mazzy? She's not... she's not on drugs is she?"

"No! Well, I don't think so. I don't know. She's becoming more and more distant, not talking to me. We just had a huge fight. It was terrible."

Lucy saw Jack through his bedroom window happily coordinating his socks by color. He looked up and caught Lucy's stare. The look of joy on his face at seeing her made her heart ache for long ago, when he and Kennedy were little, inseparable. He waved vigorously, and Lucy smiled weakly and waved back.

"What happened, Lou?"

"I don't know. It's like it came out of nowhere. We went to breakfast and she was so quiet, not herself. One minute I was telling her about my painting and the next we're in the parking lot, her screaming at me, 'Tell me about my mother! How did she die? Who was my father?' It was horrible."

"Well, what did you do?"

"I left. I jumped in the car and left."

"You left her there?!"

"She was yelling, cursing at me!" Lucy exclaimed defensively.

"And your solution was to abandon her in a parking lot?" Shelly asked in disbelief, shaking her head.

"I panicked, Shelly! I didn't know what to do."

"You know Lou, I love you, but I have never agreed with your philosophy of 'the less the kids know, the better.' This has probably been building up in Mazzy for years, and something obviously triggered it. Kennedy should have known about her past. Now Mazzy has two generations of bullshit to wonder about. Quite frankly, I'm surprised she hasn't gone off on you before now."

"Well, thank you so much, Mother of the Year, for your support!" Lucy huffed and made as if to stand up.

Shelly grabbed her arm firmly. "Old woman, sit your fat ass down!" Shelly laughed out loud at the shocked expression on Lucy's face. "That's right. You heard me. It is that approach that has gotten you into this mess. You can't go storming out on people whenever you don't like what you hear or are asked something that makes your butt hole pucker."

"You are a crass, vile woman." Lucy reluctantly sank back in her chair. "And you should talk about fat asses. How many fields of cotton had to be sacrificed to make those pants you're wearing?"

Shelly laughed again and patted her sister on the arm.

The door to the guesthouse flew open and Jack came bounding out like a Labrador puppy. He was in his forties now but still retained the enthusiasm of a young child.

"Hi, Aunt Lou! I didn't know you were coming."

"Neither did I, Jack. Surprise visit," Lucy said. Jack sat down next to her and squeezed the breath out of her lungs in a crushing embrace. The man did not know how to love or show affection in moderation.

"I wish I would have known. I told my boss I would work extra today with Saturday cleanup. I'm a good worker, Aunt Lou. Evan tells me so every day."

Lucy had never met anyone making minimum wage who took more pride in his job than her nephew. "I know you are, Jack. Evan is lucky to have you. I'll be sure and schedule my next visit on your day off."

"Okay." He stood up and leaned over to kiss Shelly good-bye. "I finished all my dishes and laundry and double-checked that the stove was turned off, Momma."

"All right, love. I'll see you in a few hours." Shelly kissed him on the cheek and smoothed down a stray cowlick on his head.

"Bye, Momma. Bye, Aunt Lou!" Jack said heartily as he strode away from the back porch. Shelly sighed and watched her son adoringly as he vanished from view.

"He seems very happy, Shell."

"I know. I would have never guessed he would be. We always assumed he would be in for a hard disappointing life, but he truly is the happiest person I know." Shelly took a bite of her lemon bar and sipped on her tea thoughtfully.

"Sometimes, when I have a mad-on over my car getting a flat or Ronnie messing up extra towels that I have to wash, I see Jack showing off his bus pass to the neighbor, bragging about how he can get to work by himself, or I catch him beaming with pride over doing his own laundry."

Shelly shook her head and poured herself and Lucy more tea before resuming her thought. "And then I think *I am such a whiner... an ungrateful whiner.* He makes me appreciate things more, Lou. He makes me a better person."

Shelly sighed again contentedly and then turned a stern eye back to Lucy. "Now, back to Mazzy. You have to tell her, Lou. Tell her about what happened to Kennedy."

"What if she goes searching for her dad, or for that Kelly? You know, she asked me if I knew him the other day!? What if she finds them and wants to become close to them and starts using drugs, too? I can't go through that again."

"Mazzy is not Kennedy. She is her own person who just so happens to not believe in taking drugs. By not talking about her mom, you might avoid the less admirable side of Kennedy, but you also rob Mazzy of knowing the amazing human being her mother was. You have to tell her. Besides, Kit would want that anyway... the good, the bad and the ugly. It drove her nuts how you kept the past such a secret. For whatever reason, right now Mazzy needs to find out more about where she came from, who she is. Tell her about Donald... about Tom," Shelly said apprehensively, waiting for the explosion. Instead, Lucy put her head in her hands and wept softly.

"I didn't want them to know ugliness… how despicable people could be," Lucy sobbed. Shelly put her arm around her sister and stroked her hair. "I was so naïve Shell, remember? It used to drive you crazy. But I truly thought I could show them beauty and peace and shield them from how life really is." Shelly handed her a Kleenex for her running nose.

"I know, Lou, but life is both. Hell, *people* are both." Shelly kissed Lucy's hair and cupped her chin in her hand. "Look at you, for example. How could someone so loving and beautiful on the inside wind up so pig ass ugly on the outside?" Shelly belly laughed and Lucy joined in against her own will.

"Why do I come here?" Lucy asked, wiping her tears away.

"Because I tell it to you like it is, and I make you laugh. Come on, you know how much I love you. Here, have a lemon square." Lucy took the little powdered square and pretended to aim it at Shelly's head before eating it.

"Yes, I do know you love me."

"And you know I'm right."

"Yes, I guess I know that too. It's so hard though, Shell. I don't even know how to start."

"Why don't you try writing it down first? Write her a letter."

"That's more your style. Speaking of which, why don't you write anymore? You were so good. I always thought you should write a book about your life, especially your younger years. You were such a wild child."

"I've toyed with the idea, but I always come back to this: why would anyone care about the details of *my* life? I'm not famous, nor have I slept with anyone famous to my knowledge. I haven't survived a life-threatening catastrophe through my iron will to live coupled with my acquired Girl Scout skills. I haven't set any world, or even local, records. I'm not exceptionally smart or beautiful, although I am smarter than the average bear and have been told I'm easy on the eyes. I'm not a gold-medal Olympic athlete. I am, however, quite proud that during a short-lived attempt at quitting smoking, I jogged a 3k Avon run without keeling over from an asthma attack. I have never been President of the United States, my high school class or even the PTA. Shoot, I have never even been a card-toting member of the Stepford Wives PTA. I abhor those stuck-up bake-sale Nazi bitches." Lucy laughed so hard, she shot tea out of her nose, which in turn caused Shelly to double over in a fit of giggles. Once they both regained their composure, Shelly jabbed her finger at Lucy accusingly.

"And quit changing the subject! All joking aside, Lou, whether you write it in a letter or send a singing telegram, you need to tell that poor girl. She deserves to know."

Mazzy's butt was numb from sitting on the blue bathroom tile. Four hours of Nirvana and John Meyer blasting on her headphones had her ears ringing, and the extra-large anti-tobacco candle had lost the war early on. The bathroom had long since turned into a walk-in ashtray.

She knew it was weird having an entire apartment at her disposal and choosing to hole up in the bathroom, but the comforting habit was hard to break. Initially not wanting her apartment to smell like smoke, she would go into the bathroom and blow the smoke out the window. When the occasional smoke turned into stress-driven nicotine binges, she started bringing her iPod in with her to relax. The small space was womblike in its comfort, and even after she had given up on preserving the new-apartment smell and began smoking in the rest of her home, the little blue bathroom had already turned into her little sanctuary.

Her eyes burned from smoke and tears and her hand was cramping from scribbling her tangential angst in her battered notebook. Once she felt satisfactorily purged of one raw emotion, she would suddenly become overtaken by another: depression, bitterness, anger, longing, remorse. She had never felt so mentally twisted in her entire life.

Having lost all sensation in her behind and right hand, she finally pulled herself up off of the floor, nuked some extra-buttered popcorn, popped open a beer and sat down in front of her TV, where she proceeded to get plastered while watching a five-hour South Park marathon.

Alan had been calling her for two days, leaving voice messages until her mailbox was full. He didn't really expect her to answer the phone, but he kept trying. The look on her face when she had driven away with Abby from the doctor's office haunted him. *But she had been in the building for such a short time. Maybe she had changed her mind, backed out at the last minute.*

He went to the Starbucks near her apartment, hoping to "accidentally" run into her, but she wasn't there. He ordered a small coffee and was walking out the door when he nearly collided with Abby.

"Oh, hey," he said awkwardly.

"Hey," she replied quickly and brushed past him. They both froze and turned to face each other.

"Have you..." they said simultaneously before pausing.

"Have... have you talked to her?" he asked cautiously.

"I haven't heard from her, Alan. I've called. I've knocked on her door. Nothing. Look, I know you're mad at her, but you still have a key. Would you please go into her apartment and check on her? Or give me the damn key and let me do it. I know it's only been two days, but I'm worried about her. We've never gone more than a day without talking to each other, and I haven't heard from her since, well, you know."

His heart sank. *She went through with it.*

Anyone could see that Abby was genuinely distraught about her friend's whereabouts. Alan also knew that if she wasn't seriously concerned about Mazzy, Abby would have sooner spit in his face than talk to him.

"Yeah. I'll go there now," he said.

"Please call me and let me know if you find out anything." Abby was clearly uncomfortable with asking Alan for any favors, but in this case, she would swallow her pride.

"I will. I'm sure she's fine. We'll find her."

Alan went to Mazzy's apartment and knocked on her door. No answer. He knocked harder. Still no answer. He used his key and entered slowly, calling out her name. Her apartment was a mess and reeked of smoke. It looked as if she had been holed up in there for days. Nuker popcorn bags and empty beer cans littered the beige carpet along with dirty clothes and photo albums. He went back to the bedroom, and then checked her bathroom, half expecting to find her lifeless body under a pile of Capri cigarettes, but she wasn't there.

Alan saw her poetry notebook on the bathroom counter next to an empty pack of cigarettes and a candle that had melted all over the sink. She was never serious about writing, but would scribble in her notebook madly when she was either very depressed or angry. She always said she couldn't write if she was happy. Love poems made her gag.

Knowing he was violating her privacy, but desperate for answers, he flipped through to her last entry.

Did someone take my baby's hand?
A hand I never held
Or was it left back in my womb
Later to be expelled
Did my flesh have conscience soul
And walk into the light
Or was it just a seedling
Without a form, without a right
Please forgive me
If I was on my deathbed
And had one wish to use
I'd wish to know my tiny soul
Was bathing in heaven's hues
Please forgive me

Alan was flooded with emotions. He threw the notebook in the tub and sank to the floor. He wept for his baby. The anger swelled in him all over again towards Mazzy for taking their baby's life. It mixed with his love for her and twisted his heart into knots. He wanted to hit her, shake her, hold her and stroke her hair. He felt her pain and wanted to rub her nose in it and take it away at the same time.

He pulled himself up and wandered around her apartment aimlessly, reminders of happier times at every turn: an old-fashioned black-and-white photo taken of them at the L. A. County Fair, the Breakfast Club DVD they watched twenty times that she never returned to Hollywood Video, his USC sweatshirt that she liked to sleep in tossed on her bed, framed tickets to a U2 concert, his sleeping bag that he never took home from their last camping trip. *Wait, where is her sleeping bag?* He searched in the back of her closet. Her sleeping bag, their small dome tent, her hiking boots … gone. *What the hell is she thinking taking off camping by her self?* He had a bad feeling. As he ran to phone Abby and let her know that he was driving up to the mountains to look for her, Mazzy was hiking toward Cold Water Lake, in an attempt to clear her head, feeling a little light-headed and starting to slowly hemorrhage internally.

Mazzy loved the outdoors. Los Angeles was the only place in the world where you could go surfing in the morning, drive two hours, and then be in the mountains hiking by noon. Not that the Angeles Forest ranked up there with Yosemite or the Rocky Mountains, but at least you could climb above the smog line of L. A. and get some fresh air, which was exactly what she needed. She felt like she had consumed more alcohol and smoked more cigarettes in the past week than she had in the previous six months combined.

She knew she had taken wallowing in self-pity to a new and exceedingly low level when she had caught her own pathetic image in the mirror Monday morning: she was sporting the same sweats that had obtained a dark blood stain in the crotch two days ago from a maxi-pad overflow and had a dark smudge on her mouth from fishing cigarette butts covered in ashes out of the trash to smoke when her reserves had been depleted. Her hair was nappy and looked like a poor man's clown wig. She was Side Show Bob after hitting rock bottom from a fallout with Crusty the Clown, so pitiful not even Bart Simpson would have the heart to laugh at her.

I have to get away. I have got to yank my head out of my ass and pull my shit together. She had called Rex and requested a few days off, which he gave begrudgingly, took a quick shower, threw her gear into the car, and then headed to the mountains. *I will commune with nature… then go back and deal with my nasty apartment.*

The only other living soul at Cold Water Camp Ground when she arrived was a small brown-haired mutt huddled by the port-a-potties. He was scrawny and his faded fur was matted into gnarled rats' nests.

"Damn, Scrappy Doo. You look worse than I do," she said.

He watched her carefully as she pitched her tent, assessing if she were a possible friend or foe. By the time she had finished and was starting to feel slightly dizzy, he had inched his way to the fire pit. She sat down on her portable camping chair and drank some bottled water, thinking she might be dehydrated.

"How about you? You dehydrated, too?" she asked the dog.

He merely stared in response, apparently unclear as to what her intentions might be. Mazzy took a plastic cup from her bag, filled it with water and set it next to her tent.

"There you go. No poison, buddy, just water."

She hitched her backpack over her shoulders and set off up the path toward the lake.

Alan had always been proud of his perfect driving record, but today, he couldn't give a shit that this female cop with a chip on her shoulder was going to increase his insurance premiums. What pissed him off was that she had something to prove and was hell-bent on making him acknowledge her indisputable authority. After clocking him at a dizzying 65 mph, she added lack of a seatbelt and failure to signal for good measure.

"But I DID signal," he tried to argue.

"One blink of the light does not equal proper notification of your intention to change lanes," she countered in a stern voice.

If this bitch was getting laid properly at home, she wouldn't have even glanced my way, he thought in an uncharacteristic fashion. *And if she lost a square fifty, maybe she would be.*

She handed him his ticket and told him to have a nice day before waddling her ample ass back to her squad car. Alan suddenly had a vivid visualization of Cartman screaming, "RESPECT MY AUTHOR-I-TAAAY!" and would have laughed out loud if he weren't so angry. He merged back onto the freeway and headed toward Mazzy's favorite camp ground.

She hiked slowly, breathing in the smell of pine and listening to the bird's calming melodies. Occasionally, she thought she caught the sound of something small scrambling in the bushes behind her, but dismissed it as a nosy squirrel. She passed two women in their late forties making their way down from the lake, talking animatedly about a peak they were scheduled to conquer with the Sierra Club next weekend. They acknowledged her with quick nods, unable to let up their stream of conversation to say hello, and Mazzy returned with a courteous smile.

The dizziness had not abated, so she faithfully kept downing water in large gulps, certain it would render a cure. When she reached the lake, doubled over from the effort to keep from peeing in her pants, she kicked herself for not bringing toilet paper and was forced to drip dry behind a bush.

After relieving herself, Mazzy sat on a boulder and gazed across the lake's smooth surface. She picked up a stone, tossed it in the water and tried to keep count of the ever expanding ripples; one turned to two, two turned to three and so on, until they eventually reached her on the shore and she could no longer pinpoint their origin.

Suddenly, her vision began to blur. She rubbed and then blinked her eyes, but the dark lake remained hazy and out of focus. She stood up and was struck with feeling of extreme gravity, as if she had twenty-pound weights on her arms and legs.

Jeez, what the hell is wrong with me?

Deciding it might be in her best interest to head back to camp, Mazzy turned toward the path and nearly fell. She grabbed the closest tree and clung to it, smashing a wayward trail of ants in her unknowing grip. Her vision tunneled and she felt building pressure behind her eyes and forehead. The bird's clear crisp song sounded hollow, as if it were traveling to her down a long corridor instead of floating above her in the trees. She closed her eyes and took a deep breath.

There was no kidding herself anymore; this was not dehydration. Something was horribly wrong. She wracked her brain to try and remember what the nurse had said about possible complications, but found it exceedingly difficult to think. With a trembling hand she checked her cell phone, but there were no bars. She had seen no other living souls since she passed the two women earlier. Mazzy had to go back to the campground and find help.

She headed back down the path with deliberate steps, pacing herself for the two-mile trek back.

Alan pulled into the deserted campground and breathed a sigh of relief when he saw Mazzy's lone Neon. He parked next to it then trotted up the short path to the fire pits. The area seemed deserted, bar a few ragged squirrels, and the isolation mixed with gloomy overcast made for a depressing setting.

As he rounded the last corner, he thought his mind was starting to play tricks on him as the moronic sound of Beavis and Butthead met his ears. He spotted Mazzy's tent and realized that the brain dead laughter was not emanating from a portable DVD player, but was instead coming from two punk kids entering her tent.

"What the hell are you doing?" he demanded. "Who are you?"

The two juvenile delinquents froze as Alan came charging up behind them.

"I said what the hell do you think you're doing?"

Alan towered the boys by a good foot, and when they turned slowly to meet his angry stare, their bloodshot eyes widened with fright. They couldn't have been more than fifteen years old.

"Um, uh…" they stuttered in confusion. "We were just, uh, looking for food, man."

"Let me guess… the munchies set in?" Alan said with disgust. The two resumed their imbecile-like laughter as affirmation. "Get the fuck out of here. Don't let me find you anywhere near this tent again," he said threateningly.

"All right, man. It's cool… it's cool." They turned and sulked off towards the path back to the parking lot.

Alan stuck his head in the tent and saw Mazzy's faded sleeping bag and mini ice chest filled to capacity with bottled water and turkey sandwiches. He checked the fire pit and found no signs of a recent fire. *She must have just arrived this afternoon.*

"Mazzy!" he called out, but there was no response.

He knew where she had to be, and come hell or high water, he was going to find her and tell her she was crazy for coming out by herself in the middle of December. To hell with independence and women's lib, he thought to himself, as he jogged up the trail toward Cold Water Lake.

Less than a mile away, Mazzy swayed and stumbled over a gnarled tree root. She hit the ground hard and sent her backpack flying into the nearest tree. The pressure in her head was mounting and the increasing dizziness kept her slumped on the ground, unable to stand. Gripped with the fear of being unable to make it back to camp and find help, she began to weep.

What if no one found her? Was this some kind of karma payback? Was she a worthless person? Maybe that's why her father never cared to know her. Perhaps her mother had even known at the tender age of two that her daughter was destined to be a horrible human being.

Random illogical self-loathing mixed in her spinning mind with growing hopelessness and despair. She closed her eyes and wrapped her arms around herself tightly in an attempt to soothe herself and prevent herself from simply falling apart.

A warm wet tongue licked her face. She opened her eyes and saw Scrappy Doo, panting and staring at her with a sad, pleading look on his furry face. He nudged her arm and started to whine.

"What do you want from me?" she cried. "I can't take care of you! I can't help you… just go away! Please, just go away," she begged, but the dog remained. He curled up at her feet but she didn't have the strength to shoo him away.

Her hysterical sobs soon became uncontrollable and she began to hyperventilate. Shadows crept into her peripheral vision until there only remained a faint light at the end of a long dark tunnel. She thought she felt herself slipping away, ceasing to exist, until all that remained was a voice, Alan's voice, telling her to hold on and that he loved her, as the light flickered out and she fainted, unbeknownst to her, into his arms.

Lucy stared at her typewriter. She was too old to learn how to navigate a computer, and her handwriting left something to be desired. A CSI technician would be put to the test to decipher her chicken-scratch. As technology marched brazenly forward and she remained stubbornly dedicated to her ancient Smith Corona, parts and ribbon were becoming increasingly difficult to obtain. The only typewriter repair shop within a fifty-mile radius had closed its doors last spring, and she feared she would eventually have to resort to Morse code.

She sipped the last of her Merlot and proceeded, unaware that miles away her granddaughter was being rushed to the emergency room.

Dear Mazzy,

First of all, let me apologize, not only for leaving you in the parking lot, but also for not telling you what you needed to hear. You threw this old woman for a loop, and I didn't handle it well at all. I don't blame you for not answering your phone when I called.

Let me also apologize for lying. While it wasn't technically a lie, it was still a Clinton fib nonetheless. I don't know a woman named Kelly Judd, but I do know a man by that name. He was your mother's friend.

But I'm getting ahead of myself. (I'm not a natural writer like your Aunt Shelly.)

Please know this: I kept my fool mouth shut not to hurt you (or your mother), but to protect you, to shield you. I suppose if the path to hell really is paved with good intentions, I'll be first in line for a nonstop first-class trip to see that spade-tailed bastard. You have a lot of questions about who you are, who your mother was and where you both came from. I will answer them all.

Let me start by telling you what I think you need to hear most.

The day you were born was the happiest day of your mother's life…

Kennedy

Kennedy realized that she didn't believe in the Bible the day her daughter, Mazzy, was born. One look at her perfectly rounded head and peach-fuzzed body confirmed it. WE ARE ALL BORN SINNERS, IMPERFECT. That was a lie and she had the proof swaddled in her own tattered yellow receiving blanket. Just let any one of those Bible thumpers from Narcotics Anonymous try and tell her otherwise!

The concept that everyone was signed up for the Tainted Sinner's Club from birth had never given her a sense of solace back when she was pouring sweat and diarrhea on the detox unit of United Recovery Rehab. Although, the thought that she, Kennedy Dawson, could be on the same mortally defective level as Julia Roberts or even the saintly Marcia Brady was a comical one.

In one of her more hallucinatory moments of detoxification (or had she just been dreaming?) she actually *was* Marcia Brady. All of the members of her high school football team were gathered around her hospital bed watching her cook with a silver baby spoon and a Zippo lighter saying, "Groovy!" and "That looks swell!" A familiar tune drifted through the window, and she looked up just in time to see Davy Jones climb through it, humming "Daydream Believer." Wearing a pair of hip hugger bellbottoms and looking dreamy, he floated to her bed and ceremoniously handed her a syringe like a sacrificial offering. "I'm the president of your fan club!" she told him proudly. Just when she had her pink tourniquet ready for action, her sister, Jan, who looked suspiciously like the unit charge nurse, burst into the room crying, "Marcia, Marcia, *Marcia!*"

It hadn't been easy getting into United Recovery. There had been a two-month waiting list for the ten-day detox program, and they didn't accept pregnant women for liability reasons. By the time Susan, the admissions counselor, had called her with the good news that she could come in the next morning, she was over four months pregnant with Mazzy and barely beginning to show. She easily hid this from everyone (except a select few friends) with extra large sweatshirts and leggings.

The night before, Kennedy had stayed at her mom's house in the spare room under her aging yet watchful eye. Her mother, Lucy, was in her forties and not wearing it well. Years of struggling as a single mom trying to overcompensate for the lack of a father had taken their toll.

"It's a good thing you're doing for yourself, sweetheart. You deserve to be healthy, and I'm proud of you for going through with this."

Little did her mom know that Kennedy would never get off the shit for herself, or to make her mother proud. It was all for the baby growing inside her, the tiny light she could feel struggling to survive, swimming upstream against the steady current of heroin. Though she had yet to see her face or caress her tiny feet, Kennedy was willing to go through months of agony to ensure her safe passage into the world. Aside from being the *right thing to do*, which she had never really been concerned with before, she wasn't sure why.

The next morning they both sat in the windowless admissions office with the intake counselor. Kennedy counted the wood panels on the wall while Lucy told the counselor that Kennedy had been a good girl, but had gone bad when she started dating that bastard boyfriend of hers. *Gone bad.* Like an egg that had cracked on the way home from the grocery store and then sat in the refrigerator for too long, emanating a rotten smell from the back of the otherwise clean Maytag. As she sat next to her weeping mother, feeling the dwindling effects from her 'farewell' hit she had sneaked in the bathroom earlier that morning, she envisioned herself in the shape of a large egg with a maze of oozing cracks all over her body/shell. Kennedy Dumpty sat on a wall. Kennedy Dumpty had a great fall. All good intentions from family and friends couldn't put Kennedy together again. Ha ha.

When it was time to go, she practically had to peel her mother off of her. Ten hugs and twenty be-a-good-girls later, she was marched into the bathroom to hurdle her next obstacle: the mandatory urine test to determine your fertility status. She had heard that during admissions a nurse actually stands in the bathroom with you while you pee, making it difficult, but not impossible, to smuggle in contraband urine. Kennedy had her friend Tracy pee in a small plastic tube before she went to her mom's house the night before and carefully inserted it with K-Y jelly up her rectum. Everyone thought she was walking funny from withdrawals. Luckily, the nurse assigned to watch over her was young and easily embarrassed, making the switch relatively easy. While Nurse Bonnie was making idle chit chat and staring at a fascinating crack in the ceiling, Kennedy reached down, carefully pulled the tube out of her butt, popped the top and poured the contents into the regulation specimen jar. The difficult part was reinserting the tube.

Susan relieved the blushing Nurse Bonnie and led Kennedy to her cluttered office, gesturing for her to take a seat.

"Right then. I just need to ask you a few questions about your history and drug use."

Susan clucked her tongue and began to scan the avalanche of paperwork on top of her desk. "Ah, here we are!" She grabbed a questionnaire from the bottom of the pile and pulled a pen out of the tangle of red curls pulled

behind her ears. Kennedy wondered what else she might have hiding in
her hair.

"All right then. What is your full name?"

"Kennedy Dawson."

"Your *full* name dear."

"Still, Kennedy Dawson."

Susan looked at her quizzically.

"No middle name?"

"No."

"Hmm. Okay then. Your date of birth?"

"August 28, 1964."

"When is the last time you used?" Kennedy froze. She found it hard
to meet Susan's eyes.

"Uh, last week sometime."

"Okay," the counselor said slowly, "What did you use?"

"Heroin," Kennedy mumbled.

"Is that your drug of choice?"

"Oh, I guess."

"How often do you use heroin?"

"Not a lot."

"How often is not a lot?"

"Um… once, maybe twice a week."

Susan set her pen down.

"Look, we can't help you if you're not honest. No one is here to judge
you or make you feel bad." With that said, she picked up her pen again.

"Now, how often do you use heroin?"

"Every day. I use every day, okay?"

Susan spent the next thirty minutes asking her questions ranging from
her parents mental history to how many guys she'd ever fucked and what
protection she'd used if any. It was humiliating.

Next came the inspection for contraband items. Susan unzipped
Kennedy's prehistoric Samsonite and then proceeded to take out every
piece of clothing, makeup and toiletry item contained, palpating each
one with a latexed finger and a suspicious eye. Kennedy's large silver and
turquoise bracelet was deemed a potential weapon. The Raider's t-shirt
she usually slept in and the red bandana she used as a headband were
considered gang-affiliated clothing. These things were confiscated and
put in a bag labeled with her name to be given back at discharge. Susan
then handed her a hospital gown and slippers.

"What's this for?"

"Everyone wears them when they're admitted, dear. You can go change in the bathroom."

"But what about my stuff?" Kennedy asked in disbelief.

"You'll get them back in a few days."

Kennedy sulked into the bathroom and exchanged her fuzzy pink sweatshirt and warm leggings for a dingy hospital gown. It was bad enough watching someone finger her things as if they were biohazardous waste, but having to discard her comforting clothes for a sterile hospital gown made her feel diseased.

"All changed? Right then, on to the detox unit."

By the time she had finished with the intake process, taken the hour-long grand tour (which consisted mainly of lengthy rules and regulations), and settled into her drab room with her comatose roommate, the first withdrawals began to seep into her bones. By the time the med nurse showed up with a Dixie cup filled with pills, she was curled up in the fetal position on her bed praying that the sharp pains in her stomach were indeed the ever-dreaded diarrhea and not the baby in distress. She downed them gratefully and didn't even ask what she was taking.

How the hell did I get here? She wondered. But hers wasn't a unique or even interesting journey into heroin. What started out as casual weekend partying in high school – an all-night drinking binge here, a few joints there – evolved into experimentation during her first year of college with her boyfriend Bob – pot to chill out, coke to liven up for exams. Heroin was the last frontier that had to be explored as Kennedy and Bob aspired to become the Lewis and Clark of the pharmacological world.

Six months and hundreds of expeditions later, she was hooked. She wasn't homeless or ripping off liquor stores (yet). She was still in school (though close to flunking out). She still had her job at Sears (but had been written up multiple times for absences and was on the manager's shit list). She was nowhere near the notorious Rock Bottom, but she was definitely starting the denial-bound descent.

Until pink. Not a pink slip or even a pink elephant with wings floating in front of her hazy eyes singing "One Hundred Bottles of Beer on the Wall." No, nothing that surreal. It was much simpler.

It was one thin pink line.

"I thought you were on the pill," Bob had said.

"I am. I must have missed one." The plastic wand with the pink line in the easy-to-read window verified that understatement.

"Oh that's just great. Fuck! Where are we going to get the money for an abortion? I still owe Benny a wad for that last score." That same score was gone, and its absence was turning Bob into a grouchy prick. Kennedy had slammed the last of it that morning after discovering she was pregnant while Bob was at his lit class.

"Well I'm not paying for the whole thing. You're the dumb ass who missed a fucking pill."

Bob had been losing more and more of his charm over the past month or so, and as she studied the vein bulging out on his forehead, it occurred to her that his looks were slipping a bit, too. His tan skin had turned sallow, and he had dark circles under his eyes.

"Well, I wouldn't have missed the God damn thing if Benny would have shown up on time at the park that one night. I was out there in the cold for two hours waiting for the fucker. Then I had to stay up all night cramming for that trig midterm, and I was exhausted! I didn't remember my fucking name more or less the God damn pill!"

"Let's not get into it about that again. Look, I'm sorry I yelled. I guess I'm freaked out, that's all. Let's just make the arrangements and get this over with. I can always hit up my folks for school supply money again." He walked over to where she was flopped on the couch and knelt in front of her, burying his head in her lap. She played with his blonde curls and wondered what he would look like bald.

"They must think you eat erasers and wipe your butt with notebook paper by now."

Bob laughed. He grabbed her hands and kissed the tips of her fingers, then went in the bedroom to call his folks, for the umpteenth time, with a song and dance. Two weeks and one money-gram later, Kennedy was on her back in Dr. Meade's office confused and scared out of her mind. *This is just a procedure. Yes, a procedure to take care of a problem, that's all.* The nurse took something that looked like a vibrator and inserted it in the place that got her into this whole mess to begin with.

"Just relax, dear, it's an ultrasound. We just need to make sure that you're not farther along than you think you are." The nurse was looking at a monitor that was angled away from Kennedy when an overwhelming itch on her left calf attacked. She knew she was supposed to lie still, but the urge to scratch the hell out of her leg consumed her. She half sat up, turned to the nurse and said, "I'm sorry, but I have an itch...," and that's when she saw the monitor. It was pulsing, rhythmically, in a beat. A *heart beat.* A little white light on the screen. Kennedy gasped.

"Is... is that my baby?" Until then the baby was just a concept, a problem that had to be taken care of. But now, it was a light. A beacon, streaming out to her in the dark sea of her mind, sending an S.O.S. for help.

The nurse pulled the vibrator apparatus out and gently pushed Kennedy back down on the table.

"You just try and relax, and I will go get the doctor now."

But when the doctor walked into the room five minutes later, all that remained of Kennedy Dawson was the paper sheet she had been lying on and a hastily discarded hospital gown.

"Are you crazy?! Not only did you leave, you didn't even get back the $300?" Bob was pissed. He had just finished a robust line of coke, which wasn't helping his mood. White powder was caked to the inside of his left nostril which was flaring in anger.

"I couldn't do it. I saw her, Bob. I saw her little heart beating. I just kept hearing a voice in my head saying, 'Run! Run!' So I did."

"You are marching your ass right back down there as soon as I call and reschedule. You are not going to ruin my life with your emotional woman crap, Kennedy! My parents would shit a brick." There was that vein again on his forehead. Bulging, threatening to burst.

"What do your parents have to do with this?"

"Well, let's face it. They pay most of the bills here. You think they'll keep floating me checks and paying for school when I bring home a baby that's black?"

"Oh, but getting a piece of ass that's half black is fine as long as Mommy and Daddy don't know? That's why you didn't want them to come out and visit last summer, isn't it? You didn't want them to see me?!" Kennedy was sick to her stomach with the realization.

"Think what you want. I don't want a baby right now, black, white or otherwise."

It was so simple then. No struggling with decisions, no heart-pull of emotions. She stood up, walked to their bedroom and started packing her clothes. Bob was infuriated that she wouldn't answer him, wouldn't even look his direction. She finished packing all the essentials, then turned to him and said, "Good-bye, Bob," and walked toward the door. He jumped in front of her and shoved her backwards, hard, sending her bags across the floor and her rudely on her ass. He towered above her, screaming down a hail of anger and spit into her face.

"You WILL listen to me, you fucking toe rag! Who do you think you are making - OUFF!" It was a cross between an ouch and the sound you would make if all of the air was sucked out of your chest. She was pretty sure that after lodging the tip of her boot in Bob's crotch, he wouldn't be impregnating anyone else for a while. He toppled over to a quivering heap of sobs on the floor. Kennedy picked up her bags and walked calmly out the front door. She never saw him again.

Sitting on the toilet in detox, she couldn't believe that her stomach had anything left to evacuate. Just when she thought she had nothing left to give the porcelain alter, her body would offer up another sacrifice. Her rectal sphincter was so sore that it felt like someone rammed a hot poker up her ass.

Knock, knock. "Are you going to be in the can all day?" Aah, the comatose roommate lives.

"I'll be out as soon as I can." *Soon as I can, get it? I'm in the can and...*

"Fuck, never mind." Kennedy heard whispering outside the bathroom door followed by retreating footsteps.

Twenty minutes and half a roll of toilet paper later, Kennedy emerged to find not only her roommate gone, but also twenty dollars from her purse. She marched up to the nurse's station - or so she thought, but she was so sore that it actually looked more like an indignant waddle - and lodged a complaint with the shift charge nurse.

"Someone, I think it was my roommate, stole twenty dollars out of my purse!"

Nurse Vivian, a heavy black woman with a Jamaican accent that Kennedy was pretty sure was a fake, was writing in a chart. Without even looking up from her work, she said, "That's impossible."

"It's not just possible, it's probable. I had twenty dollars in my purse before I went to the bathroom and now I don't. Seems pretty fucking possible to me!"

She finished what she was writing, closed the file, put the cap back on her pin and stood up to look Kennedy in the eyes. "No darlin, it's not. Ya see, ya signed a paper stating that ya agreed to all da rules, including da rule about no money allowed on da unit. If ya had money to be stolen, you'd be breaking da rules, wouldncha?"

It was hard to argue with logic like that.

With that settled, Nurse Vivian grabbed the intercom mike and screeched, "SMOKE BREAK!" over the loud speaker, then went to the hall closet to get the cigarette cart. Kennedy wasn't a smoker, but she could sure use a break. She decided to go out on the patio with the others and get some fresh air to calm her down. *Now where was the patio again?* She was finding that she should have paid closer attention to that tour of the unit and its multiple rules.

She didn't have to wait long. The hallway turned into a scene from "Night of the Living Dead." Pale, sweaty, hospital-gown-sporting zombies poured out of their rooms and flowed down the hall, beckoned by the call of the cigarette. They were joined by fully dressed, agitated, dried-out vampires who were thirsty for something more than nicotine. Kennedy followed their general direction of migration and the strong stench of ashtrays.

At the end of the hall, the monster mash procession turned left and then came to a halt. Everyone was standing in a long line in front of a med-cart which contained each patient's smokes. Nurse Vivian had the honor of dispensing them, one at a time, to each patient, then igniting them with the unit lighter that was kept under lock and key. Kennedy was making her way past the line toward the open doors to the patio when a rough hand reached out and grabbed her.

"Wait your turn, bitch!" a short muscled man in a white-wife beater tank top spat at her.

"Yeah, back of the line!" her klepto roommate chimed in. She had yellow skin and tar-stained teeth to match. Kennedy wanted to kick her head in for taking her money, but she wasn't a stupid girl. She knew that being a green-eyed, light-skinned malatto in a sea of hard Latina's and robust ghetto hood rats put her into a position of having no allies but plenty of enemies while this jaundiced chica had back-up, including the man, named Rico, who had just spat in her face. He currently had his hand placed possessively on the roommate's huge ass.

"I don't smoke. I'm just going out on the patio, so back off and keep your fucking hands off me!" Can't appear to be a total wimp either. She jerked her shoulder away from the wetback pimp and marched through the hazy corridor and through the doors to sunlight. Kennedy found an empty chair in the far corner before anyone could stake a claim on it. She was hoping to get a little fresh air, but all she could smell were the cigarette ghosts of addicts past and present. She closed her eyes and tilted her weary head toward the sun, trying to catch a few rays. *Aah, to be at the beach right now instead of here with these scum bags.* Her face suddenly turned cold. A cloud passing in front of the sun maybe? She opened her eyes. Nope, just Jaundiced Chica's huge ass staring her directly in the face. What a surprise that it was big enough to block out the sun.

The small patio was packed, with standing room only. From her viewpoint on the dilapidated chair it was a sea of elbows and assholes. *Tsunami warning! Red alert!* Uh oh, time to go.

As Kennedy tried to pull herself up off the chair, a dizzy spell hit her full force and she fell forward into that mass of cellulite, face first. Chica shrieked and Kennedy staggered to the side, falling into the chain link fence that circled the perimeter of the patio. As she tried to steady herself a tidal wave of nausea hit. In a flash the roommate was in her face yelling at Kennedy.

"What are you, a fucking dyke? You stupid bitch! I'm gonna kick your ass, you..." and on and on she ranted. The zombies and the vampires, startled out of their trances, all crowded around to see what the commotion was. In true schoolyard fashion, people started shouting "Fight! Fight!" and "Kick her ass!" Chica, egged on by crowd support, started to shove Kennedy into the fence, making the nausea worse. The loud noises and the stench of smoke and body odor combined with the heat and that fat angry face spewing hatred at her was more than she could take.

"Gonna... be... sick," was all she could manage as a warning. A stream of projectile vomit came shooting out of Kennedy and hit the chica directly in her screaming cavernous mouth. It shot up her nose, covered her face and splattered her yellow T - shirt.

Then there was silence, a deafening silence that stretched on for days. The clock stopped ticking, the birds stopped singing and the smokers stopped smoking while Kennedy and the roommate stood toe to toe, staring at each other in wide-eyed disbelief.

"What's going on out here? What's all da shouting about? Who..." Nurse Vivian spotted the epicenter of the quake and made a beeline for the two frozen women. Immediately assessing who spewed whom and the odds of her making it out of the courtyard alive, Vivian grabbed Kennedy by the shoulders and led her quickly back toward the unit. The abrupt movement broke the spell that had been over the crowd, and they all began to howl in laughter. Jaundiced Chica, whose name was Estella, looked around in horror. The same people who had been cheering her on two minutes earlier were now pointing at her and having a good hearty laugh at her expense. She even spotted Rico, who had slipped away immediately after she had been defiled. He was at the far corner with a smirk on his face and his hand on another girl's ass.

"What the fuck are you assholes laughing at, huh?! Get the fuck out of my way!" Estella had no problem clearing a path to the door since everyone was keeping a good five feet away from her stinky self.

Kennedy was cleaning herself up in her bathroom with the help of Nurse Vivian. She was weak and terrified and desperately wanted to go home and snuggle up to a movie and a long needle. The urge to use was *painful*. She didn't truly realize how badly she needed it until she couldn't have it, until it just wasn't an option anymore (or was it?). Over the past few months, she had stopped using to celebrate a holiday or a friend's promotion, but instead started using when she flunked a test at school or got reamed out at work for being late on a daily basis. Or when she found out she was pregnant.

The baby. Oh please let the baby be okay. She started to weep.

"There, there girl. You all cleaned up now," Vivian soothed, wiping the last curdled chunk of puke from Kennedy's nose. "No need to cry. Ya good to go now."

"I want to go home, Vivian. I just don't belong here with these people. I need to go home. I'm not like them. I'm not some gang-banger. I go to college!"

"These people? Ya want to use is what ya want, girl. And so do these people here. Ya have that in common with them. Ya think you better cause ya go to school? Ya'd ram a needle up your arm just as quick as Estella. Don't kid yourself. Now go get your things. I think it would be wise to put ya in another room."

Vivian set about picking the soiled towels for the laundry while Kennedy walked to the closet to collect her things. She was bending over to collect her shoes when Estella stabbed her from behind. Kennedy felt a sharp pain in her right butt cheek and then heard Estella shriek as Vivian tackled her to the floor.

"Dr. Strong! Dr. Strong!" Vivian shouted, which must have been staff code for help because within seconds the room was swarming with nurses and counselors. The last thing Kennedy saw before she fainted was blood trickling down her leg into her slipper.

"Wake up. Wake up, girl."

She opened her eyes to find the sympathetic face of Nurse Vivian staring down at her. She was in an examination room lying on her side.

"Ya fainted and were out for a bit. You okay now."

"What happened?" She tried to roll over but Vivian stopped her.

"Ya don't want to do that. Ya have a nasty wound on your rear from Estella. Lucky for you though her aim was bad and all she had was a fork from the dining room. Ya have a couple stitches, nothin' major." Kennedy could feel the painful throbbing in her ass now.

"Where is she? Where is Estella?"

"She on her way to jail now. You'll have to make a report with the police later."

"Jesus." She cradled her stomach and closed her eyes. Thank God she had been bending over and not facing the other way.

Nurse Vivian stared at her, unblinking. "Ya want someting for da pain? Ya still allowed meds for the next three days, ya know."

She knows. Vivian knows about the baby and she isn't saying anything.

"Sure."

Without hesitation Vivian got up and walked out of the room. Two minutes later, she returned with a pill in one hand and a Dixie cup of water in the other and handed them to Kennedy.

"Thank you." She popped it in her mouth and drank the water.

"I'll leave ya to rest now." Vivian walked out of the room and closed the door behind her. Kennedy spat the pill into her palm and then shoved it under the mattress. She had maneuvered it in the empty space in the back of her mouth where one of her molars used to be.

No more meds. Not even a Tylenol while her baby was inside her.

On day five of her stay at United Recovery, Kennedy awoke to find her suitcase at the end of her bed. *Finally, my own clothes.* She never could understand why patients had to wear drafty hospital gowns for the first four days of their stay. She was grateful to have her personal belongings back, though, and she gingerly rolled off the bed to get her suitcase, mindful of the two stitches that still smarted her ass. She carefully pulled on black leggings and a maroon off-the-shoulder sweatshirt and walked over to the window, feeling a bit more like herself again. Her muscles still ached, but at least the diarrhea and stomach cramps had stopped, allowing her to walk like a homo-erectus again. She drew back the heavy orange curtains and peered down below.

The detox unit was on the top floor of one wing of United Recovery. The rest of the facility was a ninety day residential rehab. It was an odd setup: three buildings set like a horseshoe around a square courtyard with a pool in the middle. Kennedy could see a few rehab residents tanning on lounge chairs while others splashed around in the blue water, laughing and tossing a beach ball like they were at a hotel on vacation.

It turned out that the facility actually had been a hotel about a dozen years earlier. One of the counselors had told Kennedy that in 1971 United Recovery had indeed been a happening hot spot that catered to big shots in the movie industry looking for a good time and a bit of discretion. This would explain the horrid wood paneling and heavy velour drapes in all of the patient's rooms that reminded Kennedy of bad '70s porn. In the early '80s, low-income housing and a new welfare office sprang up in the neighborhood, driving the movie moguls to the more glamorous surroundings of Palm Springs and leaving the hotel to be overrun by $10 crack whores and Raul, the local drug-pushing pimp. In 1982, a hair-products guru bought the hotel and turned it into United Recovery in honor of his beloved son, Chase. According to the well-orchestrated press release, "Chase's brief experimentation with drugs resulted in a tragic accidental overdose," - sorrowful pause while bereaved father wipes a tear from his eye - "So, in his memory, I dedicate the new United Recovery Rehab so that other naive souls like my son can choose a different path."

In reality, his beloved son had been a thorn in his ass for years. Back before it was chic to say "My son is gay. Yes, I love and support my gay son!" Chase's flamboyant exploits and drug abuse had put Daddy's PR people in spin-control overdrive. Rumor had it that Chase was up to his eyeballs in debt to Raul and was a regular at the hotel. When he was found facedown with both kneecaps broken, bleeding from the rectum in the same pool that Kennedy was gazing at now, it came as no surprise to anyone, least of all his father. In one last PR bonanza, he greased the palms of the local authorities who had been on the scene and bought the hotel, promising continuous fat donations to keep it up and running as a rehab, providing job opportunities to the local community.

Say no to drugs but yes to my new line of hair gel, Kennedy thought to herself as she left her room and strolled down the hall toward her morning group.

"Ya missed breakfast, girl," said the unmistakable voice of Nurse Vivian from behind Kennedy. She turned around to find her holding an apple in one hand and a carton of milk in the other.

"Morning, Vivian. Yeah, I'm not hungry. Thanks, though."

"Dontcha think ya need to eat?" She eyed Kennedy's stomach. "Dontcha think ya need da vitamins?" Without waiting for a reply, she thrust the milk and apple in Kennedy's hands and walked away.

"Uh, thanks," she muttered guiltily before scurrying off to the group room.

Carlos, a unit counselor, had already started his sermon. Kennedy quietly slipped into a seat at the back, trying to draw as little attention to herself as possible. She surveyed the room of primarily Hispanic males covered in tattoos, one scrawny white man who she predicted wouldn't last two days, two dark African American women just daring Kennedy to look sideways at them, a young Latina and an Asian woman who constantly mumbled incoherently to herself while rocking back and forth in her chair. *What a motley looking crew.*

"If your homeboys are using Rico, how do you think they're going to support your recovery, man?" Carlos was a recovering heroin addict who, with the help of God and Bill W., had been clean for ten years. His previous affiliation with a notorious Riverside gang gave him credibility with most of the patients at United Recover.

Rico apparently wasn't one of them.

"That's bullshit, man. My homeboys got my back. You sound like my fucking P.O., man." Rico replied, sitting in the front row next to the petite Latina who had the biggest hair Kennedy had ever seen. "My boys are me familia."

Parole officers. Me familia. *Screw this.* Kennedy slipped out as quietly as she came in.

Out in the hall, she could hear rebellious moaning coming from the cafeteria at the other end of the unit. She sneaked past the nurse's station, munching on her apple and keeping a watchful eye out for Vivian, leery of yet another lecture on the benefits of gang-banger junkie rap sessions. As she neared the cafeteria, she could hear a man butchering the hell out of one of her favorite rock songs. She peered in the doorway and saw the unit's abused radio sitting on a table near an open window. It had graffiti all over it, proclaiming that someone named Renee had indeed been here. Its rusted antenna was bent in two places and leaning back, threatening to finally just give up and topple out the window, leaving the fine listeners to fend for themselves in a sea of A. M. radio.

A young man was sitting in a wheel chair next to the blaring Panasonic transistor of the damned, howling along with the song and tossing his dark wavy hair back and forth to the beat. He had a strong, square jaw with broad shoulders to match and forearms like Popeye the Sailor.

Nurse Bonnie hurried past Kennedy, almost knocking her over, and into the cafeteria looking quite flustered.

"Here you are! You said you'd be right back!" she chastised him like a child. "You were supposed to take these meds a half-hour ago. Honestly, Kelly, you're going to get me into trouble!" She stood next to him with one manicured hand on her hip and the other holding a small paper cup full of pills.

Kelly deftly maneuvered his wheelchair around to face her while belting out one of the songs more sexually explicit lyrics. Nurse Bonnie turned crimson and looked like she would faint. The scene reminded Kennedy of a cartoon she once saw where a male robin was serenading a group of twitterpated girl sparrows screaming, "Frankie!" They all giggled hysterically with pink and red hearts floating above their heads before rolling their eyes back in their sockets and keeling over. Kennedy could practically see the same animated hearts bobbing around Bonnie's blonde head as she handed Kelly his pills.

"What, no water?" he asked coyly. "You wouldn't want me to choke, now, would you, Bonners?"

"Oh, no, I'm sorry. I'll get you some." She poured the pills into his hand and trotted over to the sink. She ran the tap while he ran his eyes up and down her backside. When he was finished with his appraisal, he spotted Kennedy lurking in the doorway and gave her a wink. She gave him the bird in return.

"Here you go. Drink up," Bonnie said, leaning over more than was necessary and handing him his water. He took each pill, one at a time, and passed them slowly between his full lips, then threw back the water like a tequila shooter. After smacking his lips he opened his mouth wide and fluttered his tongue to show he had swallowed all of his pills like a good boy.

"Thanks, Bonners. You're an angel."

"No problem. Do you need anything else?" she asked eagerly, like a Golden Retriever ready to please. "Are you okay?"

"All the better for seeing your sweet face," he said, grabbing her hand and giving it a squeeze. Bonnie smiled shyly and strolled toward the door. Upon spotting Kennedy, she looked at her as if only seeing her for the first time.

"What are you doing there? Shouldn't you be in group?"

"Shouldn't he be in group?" Kennedy countered.

"You need to stop worrying about other people's recovery and work your own program," she said, turning Kennedy around and marching her back down the corridor. "Come on. I'll walk with you." She could smell perfume lingering on Bonnie's uniform. That new one from Liz Taylor perhaps.

"Who is that guy?"

"Who, Kelly? He's a new patient. Came in yesterday," Bonnie emitted a slow sympathetic sigh. "Poor thing."

"Why poor thing?" Kennedy could hear him belting out the Doors now behind them in the cafeteria.

"Didn't you notice he's in a wheelchair? What a waste," Bonnie lamented.

"A waste? A waste of what? A waste of a perfectly good junkie or a waste of a perfectly good-looking bachelor?" she replied. Bonnie stopped dead in her tracks.

"Group, Kennedy! Now!" Bonnie commanded before storming off to the nurse's station.

One of Kennedy's less endearing gifts was her natural ability to strike a nerve in others, usually with as little tact as possible, hitting so close to home that people felt as if they had just been caught naked in their office doing the cancan and singing "Come to the Cabaret." Not out of spite or for the mere sport of it, mind you. She wasn't a cruel person. But what other people considered playing ignorant for the sake of politeness – "Why no Mary, you don't look fat in horizontal stripes at all!" - Kennedy considered fraudulent. In most situations that called for false social graces, silence was as nice as she could get, but this place with its arbitrary rules was pissing her off and she could feel what little grace she might have on reserve dwindling.

Group was now over. Patients were walking into the hall and anxiously eyeing the clock in the nurse's station, impatiently awaiting Nurse Vivian's booming announcement for smoke break. God forbid the staff call it 30 seconds past the scheduled time... people would be pounding their hands on the counter in protest. Kennedy could never understand the draw to smoking. Possibility of cancer and you don't even get high? Screw that.

Kennedy felt something bump into her leg. She turned around to find Kelly's cocky face smiling up at her.

"Pardon me, miss."

"What do *you* want?"

"Just trying to get by."

She knew damn well he was no novice at maneuvering that thing and could go around her. Hell, he could probably pop wheelies with it.

"So go around."

She wouldn't budge. She hated guys like him, cocky bastard, wheelchair or not. He was that kid in sixth grade that could get away with talking in class and the teacher would say, "Now Johnny, save that for recess," but give you a detention for the same thing. In high school, he would charm the pants off you (literally) one Saturday night when his date was home sick and then just throw you sly winks the rest of the school year. He was also that jerk in the bar who would refer to the women as "talent" as in "Not much talent here", or if the bar was crawling with big tits in mini skirts "My, the talent level is high in here tonight!" But what she hated even more were the stupid twits like Bonnie who fell all over themselves like little girls when they graced them with five seconds of their attention. Disgusting.

"Damn bitch, why can't you just move yo ass?" inquired one of the black girls that had been giving her death glares earlier during group. "Yeah," chimed her friend, "you think you own this fucking hallway?" The two had been standing a few feet away from Kennedy, bored and looking for some shit to stir.

"Ladies, ladies. I was just giving her a hard time," Kelly said smoothly, not giving Kennedy a chance to smart off and get her ass beat ten ways till Tuesday. "Although I must admit, I'm flattered you fine young women would come to my rescue like that. How about escorting me out for a smoke?"

"Yeah, aight sugar." The two of them gruffly shouldered past Kennedy and walked on either side of Kelly down the hall just as Bonnie was shouting "Smoke Break!" over the loud speaker.

"Kennedy, may I see you for a minute, please?" Carol, another unit counselor, inquired.

"Sure, why not?" Kennedy followed her to her tiny office that looked like a converted janitor's closet. At five feet tall with heels on, Kennedy supposed she didn't need much space anyway. There was just enough room for a small metal desk, a narrow bookshelf and an extra chair. The walls were screaming with twelve step cliché posters: Easy does it! One day at a time! She even had a special glass case mounted above her desk with years' worth of sobriety chips. This woman ate, shit and slept recovery. Kennedy wondered what Carol would have done for a living if she hadn't been an addict.

"I notice you haven't been coming to groups. Groups are part of the recovery process here, Kennedy. You have to work your program."

"So everyone keeps telling me." Kennedy spotted a framed picture of a little boy no older than five or six years old on top of the bookshelf. He had Carol's dark curly hair and almond-shaped eyes.

"Why are you here?" Carol asked pointedly.

"To enjoy the ambiance. Why do you think I'm here?" Kennedy countered.

"I honestly don't know," Carol said thoughtfully.

"To get off drugs, obviously."

"And what have you done to achieve that besides not use?"

"What?"

"There is a difference between being sober and in recovery and 'just not using.' Ever heard of a dry drunk? Recovery is a lifelong process that takes hard work and brutally honest introspection."

"Whatever." Kennedy cast a bored eye at the ceiling. Carol sighed.

"Well, maybe you aren't ready. Maybe you haven't lost enough in your life yet."

"You think you know everything just because you have a bunch of stupid chips in your case? You don't fucking know me," Kennedy spat defiantly. "Let me ask *you* a question. What the hell did *you* lose that makes you such a damn expert at loss-inspired motivation?" She jumped out of her seat before Carol could reply. "On second thought, scratch that. I don't give a shit about hearing your sob story. Save it for your gangster groupies." Kennedy stormed out the door into the hall almost colliding with Kelly in the process.

"Easy, edgy. Slow down," he chided.

"Aren't you supposed to be smoking, asshole?" She brushed past him and headed down the hall toward the cafeteria.

"My, my! So much hostility for such a young lady!" He followed on her heels.

"Jesus H. Christ. Isn't there someone else you can go bug?" Flustered and not paying attention to where she was going, Kennedy ran right into the corner of a dining room table with her hip. She cursed in pain and took a seat near the window. *I have to pay attention…that could have been my stomach instead of my hip.* She lightly rubbed her stomach absentmindedly for the briefest moment.

"Ah, the rabbit done died," Kelly said knowingly as he wheeled himself up next to her.

"What did you say?"

"The rabbit done died." Kelly looked at her stomach. Kennedy froze. *How could he know that? There is no way he could know that!*

"I don't know what you're talking about," she replied with as much nonchalance as she could muster.

"Maybe not, but did you know that in 1927 it was discovered that by injecting a female rabbit with a human female's urine, you could find out if she was pregnant or not?"

She stared at him with bewilderment.

"Most people think that if the woman is pregnant, the rabbit dies," he continued undeterred. "If she isn't, it lives. When in reality the rabbit always died. Doctors had to cut the rabbit open to check out its ovaries to see the results. I saw this one episode of M*A*S*H where Hot Lips thought she was pregnant. They borrowed Radar's rabbit for the test and instead of killing it and then opening it up, they anesthetized it, looked at the ovaries, and then sewed her back up good as new. So really, they didn't have to kill the rabbits, but who the hell gives a shit about a rabbit?"

"So was she?" Kennedy asked.

"Was who what?"

"Hot Lips. Was she pregnant?"

"Surprisingly, no, even though she was probably screwing the entire surgical team." Kelly gave her a shit eating grin. Kennedy laughed begrudgingly. "You know, you were pretty harsh on poor little Carol."

"Heard that, did you? What, were you just eavesdropping outside the door waiting to trip me and then enthrall me with tales of bunnies and piss?"

"You were yelling at her. I think the entire unit heard you." He pulled his wheelchair up to an abrupt halt next to her. "And, yeah, I was waiting to enthrall you." Kennedy felt like a doe trapped in the headlights of his intense stare. He finally backed away and rolled toward the radio at the other end of the table.

"She lives for this shit, you know. Touching the lives of addicts like us puts the milk in her Cheerios." Kelly popped a quick wheelie. *I knew it.*

"I'm not responsible for being anyone's milk, Cheerios or any other assorted breakfast food. Why do you care anyway?"

"I talked to her for a while yesterday when I got here. You might find you two have a bit in common." He gave her a relaxed smile. *Too relaxed.*

"You know, you look pretty calm, cool and collected for someone who is supposed to be two days into heroin detox. It is heroin, I assume?" She continued on without waiting for a reply, "One would almost think you weren't truly detoxing at all."

Kelly clicked his tongue like a disapproving grandmother as he rolled himself out the cafeteria door, shaking his head with a sly smile.

"Shouldn't you be working your own program and not focusing on others?" he said laughingly without looking back.

Yeah, so I've been told.

The next morning was ushered in with a surprise unit search. Word had gotten out that someone had sneaked a kit onto the unit and all the patients were herded into the cafeteria while the staff combed through every room. Nurse Bonnie was handed the unwanted job of keeping the inmates calm and contained so that no patient could run to their room and flush whatever evidence they were hoping to find down the toilet. Some people were too sick to care and sat with their heads between their knees while others were outraged and indignant that their personal belongings were being ransacked. Rico in particular was incensed at the supposed violation of his rights.

"This is some bullshit, man! They don't have the fucking right to handle my shit! If anything is missing, I'm suing their asses!" Rico ranted, looking directly at Bonnie, who was trying to look stern, but failing miserably.

"I heard dat! I'll bust dem bitches if any of my shit is gone. Me and my home girls," a very large black woman with protruding horse teeth proclaimed. Kennedy wondered what treasured belongings they thought the nurses wanted to steal. Skid-marked boxers with torn crotches or an extra large jar of Vaseline with black hairs stuck in it? Who were these morons kidding?

They had already been confined together for over an hour, and the natives were growing increasingly restless. She stared out the window and tried to block out the incessant bitching and whining that was growing louder every minute they went past the scheduled time for smoke break, but it was impossible. She was feeling antsy and these scumbags were wearing on her last nerve. She spotted Kelly, alone for a change, looking a bit strained himself. No female followers by his side, no charming commentary to entertain the masses. He was in the corner, looking a little pale and staring intently at his feet.

Carol appeared at the door and announced that everyone needed to go back to his or her rooms.

"What about smoke break?" someone asked.

"Please go to your rooms for now, and do not leave until we ask you to. Smoke break will be called soon." Everyone filed out of the cafeteria grumbling about their rights and made their way back to their rooms. Kennedy walked out behind Kelly.

"What, no rabbit stories today?" she called to him. But he didn't reply. He just kept on rolling down the hall.

Kennedy went to her room alone. She still had not been assigned a roommate since Estella had been escorted off to jail, and that was fine with her. At least she had a quiet place to retreat to. She sat on her bed and looked around the room at her few belongings. It didn't look as if anything had been touched during the search, not that there would have been anything interesting to find. She spotted the 'Big Book' that had been given to her at admission lying on the dresser unopened. *Nothing better to do*, she thought and reached for the book. Her hand stopped in midair at the sound of someone screaming in a rage down the hall.

"I'll kill you, mother fucker, when I get out. You're a fucking dead man!"

Kennedy ran to her door and looked down the hall along with every other patient on the unit. Rico was being escorted out in handcuffs by three burly policemen. When they were passing Kelly's room Rico tried to struggle free from the cops and lunge toward his door to no avail.

"You hear me, you gimp mother fucker?! You're a dead man!" They finally dragged him down the hall and out the door, screaming what Kennedy assumed to be obscenities in Spanish. She could hear him all the way out to the parking lot.

"Smoke break!" Nurse Vivian screeched over the loud speaker. There was an impregnated pause, an extended inhalation, then people swarmed into the hall buzzing, as if a beehive had been shaken up and then unleashed.

When you spend days on end bored, agitated and forced to examine your own ugly issues, high drama at someone else's expense is a welcome diversion.

"Why the pigs, man?"

"It was part of his parole. He had to finish the detox or go back to jail."

"They found used needles behind his toilet."

"Maybe that white boy narked him out. Mother fucker."

"Rico had some shit and didn't even kick down? Home boy should have shared." Laughter followed by more ghetto hypothesizing.

Kennedy waited for the swarm to pour out to the smoking patio and wandered the opposite direction to Kelly's room. She peeked inside and saw him lying on his bed, eyes closed with his hands behind his head. Kennedy could detect the faint aroma of vomit emanating from his bathroom.

"Hey," she called in casually. He opened his eyes and looked at her. He was sweating lightly.

"Yeah?"

"What was that about?" she inquired. Kelly managed a laugh, but Kennedy heard no humor in it.

"Still worried about everyone else's business?" he replied dryly.

"Hey, it's no skin off my ass, but the lynch mob down there is saying you narked him out. Not the best way to make friends here."

"Thank you for the unsolicited and unnecessary advice. I'll make note of it." He closed his eyes again. "You know, if that is the mob consensus and you are caught fraternizing with the nark, it would stand to reason that you too will not be making any new friends here." Sure enough, Kennedy looked back down the corridor and spotted a small group of leper nonsmokers congregating near the patio exit with mouths running a mile a minute and suspicious eyes fixed on her.

"I wasn't winning any popularity contests as it was," but Kelly wasn't listening anymore. He had rolled over on his side turning his back to Kennedy, his legs limp and exposed. The back of his hospital gown stuck to his butt with sweat. *He's been here three days and he's just now starting to kick?*

Kennedy heard Carol's voice and turned to see her enter her office. She walked over and knocked on her door.

"Yes?"

"Um, can I come in for a minute?" Kennedy stammered, barely making eye contact with her. Carol crossed her arms and stared at Kennedy, contemplating if she should open herself up for another verbal assault. She was already feeling down in the dumps and feared she might not be able to keep her professionalism intact as she did yesterday. She sensed an apology and bid Kennedy to take a seat.

"What can I do for you?"

"I'm sorry I went off on you. I know it's your job to push me to think about my issues and all that, but I'm not like these people… you know what I mean?" She searched Carol's eyes for recognition but instead found a controlled stare. "I'm like you. I'm educated. I'm not ghetto. Just because I use doesn't mean I'm in a gang or a scumbag. I don't need the same line of bullshit they do. I just need to be confined here the first couple weeks, get off the shit, and then I'm fine."

Carol sighed.

"You ran out the other day before I could tell you what I lost, Kennedy." She took the picture off the bookshelf and gazed at it intensely. "I was slamming day and night, even when I was pregnant. I would try and cut down, but it never worked. I even tried detox… approached it the same way you are now. I lasted one week sober. Jonathan was born addicted to drugs and they took him away from me at the hospital…my little drug baby." She put the picture back on the shelf. "And I STILL didn't quit. Not right away. I fought with county. I blamed everyone in the world except myself. I couldn't surrender my life to a higher power until temporary county custody turned into permanent custody. I will never have my son back. All I will have are these sporadic pictures from his adoptive mother." She reached into her purse and pulled out a wallet-sized school picture of an older Jonathan. "I just got this one yesterday. First one in two years his adoptive mom felt kind enough to send me." Carol struggled to fight back a sob. Kennedy reached out a hand tentatively towards her shoulder in condolence but Carol waved it away, regaining her composure.

"I'm so sorry, Carol. I didn't know."

"Why would you?" She wiped away a tear that was threatening to spill over and sat up straight. "You're right, Kennedy. You are like me... or like I was. I thought I just needed to stop taking drugs and that would be it. Sweat it out a bit, and then be done with it. I couldn't admit that it was a disease I had. A disease I would have my entire life that could either be active or in remission. I have been sober for seven years now, but I am still an addict. Always will be. You can't *control* the use. That is a mind game you will forever lose. You have to surrender, to give up control to something bigger than yourself." Carol looked at Kennedy as if examining an interesting painting. "I don't know why you're here... court ordered... make momma happy. I don't know. But I do know that this stay at detox is a waste of time if you don't start listening to others and doing some work." She leaned in closer toward Kennedy. "If you don't need this and if you have all the answers, then why are you really here?"

Kennedy was silent. She couldn't take her eyes off of the photograph in Carol's hand with its generic blue background and contrived pose. Two years' worth of scraped knees, Disney movies, dodge ball, McDonald's french fries, stickers, grass stains and Kmart denims gone by, and all Carol had was this one second snapshot of her son's life. The thought of it made Kennedy's throat tight.

"Group starts in fifteen minutes. I encourage you to go. Even if you don't participate, go listen." Carol took the picture, inserted it in a ceramic frame with baseball designs around the edges she pulled from her desk and set it on the windowsill. Kennedy left without saying a word.

Later that evening, Nurse Bonnie found Kennedy in her room reading the Big Book.

"You have a phone call."

"I thought we weren't allowed to get phone calls."

"It's your aunt." Kennedy immediately jumped out of bed. Aunt Shelly wouldn't be calling her here unless it was an emergency. She followed Bonnie to the back of the nurse's station and was led to a small side room with no windows that only contained a rotary phone on a table. Bonnie dragged a chair in for Kennedy and closed the door behind her as she left.

"Aunt Shelly?"

"Hey, Kit. How are you making out in there?" Her voice was strained and she was sniffing.

"I'm fine. Don't worry about me. What's wrong? Is Mom okay?" Kennedy felt sick to her stomach.

"She's going to be fine, honey. She's been in an accident."

"Oh my God! What happened?!"

"Now, Kit, calm down. I wasn't even going to bother you with this, but I wasn't sure when you were getting out of there and I didn't want you to go back home and wonder where your mom was."

"What happened?!" Kennedy insisted.

"She lost control of her car on the freeway. She was coming back down from visiting me in Victorville. Someone cut her off and she swerved to the left into the hill. Flipped her car. Luckily she was wearing a seat belt. She has some glass stuck in her head and they had to shave half her hair off. Well you know how happy she was about that. Couple broken ribs and some bruises. The state trooper said it was amazing she walked away from it. She has some mending to do, but she'll be fine."

"Is she in much pain?"

"They have her pretty well doped up. Her major malfunction is that hair of hers." Lucy had grown her hair for years, taking great pains to take care of it. It hung to her lower back, light brown with silver streaks that made her look like an aging hippie.

"She must be devastated. Poor Mom. I have to come see her," she said without hesitation.

"No! She made it very clear she doesn't want you leaving till you are discharged, and even then she wants you in aftercare…some kind of treatment. She will refuse to see you if you leave, Kennedy. She wants you healthy."

"But, Shelly, I feel fine now. I want…"

"NO, KENNEDY! In no uncertain terms are you to leave that detox unit, young lady. If you really want Lou to feel better, then stay there and do what you are supposed to do." Kennedy tried to interrupt, but Shelly cut her off. "I have told the staff there that they are to call me the day before you are discharged and I will come get you. You can see your mom then." Kennedy knew better than to argue with her mom or Shelly. She begrudgingly relented.

"Then tell her I love her and I hope she's okay. I'll buy her a hippie wig for her birthday."

"I will, Kit." Shelly laughed.

"Aunt Shelly?"

"Yes?"

"You promise she's really okay, or going to be okay?" Shelly was touched by the scared little-girl tone in tough little Kennedy's voice. Her niece was usually one hard nut to crack, not one to show softer emotions.

"I promise. Besides, do I ever blow smoke up your ass?" Shelly joked.

"No. You tend to inhale, not blow." Kennedy countered.

"Too true. Damn cigarettes." Shelly paused. "Tell you what. If you make it through rehab, I'll kick these stinky things. I'll quit with you. I want you to stay that much, Kit."

Kennedy was stunned. She knew how much her aunt loved her smokes.

"It's a deal."

"Good. Gotta run now. Love you, Kit. I'm proud of you."

"Thanks. Love to you and Uncle Ronnie and Jack. Kiss Mom for me."

"I will. Bye, Kitty."

"Bye, Shelly."

Kennedy hung up the phone and sat for a while trying to imagine what her poor mother looked like with half of her hair gone and glass sticking out of her head. The image made her weep. She wished she would have asked what hospital her mother was at so she could call. *Yes, only to call*, she kept telling herself.

How many eleven-year-olds could say that they were someone's muse? Not many. Especially a muse that inspired great works of art like "Rainbow Rip Tide" - or so Kennedy kept telling her cousin, Jack, over and over again.

That was the great thing about Jack. He was an eager listener. Not much in the response department, but he loved it when anyone would talk to him.

"Did you see the mermaid sand sculpture Turk did yesterday, Jack? That was me! Turk told me it was." Kennedy was leisurely strolling the Venice boardwalk with her cousin while her mother painted and Aunt Shelly went to the market for yet another supply of peanut butter and bananas, Kennedy and Jack's main dietary staple for the summer.

"Wow! I like sand."

"I know you do. Did you see it?"

"I think so." Jack lied. He had no idea what Kennedy was talking about but lived to make her happy.

"Well, you're going to see it for sure today. He's going to do another one." Kennedy loved staying with her aunt in Venice Beach for the summer: warm breezes that carried the exotic smell of incense, the drum circle that would start in the afternoon with one or two bongo players and culminate with thirty musicians around a bonfire till midnight (according to her neighbor Len… Kennedy wasn't allowed out past dark), handmade exotic wraparound skirts, local artists who sold their work on the boardwalk, out-of-work musicians who sang for spare change and Turk, the convertible-owning surfer hottie who made sand sculptures on the boardwalk for donations.

"Ice cream! I want ice cream!" Jack had spotted a vendor on the corner and was jumping up and down.

"You just had one an hour ago!"

"I want more. Please, Kitty." Poor Jack could never pronounce Kennedy's name as a young child. Kitty was as close as he ever got and it stuck.

"Okay. One more, but don't tell your mom." Jack had a bit of a weight problem. Aunt Shelly would have a fit if she knew Kennedy was feeding him ice cream. She scrounged some change from her brown faux suede purse and handed it to him. He clapped his hands with glee and made a beeline for the vendor. It was hard for her to believe that they were the same age, birthdays only months apart. She wished he was normal. Not for her sake or embarrassment, but for him. Jack was a sweet person, and even at the tender age of eleven, she knew that people could be less than kind.

Kennedy surveyed the boardwalk for Turk and saw him under a palm tree working on his next piece of art. She admired his tan chest and developing adolescent muscles, sweaty with his effort. Many a day she had spent dreaming those strong arms would be wrapped around her instead of his ever present surfboard. Jack was busy waiting in line with a bunch of kids for his rocky road single scoop, so she trotted over to him.

"Hi, Turk." He flipped his blonde bangs out of his eyes and tilted his shades up towards her.

"Hey there, Mr. President." Kennedy hated it when most people made that obvious reference to her namesake, but from Turk, it had more of an intimate feel. The fact that he would grace her with any term of endearment made her blush.

"Whatcha making? Another mermaid?" *Oh please, oh please, let him make me!*

"Hmm. I don't know yet," he said lazily. "I'm waiting for my inspiration to hit." He took off his glasses to reveal eyes as blue as the ocean that he surfed every day. "I take it you liked the little mermaid I made for you the other day?"

"Yes. Very much." The sand sculpting had had Kennedy's full lips and wild curls.

"Well here comes some inspiration now," he said provocatively, looking past Kennedy. Kennedy turned around to see a bikini clad girl with the longest hair she had ever seen. It was light blonde, straight and hung past her behind. She also had the biggest boobs Kennedy had ever seen.

"What have we here? Competition?" the girl asked playfully before hopping in Turk's lap. They both laughed and then kissed each other with tongue. Kennedy wanted to jerk that long hair out by its roots.

"This is my little friend, Kennedy. I used her for the mermaid," Turk said while stroking the top of bikini girl's thighs. *Little friend?*

"Oh, the little mermaid! Cool! Nice to meet you honey," she said genuinely. "I'm Star." Kennedy stood with her jaw agape. *I will not cry. I will not cry!* "Nice to meet you," she finally managed in a tight voice.

A cry of anguish split the air from the direction of the ice cream vendor. Kennedy turned to see three boys, a couple years older than her, circling around Jack who stood with his cone splattered on the ground before him and his shirt pulled up over his head. The boys were pinching his white flabby stomach, leaving red marks all over him. He was sobbing hysterically while the boys were sneering and telling him - Go on, fat ass! Lick it up! Kennedy ran toward them, screaming for them to stop.

"Knock it off! Stop it, you jerks! Leave him alone!" She pushed past one of the boys and pulled down Jack's shirt, trying to cover his exposed flesh that was red and angry with scratch marks. She looked at his snotty nose and splotchy face. His eyes were wide with terror and he was shaking uncontrollably. "It's okay, Jack," Kennedy soothed. "Come on. Let's get you cleaned up." She started to pull him away toward the bathroom.

"Looky here, the retard has a nigger girlfriend!" one of the bullies said, making his two buddies howl with laughter. "Hey, retard. Don't you know those girls are dirty?" the ring leader said before taking his vanilla milkshake and dumping it on Kennedy's head. "There you go, lick that up, retard! Do it!" On cue, the two buddies grabbed Jack and started to shove him toward Kennedy.

Kennedy snapped. It would frighten her later to think back on it, how she actually heard a 'snap' in her head and then attacked that boy with swift and blinding violence. She had no idea she even knew how to fight, especially with a boy that stood a good five inches taller than she did. As it turned out, that boy had not anticipated she knew how to fight either.

She flew at him and punched him in the nose, not enough to break it but enough to set him seeing stars of pain. Before he could react, she kneed him in his balls, and he doubled over groaning. Then, as he was bent in agony and his two cronies were in shock, with adrenaline-induced strength, she kicked his head like it was a football and she was going for the extra point in an already cinched victory. He wound up on his back with a bloody nose, cupping his crotch in his hands and whimpering. Kennedy was breathing hard and shaking with rage and fear, vanilla milkshake dripping down her frizzy curls. The two buddies, not wanting their asses beat by a girl, let go of Jack, then tucked tails and ran. Jack stared at Kennedy in awe, the same way he looked at Wonder Woman on television when she used her lasso of truth on a villain. Turk and bikini girl ran up to the scene.

"Holy shit!" Star exclaimed.

"Helluva kick, Mr. President," complimented Turk with a chuckle. "Remind me never to piss you off."

Kennedy took off down the boardwalk, running into tourists and stumbling over a particularly large pit bull that threatened to rip the back of her skirt off in retaliation. Snapping teeth missed her hem by an inch. Embarrassment, tears, milkshake and rage blinded her. She ran until she was out of breath and had a stitch in her side, then collapsed on a bench some two blocks from her aunt's house. She wanted to disappear, just melt into the hot sand and cease to exist. After regaining a little composure, she trudged down to the water's edge where the waves met the beach. She lay down on the wet sand and remained there, letting the salt sting her eyes and the waves wash over her. Her mother found her an hour later pruned and red-eyed.

"Kennedy? Good lord, honey, come here." Kennedy looked up and saw Lucy standing above her with a worried face and a dry towel. She started to cry all over again. Lucy gently pulled her up and wrapped the towel around her cold shoulders. They walked up to dry sand and sat down.

"Oh, Mom, I left Jack! Did he come home? Is he okay?"

"He was escorted home by a nice girl named Star. He was still pretty shaken up. After Aunt Shelly got him into the shower, Star told us what happened." Kennedy hung her head in her hands.

"I'm sorry, Mom," she sobbed.

"What in the world do you have to be sorry for?! I'm proud of you. I'm the one who is sorry." Kennedy looked at her mother in bewilderment. She was convinced Lucy would be ashamed of her behavior and Aunt Shelly would never forgive her for leaving Jack. Lucy was staring out toward the ocean with an odd mixture of sadness and disdain.

"I don't understand. What did she tell you?" Kennedy thought that perhaps Star, out of well-earned guilt for stealing Turk, told her mother that she had saved Jack from a burning building or on coming traffic.

"Star told us about those horrible boys," she said bitterly, "what they did to Jack, what they said to you." Lucy turned to Kennedy and looked at her with fierce pride. "And then what you did to them. My girl's a fighter." Kennedy's jaw dropped.

"I thought you would be mad. You always told me that fighting was low-brow and uncivilized."

"It is. But what those boys did was worse. It was barbaric, inhumane. Baby, I don't want you to ever start a fight. But sometimes, you don't have a choice but to finish one. And a word of advice, if you fight a man, you better make sure you hit them hard and fast to where they can't get back up, just like you did."

Kennedy could not believe the words were coming from her mother's mouth, her peace-loving nonviolent mother. The same mother who had just read Kennedy the riot act last week for killing a spider in the kitchen because she was taking the life of another living creature.

"Why did you say that *you* were sorry?" Kennedy asked timidly. She wasn't sure she was ready for the answer from this stranger who had invaded her mother's body.

"I'm sorry… I'm sorry that people like that exist. I'm sorry that I brought you into a world with hate and cruelty and that you have to be exposed to it. I'm sorry that you're getting older and I can't protect you from people like that anymore." Tears started to well up in Lucy's eyes.

"It's okay, Mom." Kennedy hated to see her mother cry.

"No, it's not. It's far from okay." Lucy cupped Kennedy's chin in her hand and looked at her face lovingly. "When I was pregnant with you, all I could think about was the beauty I would show you in the world. The beauty and love that you represented to me." Lucy sighed and dropped her hand back in her lap. "I was naïve. The world just breaks my heart sometimes."

Kennedy was confused. She didn't know what to say. It was too much to absorb in one day, especially for a young girl: seeing her cousin abused, being called *that word*, this bizarre outpouring from her mother. She sat in silence with Lucy watching the surfers.

"Mom?"

"Yes?"

"Did my Dad feel that way too?" Kennedy could feel Lucy tense up.

"Yes. I think he did."

"How did he die?"

All Lucy had ever told her was that her father had died before she was born and that the light green gem stone ring that Lucy had passed on to Kennedy last year for her birthday was given to her by him before he died, Kennedy's birth stone. She knew he was black and that her mother had loved him deeply, but all the details that Kennedy had wanted to ask - What did he look like? How did he die? Who was he? - Lucy kept locked inside. Any time Kennedy tried to broach the subject her mother would deflect the question and then remain irritable for hours.

"He died in a car crash."

"What happened?" Lucy stood up.

"I told you, he died in a car crash. Now come on, it's time to go." Kennedy cringed. She had been so close, but as usual, Lucy shut down.

Lucy saw the pained expression on her daughter's face. She wanted to tell her so much more. She yearned to tell her what a lovely man her father had been, but details could lead to questions that she wasn't prepared to answer. She couldn't bear her daughter's knowing the extent of people's hate and cruelty.

"When he sees you now, and I know in my heart that he watches over you, I guarantee that he is bursting with pride at the young lady you are becoming."

Kennedy jumped up and hugged her mother tightly.

"Thanks, Mom."

"Now come on, I want to get back before Uncle Ronnie gets home and decides to go kill those boys."

Kennedy sat in her room that evening battling sporadic muscle cramps and the intense urge to leave. She skipped dinner and the companionship of her fellow patients, who were all convinced that she was in cahoots with Kelly and his plot to frame Rico, and alternated between pacing and futile attempts at reading the Big Book. At midnight, she gave in to sleep, but was haunted by dreams of car crashes and wigs. At one point, she awoke with a start, unable to determine if it had been a bad dream or a noise by her door. Fatigue eventually overcame her and she drifted off into restless sleep. The next morning she awoke late, feeling lethargic and nauseous.

She went to the cafeteria and grabbed a few saltine crackers, then went into the morning twelve-step group late. It was standing room only. Everyone on the unit was in attendance, and the atmosphere felt hostile.

"You may not go into other people's rooms. Ever! Period! End of sentence! Not even if they are your friends. If you do, you will be put on contract. If you are caught threatening, harassing or abusing the other patients, you will be kicked out immediately." Carol was standing at the front of the group room next to Carlos as he barked out the rules which everyone had been told, but apparently had forgotten. *What the hell is this about?* Kennedy surveyed the room and saw Kelly in the back row with what looked like a fat lip. He still looked pale, but mildly improved from yesterday.

"If any of you are not interested in being here, if any of you are still banging and think this is your hood, get the hell out. Now." Carlos scanned the room looking for takers. He spotted a couple of Chicano's, two of Rico's home boys, talking to each other and throwing threatening signs to Kelly who ignored them and stared straight ahead.

"You two!" Carlos commanded. One kept staring at Kelly and the other gave Carlos a slow fuck-you glance.

"Out! Now! You're outta here."

"You think I give a fuck?" said slow-glance as he stood up and strode out the door. The other one picked up his chair and threw it toward the front, missing Carlos by two feet. He gave Kelly one last glare, then walked out the door laughing maniacally. Two large male mental-health workers followed them out to call security back-up for their escort off the unit.

"Anyone else?" Carlos asked. The rest of the patients were busy studying the floor or biting their nails.

"Now I'm sure Juan would like you all to think that he really didn't give a fuck, but I guarantee you, he will give a huge fuck when we notify his parole officer of his noncompliance and discharge from our unit." Carlos stood with his feet slightly apart and his hands behind his back, looking directly at each patient in turn. "Let me remind you why you are all here, or at least why you are supposed to be here. You are drug addicts. You are here to start recovery and to learn how to maintain your sobriety. You are not here to exact revenge, to stake your territory or pull one over on anyone." With that said, Carlos left the room. Carol picked up the discarded chair, righted it, and then spent the next thirty minutes discussing the first two steps of the twelve they were to eventually climb.

After group, Kelly stayed where he was while people brushed past him. Kennedy lingered behind and cornered him once they were alone.

"What the hell happened?"

"Well, as you saw, Miguel threw a chair and Juan…" he began.

Kennedy cut him off.

"Can't you ever just give a straight answer?! What happened to your lip? Why the paid-for-public-announcement from Carlos? And if you tell me to focus on my own program, I will fucking slap your ass out of that chair." Kelly started to reply with a smart-ass remark, but then decided against it. She had a right to know.

"Last night, someone - or *someones* - paid me a visit and gave me lip augmentation free of charge."

"Didn't you see who it was?"

"No. It was dark and I was asleep. Someone belted me and said 'You're fucking dead nark,' then left. But given that display earlier, I think it's a safe bet to say it was Juan and Miguel."

"I thought I heard someone at my door last night, too," Kennedy recalled, frightened. Her arms broke out in goose bumps at the thought.

"Yeah, I heard whispers before the group about a couple of the Latina's trying to pay you a visit last night. Vivian caught them in the hall and put them on contract."

"Fuck! What the fuck for?!"

"I warned you yesterday. Talking to me could get you into trouble."

"No shit!" Kennedy paced nervously, frantic with the thought that someone could come and attack her, attack her baby, while she was asleep. All because of him.

"What did you do?" she asked accusingly.

"I didn't do anything."

"You're a fucking liar. And now my ass is on the line." Kennedy held her stomach which Kelly took exaggerated notice of.

"Yes, asshole, I'm pregnant. I have a lot more here to lose than you do."

"I thought they didn't allow preggers in here?"

"Yeah, and I thought they didn't allow drugs in here." She stopped pacing as the realization hit her and the pieces came together. "I knew you looked way too cool, calm and collected." Kennedy thought back to Kelly sweating and losing his charm yesterday. "You didn't start to kick until you had been here a few days. You were fucking using when you got in here, heard they got wind of it then tossed the shit in Rico's room."

"I guess you got it all figured out."

"How did you get it in, since we're being all honest and shit?"

Kelly studied her for a moment then popped off the armrest of his wheelchair. The frame was hollow with enough width to fit a kit.

"Why did you come here then?"

"I only brought some shit in because I had heard the detox was too fast. I brought enough to wean myself off a little more slowly, which is exactly what I did. I only had one hit left in my kit."

"So you heard that they suspected you and you put it in Rico's room?" Kennedy shook her head in disbelief.

"Don't tell me you're shedding a tear for him. That fucker was smoking pot in his room since the day he got here. He was going out anyway," Kelly added, as if this justified his own actions. Kennedy was disgusted yet somewhat intrigued by his ingenuity. She wanted to balk, but it wasn't as if she had been completely forthcoming with staff and had abided by the rules of admission. Hypocrisy was worse than breaking rules in her book. With the ethical wind ripped out of her sails, she sat down and sighed.

"How did you get in the wheelchair anyway?"

"Climbed in."

"No, I mean how did you become paralyzed, or is that bullshit, too?"

"Anger management."

"What?" she asked with more than a hint of irritation in her voice.

"Anger management got me in this wheelchair. I was court-ordered by the think tank over in Torrance Court to take mandatory anger management classes as a term for my probation."

Kennedy laughed.

"Probation? Why does that not surprise me? I knew you were shady."

"If shady is clocking my mom's boyfriend upside his head for taking our rent money, then by all means, I'm shady."

"Oh, sorry."

"Not at all," he continued, undeterred. "So one Saturday afternoon session, everyone-needs-a-hug Becky is leading the anger-management group. She loved to set a 'happy chair' in the middle of the circle and put people in it that needed help focusing on their positive thoughts. So she starts discussing appropriate ways to express our frustrations and mistakenly picks this English guy, I think his name was Andrew, to share what he did to be sent to our little love fest. I don't think he was very much in touch with his feminine side 'cause old Andy didn't like to share. So Becky decides to remind him that he was there for nearly strangling his old lady's lover that he found her in bed with. Now I can see this guy is getting pissed, and he is a big son-of-a-bitch. So I decide to try to lighten the mood a little by cracking a joke about the English man's wife who walked into a bar carrying a two-foot-long salami and old Andy stood up and fucked the 'happy chair' right out the window."

"And how did that make you paralyzed?"

"I was in the happy chair and it was a second-story window."

"Shut the hell up!" Kennedy exclaimed in disbelief.

"True story."

"No frigging way! You must be lying! You're lying, aren't you?"

"Yeah, I am. Fell asleep at the wheel and ran into a tree without wearing a seat belt, but that just sounds like an ABC after-school special, doesn't it?" He gave her another one of his sly grins.

"You are such a dickhead," Kennedy said, laughing.

"You're too easy. Like shooting fish in a barrel." Kelly wheeled himself closer to her. "So when do you get out of here? You can't have much longer." He eyed her appraisingly. "You don't look to be in the throes of initial detox."

"I'm not. This is my seventh day here, out in three." She stretched her legs, which still ached slightly. "I feel fine now really. Mainly restless, a little achy."

"I still feel like shit. You might think I was an asshole, but I'm telling you, I wouldn't have been able to hang without my little helper I smuggled in here. I was using pretty heavy before." He took a washcloth that was stuffed in his chair and wiped a thin sheen of sweat from his brow. He tensed a bit and closed his eyes.

"You okay?" Kennedy asked. He opened his eyes and relaxed again.

"Yeah. Just some cramps. They passed." He was pale and smelled of deodorant that was working over time. "And where do you go after this?"

"To the hospital," she replied, although she wasn't sure which one.

"For the baby?"

"No. Well, yeah, that too. For my mom. She was in a car accident yesterday. I have to go see her."

"Oh shit, that sucks. What happened?"

"I don't know for sure. My aunt called last night. I want to go now but they, my aunt and mom, want me to stay the whole ten days. It's so stupid, though. What the hell am I going to accomplish here in three fucking days besides maybe getting my ass beat in my sleep?"

"Good point," he replied. "I'm glad you're staying, though. At least there will be one person here for the next couple of days who doesn't want to kill me."

"That's debatable," she said sarcastically. "What about you?"

"When I leave?"

"Yeah."

"Going downstairs to the rehab. Start physical therapy and see if I can get these fucking legs to work again." Kelly paused. "So where is the dad?"

"The baby's? I don't know and I don't care," she said defiantly.

"Does he use?"

"Oh yeah, big time. We did together." Kennedy brightened for a moment. "You know, I only really used with him and his friends. When I get out of here, it's not like I'll be surrounded by the shit like most of these other assholes. I guess I'm a step ahead of the game."

"He doesn't want to be involved with the kid?"

"No. Unless by involved you mean paying for the abortion." Kennedy pictured Bob in her mind, screaming at her with that vein bulging in his forehead.

"Sorry."

"It's okay. I have family. Besides, it'll just be me and my girl. Us against the world. I'm fine with that."

"You know it's a girl already? I thought you had to be about to pop before you could find that shit out."

"No, I just know. I know she's a girl."

"Woman's intuition?" Kelly laughed. "What are you going to name her?"

"I haven't even thought about it, to tell you the truth. I'm just worried about bringing her into the world in one piece at this point."

"I don't blame you. I'd be worried if I were you, too." Kelly smacked his leg. "I can't have kids. Not now obviously."

"Did you want kids?"

"It was never on my priority list, but once the option is taken away from you, you start to think about shit like that."

"Would you want a boy or a girl?"

"Hmm. I don't know. They both have their advantages and disadvantages." He pondered for a moment, running his hands through his hair. Kennedy was once again struck by his massive arms. "I think I would want a girl. If I had a boy the poor bastard would probably turn out like me. Yep, a girl. A daddy's girl."

"Naturally," Kennedy smirked.

"Oh, come on. If you were going to have a boy, wouldn't you want a momma's boy?" he countered.

"Hell no! I don't like momma's boys. If I had a son, I wouldn't want him to be some wimp like every other momma's boy I've known. That whole Oedipal thing creeps me out." Kennedy shuddered at the thought. Kelly smiled at her.

"I like you," he stated matter-of-factly. Kennedy glowed a little against her will, chastising herself for feeling... well, for feeling anything at all.

"Um, so, what would you name her, your daddy's girl?" she stammered, trying to steer the conversation back to safe ground. Kelly, sensing her ambivalence, decided to let her off the hook and play along with the redirection. He arched his eyebrows and rubbed his chin in mock contemplation.

"I would name her Mazzy," he proclaimed dramatically.

"Mazzy? What the hell kind of name is that?"

"I read it in a comic book when I was a kid. She was a superhero's sidekick. Kinda looked like you. Dark, wild ass hair and green eyes."

"Hmm. I like that. My little sidekick." She pictured a baby with a lasso and gold deflector bracelets and laughed. "Did she have a super power?"

"If I remember correctly, she could travel ahead in time and then back to the present day. Never backwards in time, though. She could predict the future, but never change the past." He paused and then closed his eyes again in tense concentration. Kennedy touched his hand and he looked at her. "Now, if you will excuse me, Super Mom, my bathroom calls. I'm sure you understand." He squeezed her hand briefly and rolled toward the door.

"Lock your bathroom door, Boy Wonder," she called after him. "There are villains among us."

The next morning, Kelly looked for Kennedy in the dining room during breakfast, but could not find her. Momentarily panicking as he wolfed down the last of his runny scrambled eggs, he barreled out the door and down the hall to her room, then breathed an uneasy sigh of relief when he found her curled up on her bed with the Big Book in hand.

"Decided to give in and study the faith, have you?" he asked as he rolled himself in her doorway, mindful not to enter given the newly enforced unit sanctions against trespassers.

"Speaking of faith, have you read this yet?" she asked angrily.

"Bits and pieces. Why are you all worked up?"

"This chapter here," she said as she hopped out of bed and shoved the book in his lap. "This isn't really a section to help agnostics work the program. It's a section to convert."

Mildly amused by her frustration, he took the book and scanned the pages as she paced in front of him.

"It's either A) drug or alcohol induced destruction or B) accept that there is a power higher than us, like if you don't become spiritual you are doomed to drink yourself to death with no hope. So saying that they deal with agnostics is bullshit. They're just saying you might be agnostic now, but you will cave when faced with the consequences.

"They go on to say that agnostics are vain for thinking they are the ultimate intelligence. Who's to say that we don't think there are aliens out there a million times smarter than we are? They also say agnostics should observe how stable and happy religious people are. Give me a fucking break. I know just as many jacked-up Christians as I do stable agnostics."

"I take it you don't believe in God."

"Do you?"

He closed the book and took a minute to ponder. She stared at him expectantly with her hands on her hips.

"I don't believe in God as personified in the Bible or in any organized religion. I do believe there is something out there, some universal force. I'm just not too pushed on trying to label or define it."

"Well, I don't. I don't believe in that. You live, you die, you turn to fertilizer. People can't stand the thought of that so they have to convince themselves that there is something else, a grander scheme they just aren't clued in on yet."

"And where has your way of thinking gotten you, Kennedy?" said Carlos, coming up behind Kelly and startling them both.

"It's rude to eavesdrop, Carlos. Where are your manners?" Kelly inquired with mild antagonism.

"Just because I was dumb enough to use drugs does not prove that there is a higher power," she spat. "According to this book, I can't possibly stay drug-free unless I start believing in some God or all-knowing spirit. That sounds pretty prejudiced to me."

"Let me ask you a question," Carlos started, but Kennedy cut him off as she brushed past Kelly and into the hallway.

"No. I don't need some prepackaged sermon on the graces of Jesus and how he saved your life, Carlos. Sorry, but I'm not religious."

She left the two men standing in her doorway as she sulked down the hall to the cafeteria. Carlos sighed heavily.

"Sorry, amigo. Guess she isn't tithing today," Kelly joked as he left him alone to roll down the hall after her.

He wheeled himself into the dingy cafeteria. Kennedy sat by herself at a table near an open window, holding her stomach absentmindedly.

As Kelly made his way toward her, mindful to skirt around a lone Asian woman who was missing half of her teeth and mumbling incoherently to herself, he admired Kennedy's wild beauty -- slender arms with femininely defined muscles, a shock of curly dark brown hair that snaked down her back and dared any brush to try and tame it, green eyes that locked in on you like laser beams from underneath the longest eyelashes he had ever seen. She stood out on the run-down unit like a wild orchid bursting into bloom in the middle of charred ruins.

He had given up on the idea of ever having another girlfriend. He knew a male with no use of his manhood wouldn't keep a woman around for long, even with his charm and useless good looks. Add the fact that he was a perpetually jobless heroin addict, and not too many quality women could be expected to pound on his door. Oh sure, there had been a few who had wanted someone to take care of and mother him -- ironically, other addicts like him. But when two druggies are jonesing for the last fix in the house and cash is low, love and nurturing can turn ugly fast.

There had been one girl who was straight, a cute little blond who didn't even drink or smoke. She had taken him in as her own personal charity case and was too naïve to realize, at first, that he was higher than a kite. In the end, he sent her off crying over what a bastard he was. Not having the option of makeup sex at your disposal, it's hard to keep a woman around after stealing her car payment.

After a while, he had resigned himself to a life of bachelorhood. All the more so now that he had decided to get off the shit and get his wrecked life back on track.

So when he found his chest tightening ever so slightly over the site of Kennedy sitting at the table, he mentally slapped himself. *Don't be an asshole, you stupid gimp.* He shook it off and fell back into his reliable comedian routine.

"Let me ask you a question, little miss nonbeliever," he said in his best imitation of their Hispanic counselor.

She gave him a dirty look and wan smile against her will.

"Since you so fucked up, wouldn't it be nice to know that there is some deeper meaning to your existence?" He maneuvered himself next to her, weathering her steely glare while scrunching up his face in deep thought in a perfect likeness of Carlos. "Like, maybe God wanted you to be a fucked-up little addict so that you would end up here, ensuring my continued job as a counselor and securing my paycheck, so that I can finally pay off the mortgage on mi casa in Pomona. Now that is a noble purpose, no?"

She laughed heartily, impressed by his accuracy, and smacked him on the arm.

"You're a nitwit."

"Maybe some people need to let go and think that someone else knows what their greater purpose in life is, because they are too lame to figure it out themselves." He gently put his hand over hers on her stomach. "I guess you already know what yours is."

"She *is* my higher power," Kennedy agreed.

They both smiled. She left his hand on hers as they stared out the window, gazing above the swaying palm trees to the clear blue sky.

"There you are," drawled a Jamaican accent from the doorway behind them, "You supposed to be goin' downstairs."

"Oh, yeah. I'm coming, Vivian," Kelly responded as he wheeled himself around.

"Downstairs?" asked Kennedy.

"My interview. To see if they want to let me in after I bust out of here."

"I almost forgot. I'm sure you'll charm them into an admission."

"Naturally," he purred before casting her a sly smile over his shoulder and rolling past Vivian into the hall.

Kennedy looked at Nurse Vivian and took note of her suspicious glare and folded arms.

"What?"

"You two been pretty... distracted lately, dontcha think?"

"After the warm fucking reception I've had here, you'd think you'd be glad I found someone to talk to, Vivian," Kennedy responded incredulously.

"Uh-huh. Get yourself down to group, girl. It's a topic you might want to listen to."

Kennedy sulked down to the group room and gritted her teeth while she endured the hour-long session on the reasons why one should not engage in new romantic relationships during their first year of recovery, vowing to set Nurse Vivian straight on whatever misconstrued ideas she had about her and Kelly the moment she was excused from group.

But she never got the chance. Vivian was initially no where to be found, so Kennedy went to lunch. She angrily munched on an apple by herself in the corner of the cafeteria, practicing what she would say, when a new patient vomited in his own lap, sending most of the diners scurrying towards the exit in an effort to avoid the stench and keep their own lunches down.

She was about to follow suit when LaShawnda, the ghetto hood rat who had been in her face before, complained, "Hey, what's that gimp doing downstairs flirting with dem bitches? I wanna get outta here for a while, too!"

Kennedy peered out the window to the courtyard below and spotted Kelly in the middle of a gaggle of girls, jockeying to see who could push his chair for him. She could see by the expression on his face that he was eating it up with a spoon, basking in the attention as he was fussed and fawned over by the females downstairs desperate for a good-looking diversion, wheelchair or not.

"Yo, bitch. Looks like yo man is down with some new action," LaShawnda taunted Kennedy.

She clenched her jaw and walked toward the door, not wanting to open her mouth and get into a fight. The girl started cackling, relishing the fact that she openly irritated Kennedy.

"That is a bitch when da only man you can get is a fucking gimp and you can't even keep *him*. Ha ha ha ha!"

Kennedy stopped in her tracks, and with impressive accuracy, pivoted and nailed LaShawnda between the eyes with her half eaten apple from across the cafeteria. Her junior high softball coach would have been proud. LaShawnda, however, was not impressed and leapt to her feet, hurling an empty tray that missed Kennedy by mere inches and nailed Carlos, who was just entering the room, in the chest, knocking the shocked wind out of him.

An hour later, after each girl had been hauled out to the nursing station and had given their opposing stories, they were escorted back to their respective rooms and ordered to pack their things.

"What were you thinking?" Carol asked Kennedy as she supervised her packing. "You were out of here in two days!"

"Exactly," Kennedy replied. "What the hell was I going to gain in two days? Hmm, stay here listening to this junkie bullshit and leave with my little certificate in hand that is about as worthless as the toilet paper

I wiped my ass with this morning, or leave with a dishonorable discharge and get the chance to nail that bitch between the eyes? I voted for option B," she said with a chuckle as she stuffed the last of her belongings into her bag.

Carol shook her head and handed Kennedy the Big Book to put inside her suitcase along with her dirty undies and socks. Kennedy took it from her and laid it on the dresser instead.

"Look, I got as much as I could from this place. I'm dried out now. Besides, luckily I had only been using for six months or so. I won't hang around people who use; I will focus on more important things. I'm going to go stay with my mom until I finish school, and believe me, she'll keep close tabs on me. And if I get the urge to use, I'll do one of your meditations or go jogging instead."

Carol sighed and handed Kennedy her suitcase. Her shoulders sagged along with the prematurely aging skin around her eyes, evoking a twinge of sympathy from Kennedy for Carol's blatant disappointment. She wondered if the poor woman ever got a chance to save anyone.

"Actually, Carol, you helped me most of all," she said more seriously.

"Me?" Carol laughed sarcastically.

"That day in your office. I heard you, and I refuse to suffer that loss," Kennedy said gently as she took her suitcase and headed for the door.

A dawning realization swept over Carol's face.

"The picture of your son will haunt me forever. Thank you for sharing that," she added before disappearing down the corridor.

Kennedy sat in the downstairs lobby waiting for her irate Aunt Shelly to make the drive from Victorville to come and pick her up. She did not look forward to the ass-chewing she would face during the two-hour ride back to her home in the desert. But was excited over being able to leave and see her mother who had already been discharged from the hospital and was convalescing at her aunt's home.

She heard Nurse Vivian's voice from an office off to the right instructing someone to wait in the lobby, and a moment later, Kelly rolled into view. He spotted Kennedy and broke into a wide smile until he noticed her bags at her feet. His face fell, and he wheeled himself hastily towards her.

"What the hell? I'm gone a couple hours and you're ditching me?"

"Looked like you were making new friends just fine on your own, cowboy."

She avoided his eyes and instead focused straight ahead on a dusty fake palm tree, the only décor in the otherwise stark waiting area.

"Well, fuck me, you're jealous," he said smiling. "Don't tell me you're leaving because of..." he started, but Kennedy cut him off.

"Don't kid yourself. That ghetto hood rat was giving me shit, so I nailed her in between the eyes with a projectile fruit."

"Aah. They finally got to you, huh?"

"You know what? I..." but it was his turn to cut her off.

"Look, Kennedy," he said forcefully, "I know what you saw. I will kiss every single ass I need to, patient, counselor or otherwise, to get into this rehab. I need it. I don't have a family to go back to."

His need to explain touched her. She was flooded with guilt, having acted like a jealous girlfriend when they were just... she didn't know what they were. All she knew was that she didn't like seeing him pouring on the charm to those women, and she had no business indulging in those kinds of emotions.

"What about your mom?" she asked softly.

"Stupid bitch stayed with her boyfriend. Look, I have nowhere else to go. They'll help me find placement if I complete this program."

The pleading look in his eyes tormented her.

"I'm sorry. I didn't know, and I have no right to judge you like that," she squeezed his hand and forced a smile before adding sheepishly. "I guess you better make some friends down here since the only one you had up there is out the door for assault with a deadly apple."

"Yeah, it's gonna be lonely up there for the next few days without you," he said more seriously than he had intended to.

An awkward silence ensued, and they both studied the dusty palm tree at length.

"Hey, uh, I can't have any mail or phone calls for the first thirty days, but after that, I don't suppose you'd want a pen pal, would you?" he asked with forced joviality.

"I could probably manage a letter or two," she said, brightening against her own will.

"What's your address?" he asked, searching his pockets for a pen.

"Not sure. I'm going to my aunt's for a while 'til my mom gets better, then most likely back to my mom's house. But don't worry, I know the address here."

"Kelly, let's go," Nurse Vivian called, walking up behind him and signaling their last moments together had come to an end.

"And what happened to you, girl? Why you leaving now?"

"I guess I still need anger-management groups," Kennedy replied, throwing Kelly a wink.

Vivian shook her head.

"Take care of you self, girl," she said, giving her stomach one last meaningful stare before turning Kelly's wheelchair toward the elevator.

"I will. And Vivian… thanks. For, well, you know," she stammered, unable to convey her gratitude to the woman who had saved her ass on more than one occasion on the unit.

Vivian gave a silent nod as she turned Kelly around and backed him into the elevator. His and Kennedy's eyes locked for a brief moment before the doors started to close and Kelly hollered, "Take care of your higher power, too!"

Kelly,

I'm sure by now you are settled in and have arranged for a bevvie of beauties to wheel you to and from the pool and lather you with sunscreen. I, on the other hand, am blowing up like a beached whale and can barely manage to bend over to tie my own shoes.

My mom and I just got back home yesterday from my aunt's. Can you believe it? Two damn months!! Could have come back sooner, but every time I brought a departure date up, Aunt Shelly would dig her heels in and find some new reason why we had to stay. When she started resorting to blackmail with baked goods and my mom put on ten pounds, Mom had finally had enough.

I would have written weeks ago, but I didn't have one moment of privacy up there. Between my cousin Jack wanting me to play checkers with him every waking moment and Shelly and mom too paranoid to leave me alone for five seconds, I was lucky to be able to wipe my ass without a fucking audience.

My little sidekick is doing great. Did I mention before that I hadn't told my family yet that I was pregnant? (Aren't you special? You knew before they did.) I waited until Mom and I got home before I dropped the bomb. I was expecting a seismic explosion from her, but she instead alternated between unnerving calmness and tears of happiness. I swear I never know what to expect from that woman!

I've been to the doctor, and he says the pregnancy is progressing well. Of course, he isn't the one who has to pee every five seconds, is ridiculously constipated and can't sleep worth a shit.

Okay, I just went back and read what I just wrote and came to the horrid realization that I am a fucking whiner! Let me try again...

Dear Kelly,

How have you been? Are the other boys and girls playing nicely with you?

But seriously... I hope you are doing well and wonder how you are faring downstairs. I miss your witty repertoire. ;) Write back soon. I'm dying for some intellectual stimulation.

Take care,
Kennedy

Dear Kennedy,

Greetings from Camp... Hiawatha... Food is great here, but this place is, not like detox with its sweat-soaked pillow cases!

I thought you had moved on to your next lost cause and had completely forgotten about me. I guess my counselor was right -- miracles do happen.

And yes, I miss your company also. Although I met an old guy here, Charles, who is one seriously funny mother fucker. You'd like him. He sits in group, quiet with a dead serious look on his face, then when someone is whining over petty bullshit drama, he looks them dead pan in the eye and says, "Damn, you are a punk-ass bitch, ain'tcha?" Being that he is one big son-of-a-bitch he can get away with it without getting his ass beat, but he does tend to spend a lot of time in forced solitary introspection in his room.

As far as the sunbathing goes, that would be limited since my "free" time is spent in physical therapy. Now I don't want to be a whiny bitch like you ;) but it is ass-busting. I am, however, happy to report that I stood up with a walker (for about five seconds before collapsing).

Anyway, I'm glad to hear your mom is better and that you are taking care of the little sidekick. I'm assuming that you agreed with me that Mazzy is an awesome name and will be sticking to it. So henceforth, let 'the little sidekick' be referred to as Mazzy, for ever more.

Alas, my personal torturer knocks, signaling that it is once again time for physical therapy, so I must go. But before I do, I know that you are becoming less mobile than I am right now, what with you blowing up like a whale and all, but I will be graduating in a month or so and would love it if you came to the ceremony. Contrary to popular belief, the 'bevvie of beauties' here is sorely lacking and I could benefit from seeing your gorgeous self.

Kelly

Dear Kelly,

Congrats on hauling your sexy self up out of that walker! I'm so proud of you! I'm also impressed with your staying ability in that program. I myself would have probably been kicked out already for starting a food fight.

Charles sounds like my kind of people. I can't wait to meet him when I come to your graduation in a few weeks. I called the front desk person, and they gave me the time and date. So look for me in the crowd. I'll be the one waddling to her seat.

And yes, I have decided to go with the indisputably cool name of Mazzy, much to my mom's chagrin. She accused me of using drugs again when I told her that. Not that that hasn't crossed my mind once or twice (or ten or twenty times), but I swear, Kelly, every time it does, Mazzy kicks me! The first couple times it happened, I thought I imagined it, but after six or seven more swift kicks when I was thinking about it, I couldn't blow it off to coincidence anymore. She is my higher power.

I enrolled in two summer classes at a local college and can't wait to start. My mind is slowly turning to Jell-O from TV overload. I've been helping out at my mom's firm part-time doing some light office work, but can't be on my feet too long, so I like to kid myself by thinking that kicking ass on Family Feud and Wheel of Fortune in my living room is keeping my brain stimulated.

Can't wait to see you soon.

Kennedy

Greetings Vanna,

I laughed my ass off at the thought of you screaming at the TV – The answer is cheese fondue you idiot! CHEESE FONDUE!!

I can't believe I'm outta here in a week. I went to visit the halfway house I'll be staying at and it's not half bad... once you get past the manager's odd body odor and the old guy next door, who likes to walk around with no shirt on. Did I mention that he has a profound amount of back hair? Anyway, it's wheelchair-friendly, and my physical therapist will visit me there to twist me into a pretzel. They also helped me find a part-time job doing office work a block away from the house, so yes, all of the ass-kissing was worth it ;)

I'm stoked to get the confirmation that my little buddy will indeed be named Mazzy, and that she is keeping you on the straight and narrow. Maybe I can touch your stomach next week and she'll kick me, too. I've been told I need my ass kicked on more than one occasion here.

I regret to inform you that you will not be meeting old Charles. He finally pissed off one too many people and got kicked out with another guy for fighting. Such a shame. You would have loved him.

Gotta run now. I must say that I am looking forward to seeing your crazy hair and hearing you pop off with some smart-ass comment next week.

Kelly

"Give Mommy some love before you take off with Gramma."

Kennedy picked Mazzy up and chewed softly on her little nose and pudgy cheeks, sending the toddler into overjoyed giggles.

"You're nummy," said Kennedy as she finished off with a loud kiss on her forehead. "Who's your momma?"

"You!"

"Who's the only one who gets to nibble on you?"

"You!" Mazzy squealed gleefully.

"Who's my little girl?"

"Me!"

"And who loves you the most?" she asked before handing her to Lucy.

"Momma!"

"That's right, and don't you forget it," she said in mock warning.

Lucy gathered the squirming girl in her arms while Kennedy donned her coat and Kelly paid the waitress. Their celebratory dinner had been a spicy Mexican affair, and everyone was stuffed.

"Kelly, thank you for supper, although I have a feeling my stomach will be paying the price for it later," Lucy said.

"You're welcome, my lady," he replied as he maneuvered himself with his walker over to her and Mazzy. "And also to my little lady. Are you going to be good for Gramma while I take Mommy out on the town?"

"Wanna go!" Mazzy implored, getting the drift that Mommy and Uncle Kelly were going to go have fun without her.

"Not tonight, Maz. I'll be home in an hour or two and sneak into your room for more kisses," Kennedy said, leaning in to kiss her daughter and her mother. "And thanks, Mom. I promise I won't be gone long. Just a short visit with some friends."

"No problem. You deserve it, sweetheart. You've worked hard, and I'm proud of you."

When Lucy thought of how far Kennedy had come, from the drug detox to becoming a dedicated, loving mother and full-time student, then to graduating with her degree and having a bright future in front of her, she had to suppress tears of joy.

"We'll see you in a few hours, right grand girl? Wave bye-bye."

Mazzy begrudgingly waved as Kennedy and Kelly hailed a cab and left for a graduation party.

"You know, you're getting around pretty well in that walker. Think you'll be able to dance with me tonight?" Kennedy teased as she leaned on her friend's shoulder.

Kelly sighed, wanting to take her in his arms more than she could have known and twirl her around the dance floor. While he no longer viewed himself to be a loser with nothing to offer, he continued to keep his deep love for her buried beneath their jovial sparring and dedicated sibling-like devotions. They had been "best friends" for so long now; he didn't think he could ever muster up the courage to tell her how he really felt.

They had cheered each other on through his physical therapy and re-entrance into school, to her trials and tribulations as a young mother and struggling student. He couldn't chance her not reciprocating his feelings and things becoming awkward between the two of them. She was his support, his lifeline.

"How about you sit on top of my walker, and I'll scoot you around to a slow tune?"

"Mazzy loved it when you did that to her the other day." Kennedy smiled at the vision of Mazzy laughing herself silly as Kelly hummed a Frank Sinatra tune while pushing her around the kitchen.

Kennedy's smile faded as she remembered Mazzy's sweet face dropping over watching them leave tonight.

"Knock it off. I see that look on your face. She's fine. The world won't come to an end if Mom isn't there for one evening," Kelly chided. "You need to get out once a year for a couple hours, woman."

"She just looked so sad."

Kelly rolled his eyes at her.

"Yeah, yeah. I know you're right. Besides, it will be nice seeing Sherri tonight."

"So what is this thing we're going to anyway?" he asked as the taxi rounded a corner into a plush housing estate.

"Just a small get-together. My friend from history class invited me and few others from our study group over. Said it would be low-key," her voice trailed off as they pulled up to the address.

Cars were parked on both sides of the street for blocks in either direction. Loud music could be heard blaring from within, and people were overflowing from the front door into the yard. The house looked like it was bursting at the seams, pulsating with the people within.

"If this is low-key, I can't imagine what she considers a big party," Kelly said.

"Wow. Uh, this isn't what I expected," Kennedy said, feeling a little nervous.

"Do you want to leave?" Kelly asked, noting the anxiety in her voice. "We could go catch a movie instead. Looks like this is some heavy partying," he added, noticing a small group of guys besides the garage passing around what was most likely more than an exceptionally small cigarette.

"Hey, you guys getting out here or what?" the cabbie asked crankily. He was off shift after this fare and was in a hurry to get home to his wife's pot roast.

"Yes, we're getting out," she said. "Don't worry, Kelly. I'll say hello to a few friends, maybe a beer and then we're outta here."

She hastily paid the cabbie before Kelly could protest, and then helped him out with his walker. As they made their way up the empty-beer-can-littered driveway, she had to admit, it looked much more like a frat party than a few college grads meeting for a cozy get-together.

This is no big deal. I am not the same person, Kelly is not Bob, and I am capable of visiting a few friends. She smiled.

As they entered the doorway, they were greeted by their hostess, Sherri. Kennedy imagined she must have been a cheerleader at some point in her life. Her voice and ample boobs were as bouncy as her black ringlets of shiny hair.

"Hey, glad you could make it!" she said tipsily as she hugged Kennedy's neck with one arm.

"Yeah, what happened to the small get-together?" Kennedy had to shout over a local band that was playing in the family room. Sherri looked around innocently.

"This is only, like, half, no..." she looked around more, "uh maybe twenty percent of the people I know. Come on in, have a drink."

She led them through a high-arched entryway and into an adjoining living room with vaulted ceilings where it was a tad less crowded. It was decorated in white with gold trim accents. Even the carpet was a bright white, and Kelly could see one strawberry cooler stain that was seeping into its shag fibers in the corner. He wondered if Sherri's mommy and daddy were aware of her guests' presence this evening.

Sherri asked if they wanted a drink, and when Kennedy said a beer for her but a Coke for him, she responded with a quizzical look, but obliged anyway and trotted back with the drinks a minute later.

"Okay, now, you guys have fun and I'll see you in a little bit," she said before disappearing off into the crowd.

"Why do I have a hard time picturing you two as buddies?" Kelly asked.

"I know. I've never seen her drunk. She's much more down-to-earth when she's sober, believe it or not," Kennedy answered as she surveyed her surroundings. She'd had no idea that Sherri came from this much money.

Random acquaintances from varying classes greeted Kennedy and chatted with her and Kelly throughout the evening. She enjoyed herself and loved to watch Kelly outwit others on topics of philosophy and which local bands had the most likely chance of making it big.

He was so intelligent. It disappointed and irritated her that he was limiting himself to a vocational city college when he could do so much more. In the past, she had chastised him for not wanting more for himself, but recently, she had slowly started to admit that not only did she want him to achieve more for his own gratification, but also for her and Mazzy.

Yes, she wanted a future with him. She loved him. The crush that she had battled against at the detox unit had first evolved into a close friendship and then into a deeper love. He was her rock, and he loved Mazzy as his own, and after many a late-night inner debate over whether or not to tell him, she had decided that tonight was the night.

"Would you call a cab? I'm going to use the potty, and then let's blow this popsicle stand," she said with a wink.

"The potty? Wow, you *have* needed to get away from Mazzy," he laughed.

"I know. I'm talking more and more like a toddler everyday! Be right back."

She left and made her way up the stairs, grabbing her third beer from a cooler as she went, needing a little more liquid courage for their talk on the ride home.

Kelly continued to sip on his Coke, cognizant of the fact that he was the only sober person in the room. He hated being in this type of environment, but it was only one night and Kennedy deserved to let her hair down. He knew that tempting the gods by indulging in even one beer was not an option for him. One would lead to three, three would lead to six, and before you know it, he would want to chase a twelve-pack with a needle. He had seen Kennedy drink a beer or two over the past year, and it never seemed to affect her in the same way.

Kennedy chatted in the crowded hallway with her friend Laura from Lit class, a chirpy redhead whom she hadn't seen in ages, while they waited for the bathroom.

"I'm just so glad that I will never have to take another final exam again as long as I live!" Laura exclaimed.

"Me, too. At least for a while… I don't know. I might go back for my masters."

"Arg, you can have it! I'm done."

Laura noticed a tall brunette in front of them and recognized her as a fellow classmate from her yoga class. She was painfully thin, and her long hair grazed the top of her jeans.

"Bree! Good to see you!" she exclaimed as the two girls embraced. "This is my friend Kennedy. She and I had a class with Barnes together."

Bree rolled her eyes dramatically and made a disgusted grunting sound. "Barnes. What a dickhead."

"Didn't you say you were failing his class?"

"That's one nice thing I can say about him. At least he allowed me to do extra credit, so I didn't flunk," the lanky girl retorted sarcastically.

Kennedy had heard unsavory rumors about what type of extra credit he accepted, and while she dismissed them as tasteless gossip, her curiosity was aroused.

"What, like an extra essay?" she asked casually.

"No, more like an *oral* exam," Bree replied before lighting a smoke.

"Shut the fuck up!" Laura yelled and smacked her on the arm. "You whore! He's like older than my dad!"

"No shit. I didn't think men his age could even get it up anymore," Kennedy laughed.

"I'll admit, it wasn't my proudest moment, but I was flunking his class big time, and they didn't offer it in summer classes. There was no way in hell I was about to wait another God damn semester to graduate."

"Well, here's to no more final exams and no more geriatric blow jobs!" Kennedy cheered, raising her beer up in a toast.

The other girls chanted, "Here! Here!" and clinked their bottles together in agreement.

The line began to dissipate, and the three girls went into the bathroom together. As they fixed their makeup and yelled at an impatient person pounding on the door to wait his damn turn, Bree took out a baggie of heroin from her purse. Kennedy froze, lip gloss wand in midair.

"Is… is that…" she stuttered.

"Yeah. My little party stash." Bree misconstrued the look of horror on Kennedy's face. "Oh I don't use needles or anything like that. I just snort some now and again. It's not like I'm some druggie. You want a smash?"

"Yuck. I'll pass. I hate snorting anything. Makes my nose burn," Laura said as she blotted her lips on a tissue.

Kennedy hesitated, initially startled that she was even contemplating it. Bree shrugged her shoulders and proceeded to help herself.

It's just once. Lots of people chip. And besides, snorting isn't as intense anyway.

"What the hell. We are celebrating, right?" she said before taking Bree's generous offering.

Kelly, relieved that Kennedy was ready to leave this place, was about to send a search party after her up to the bathroom when he noticed an anorexic brunette hot-footing it down the stairs, almost knocking down a couple making out at the bottom.

"Damn bitch! Where's the fire?" the shaggy-haired boyfriend snapped as he nearly toppled over on his girlfriend.

A moment later there was a glass-shattering scream from the second floor. People could be heard calling for an ambulance and general chaos ensued. Half of the crowd, red-eyed and staggering a bit, made a beeline for the exit while the other half ran up the stairs to check out the drama first hand. Kelly tried to maneuver his walker towards the stairs through the crowd, but with limited success.

"Kennedy!" he yelled, not really thinking this melee involved her, but feeling anxious nonetheless.

"Get the bitch out of my house! She fucking OD'd! My parents will kill me! Get her out!" their hostess shrieked from up above, all bounciness vanished from her demeanor.

Kelly's heart froze, stopped pumping in mid beat as all the blood drained out of his body.

Two large brutes in wine and gold football jerseys emerged at the top of the staircase carrying Kennedy gruffly down the stairs, her head lolling from side to side, blood and foam running from her mouth and nose.

"Just put her on the front lawn and tell the cops she never made it in here," one of them commanded.

"PUT HER DOWN, YOU FUCKERS!" Kelly yelled, frantically trying to block their exit.

"Look, asshole, sorry if your girl here is..." the brute that was holding her legs began before Kelly let go of his walker and nailed him across the jaw with a right hook. The effort sent Kelly flying and he landed on top of her legs.

The other guy dropped Kennedy's head on the bottom of the stairs, said "Fuck this," and took off for the front door, leaving Kelly to crawl and pull himself up next to her limp body. Her green eyes were rolled in the back of her sockets, and she was gurgling on her own vomit.

"No, Kennedy, no..." he whimpered as he wiped her mouth and turned her head to the side to try and clear her airway.

"Hold on baby, *please*. Mazzy needs you. *I need you*. Please Kennedy, I love you," he sobbed as he cradled her in his arms.

"Mazzy..." she mouthed inaudibly, unheard over the approaching sirens and Kelly's tormented sobs as he buried his face in her wild curls.

Lucy

As Lucy washed her hands, she glanced up and caught her own bewildered expression in the mirror. She heard a low rumbling from the bedroom that was the pacified snoring of her husband, naked and sprawled across the entire queen-sized bed no doubt. Unsatisfied and wide awake, she wandered into the kitchen to make a cup of tea and recount the evening's events.

She had alluded to Tom early on her desire for sex by coyly asking, "Feel up for some love tonight, darling?" A blunt approach, yes, but one that he appreciated.

"I was just wondering the same thing myself." He kissed her quickly, smacked her on the butt and trotted off to watch a baseball game on TV.

After the dinner dishes were washed, dried and put away, and Tom's work clothes were ironed, she put on his favorite pink nightie with the lace bodice and knelt down in front of him on the floor. The Cleveland Indians, his hometown team, were down by one in the bottom of the ninth, and Tom was craning his head past her to see the next pitch. The crowd went wild. Tom jumped off the couch and hollered, knocking Lucy on her rear end.

"Woo hoo! Extra innings!" He looked down and saw her. "Oops! Sorry, Lucy." He offered her his hand, and pulled her to her feet before flopping back down on the couch. Lucy demurely straightened out her nightgown and snuggled next to him. She cleared her throat and leaned forward, staring into his eyes and smiling. He smiled back at her, but not his come-and-get-me-smile, more like his I-want-sex-but-not-until-this-game-is-over smile. Her own smile faded.

"Come on, honey, and sit with me." He pulled her up closer to him and resumed his game. She sat in rejected disbelief, her libido instantly squashed. She knew he worked hard and deserved to relax, but was it that long ago when just the thought of sex with her could make him miss social engagements, not to mention be late to work? Now she couldn't even motivate him to turn off the television.

In an attempt to pacify her, Tom started touching her breasts. Not caressing or tenderly fondling, but playing absentmindedly with her nipples like they were Ben Wah balls.

Once the Indians reigned triumphant, he jumped off the couch to hurriedly lock up the house for the night before Lucy could change her mind. Little did he know that she had changed her mind a half-hour earlier when that selfish take-my-wife-for-granted-and-finish-this-game smirk was slapped across his face.

Lucy was already curled under the covers when Tom snuggled up and kissed her. She tried to get back into the mood again, but found herself repulsed by his touch and offended by his limited kiss here/rub there patented technique of trying to hurry her arousal process.

Rather than cause a scene, she shifted herself into a position that offered minimum body contact and ensured his quick release. Within minutes he was peacefully sawing logs while she was painfully wondering what happened.

The water began to boil, snapping Lucy back to her bright yellow kitchen. She took the kettle off the stove and started to pour, scalding herself a bit from the steam.

She remembered the day she got the kettle vividly. Christmas of last year. She had been exhausted from playing hostess to Tom's family for Christmas Eve dinner -- a five-course extravaganza for ten people that catered to Uncle Herman's allergy to all nuts and wheat, Aunt Edna's dislike for anything less than top-quality meat, Tom's mother Mary's insisting on upholding the annual tradition of stuffing made "the Jackson way," a recipe so complicated and secretive she had practically needed FBI clearance to read it and Jesus' blessing to cook it, and Tom's meager budgeted allowance to pull the whole thing off.

She had fallen into bed after midnight and was asleep before her head hit the pillow while Tom and his single brother Ed stayed up drinking scotch and stinking up her house with cigars long after even Santa should have packed it in for the night. She had awoken Christmas morning to the house smelling like an ashtray, Ed passed out in the tub and Tom in a coma on the couch.

When Tom awoke around noon, cranky and hung over, he gave her two presents: the blue kettle and a vacuum. He probably thought she would get much more practical use out of them than the watercolor paints she had hinted she wanted. Spending hard-earned money on silly hobbies was something only a housewife would think of, according to Tom.

She went to the fridge for some cream and found a note on the door that read, "Lucy, out of peppers and mayo still?!" *Oh shoot. I forgot them at the grocery store again.*

She took the note off the fridge and was going to put it next to her purse on top of her car keys so she wouldn't forget, but stopped. She spotted Tom's pack of cigarettes and took one along with a book of matches and headed out behind the garage. Tom didn't know about her little habit, one of the very few secrets she kept from him. She didn't do it often, but was ashamed at how unladylike she could be.

The first pull from the smoke was always so delicious, it was almost sexual -- wrapping her lips around something and inhaling, the smoke caressing the inside of her mouth, the slight burn she would feel deep inside her. She looked at the cigarette. *Well, it's about the same size. Ha ha ha ha ha.*

Oh, but it wasn't funny. It had crushed her on their honeymoon. The long painful waiting and yearning to finally culminate in finding out her husband had an abnormally small penis. No, not funny at all. She had only slept with one other man before Tom, but that was enough to clue her in on the fact that not all men were created equal.

She was raised in the old school of thought that women performed their wifely duties for their husbands without regard to themselves, that the women's self-fulfillment came from carrying the resulting child. But she had her own stirrings, her own needs that had been far from met. To voice them would be unheard of. It would show her to be the low-class floozy that Tom's mother had initially pegged her to be.

And God had yet to grace her with the fruits of her wifely labors and give her a child. So she was left with the cigarette, phallic joke that it was, and the note reminding her to do her damn job and pick up the mayo and peppers.

She took the tip of her cigarette and burned a hole through the O in mayo and watched the flame slowly spread. The circle burned wider, consuming the demand and setting her free from the task. She dropped it on the ground and poured some of her tea on it to put out the flame in the grass. She leaned back against the garage and took another hit, looked up to the moon and thought, *I feel worthwhile on the days I have cleaned the entire house, gone to the cleaners and the post office, bought fresh vegetables at the market and created a home-cooked meal from scratch, washed the dishes and brought Tom a scotch on the rocks while he sits in front of the couch cheering on his favorite baseball team. But he doesn't notice. If I went on strike, it would be noticed immediately, yet when things are done he thinks the cleaning fairy did it magically when he wasn't around while I sat on the couch eating chocolates and watching TV.*

How many errands do I have to run to be worthwhile, to have earned my keep, to feel like I do not just take up space, but am instead productive and useful - when really, all of these things mean nothing to me? What level of productivity am I measuring myself against and where did this unit of measurement come from?

It's as if I, as a woman, as an individual, do not exist. How do women spend their entire lives doing this and not throw themselves from the top of the highest building?

She snubbed out her smoke and put the butt in the trashcan, mindful to push it down below last Sunday's newspaper and out of Tom's sight. As she turned back toward the house, she heard a low moan from the Smith's back yard. She started walking slowly, ears perked. She heard it again, this time a bit louder, and froze. A gagging noise a few moments later got her moving again. She walked on padded feet to the fence that separated their properties and peeked through the wood slats.

There in the Smith's back yard, softly lit by the full moon, was the middle child of the Smith clan, Rose, on both knees in front of Sandy Ross' boy, Roy. Her head was bobbing up and down rhythmically and Roy's hands were entwined in her curly blonde hair, guiding her movements. He was watching her with an intensity that Lucy had never seen before.

Lucy heard Rose wretch slightly and saw her start to pull her head back, but Roy was unyielding with his grip on her hair and pulled her back down again, faster this time. He whispered something that Lucy couldn't hear. Lucy's heart was pounding. She wanted to turn away, but the tingling between her legs kept her feet planted, ashamed and excited. She heard Rose whimper and saw Roy's body tense until he moaned, 'Oh God. Oh, hell yes.'

Rose's whimper turned to gagging until Roy finally released his fingers from her golden curls and pulled up his pants. Rose was kneeling on the grass, spitting and wiping her mouth. Before she could even stand up, Roy said, 'Thanks. I'll call you sometime," and strode away. Rose stood up and looked after him for a moment, then walked out of Lucy's view.

Lucy's mind raced as she quietly made her way back into her house. She was shocked at the behavior of the neighbors' children and her inability to look away, appalled by the boy's disrespect of such a nice young girl and more sexually aroused than she had ever been in her entire life. God, what the hell was wrong with her?

She locked herself in the bathroom, sunk to the floor and wept.

Tom hated it when Shelly called. The phone would ring and Lucy would be off to the bedroom phone like a shot under the pretense of not wanting to disturb him while he watched the news, but he knew better. Shelly was a little hippie whore who wanted to corrupt his sweet wife. He had hovered around the bedroom door more than once trying to hear what was so God damn funny to have Lucy cackling like an idiot.

During their first year of marriage, Tom had slowly weeded out her friends -- first, by keeping her busy with wifely errands and chores, and second, by having her every spare minute spent with him and other couples. Janice would call to meet for lunch, but sorry, Lucy and Tom were going to a potluck at Dick and Betty's house. Glenda would drop by for a cup of coffee, but Lucy was running out the door to meet Tom, his boss and the boss's wife for drinks. After two years of, "Sorry, I'm busy today but call me later!" the phone stopped ringing.

It wasn't as if he didn't want her to have friends. She had a dozen or so hens, hand picked by Tom himself, to share recipes and coupons with. There were plenty of his friends' wives that he found perfectly acceptable and that Lucy enjoyed attending social engagements with.

And besides, it's not like he hung out with single male friends anymore either. So why then should she continue to associate with single women who were either desperately looking for a man to marry, or those communist bitches protesting the war and pretending to give a damn about a nigger's right to vote?

Lucy was too naïve and easily influenced in Tom's opinion to be around people like that, especially women. And how close had those friends really been if they stopped calling?

Except for Shelly. She was the one person Lucy found time for. No errand on earth would keep her from talking to her one and only sister. Tom had hoped she would eventually get so caught up in her own pot-smoking orgy in California that she would be too stoned to pick up the phone anymore.

But here it was, Monday morning at the crack of dawn, and Lucy was locked in the bedroom on the phone again. She didn't even butter his toast or bring in the morning paper before scurrying down the hall. Tom had a good mind to get rid of the extra phone and make her talk in the kitchen in front of him.

But enough dwelling on the negative. The Indians had won, and he was still relaxed from Sunday night sex. Plus he was going to work as the new assistant to the vice president today, which included a bigger desk and a nice raise. Life was good.

He sipped the remains of his coffee and yelled down the hall that he was leaving. He adjusted his tie and gathered his keys as he waited for his wife to give him a farewell kiss and wish him good luck with his new position.

A minute later, Lucy popped her head out of the bedroom and briskly said, "Okay honey. Have a nice day." She shut the door quickly, before he could respond.

Tom grumbled under his breath and stomped out to his Buick.

"I can't believe you're calling at 7 a.m.! Isn't there a three-hour time difference? My lord, it must be four in the morning there. What would cause you to wake up so early, Shell?" Lucy spoke softly in case Tom ran back into the house for something.

"I haven't gone to bed yet, Lou." Lucy could hear a man in the background say something in Spanish that made Shelly giggle.

"Who was that?"

"Francisco," Shelly pronounced with a roll of her tongue, "and he was just leaving, weren't you, mijo?"

Lucy heard kissing and a light slap followed by a giggle. "Adios."

"Jesus, Shelly. Did you just have sex with him? And he's a … Mexican?"

"You caught me. I admit it. I have been having wild sex with a tall dark and handsome Latino all night," Shelly said dreamily.

"Is he your boyfriend?"

"Boyfriend, friend… you are so hooked on labels. You need to loosen up, Lou. You've been in Ohio too long." Shelly lit a cigarette. "Speaking of narrow-minded, backward thinking, how is Tom?"

"You're terrible!" Lucy chuckled in spite of herself. "He's…" a vision of Tom laying on the clean side of the bed and leaving the wet spot for her last night flashed in her mind, "He's fine. Oh, he got a promotion last week to assistant to the vice president!"

"Does that mean he gets to hold the VP's pecker while he takes a piss?" Shelly howled with laughter.

"Honestly, Shelly! Do you have to be so vulgar? I'll not have you talking about my husband that way." Lucy wanted to tell her sister that she had had thoughts along those same lines, but couldn't bring herself to openly disrespect Tom. Shelly had enough ammo against him as it was.

"Okay, okay. I'm sorry. Tell him I said congratulations."

"Thank you. I will," she replied in a tone more wounded than she actually was. "And how is your job going? It must be so exciting to write for a newspaper, to have people read what you have to say and take note of it. I envy that."

"It's just a local rag, Lou, nothing to get worked up over. And if you want to write, why don't you? Jesus, you're college educated, top of your class, and you spend your days ironing Tom's shirts and bringing him drinks! Women have a right to be more than just their husbands' indentured servants and brood mares."

"I would have to have a few ponies to be a brood mare, wouldn't I?" Lucy said bitterly.

"Oh, Lou. I'm sorry. I didn't mean to... I just meant," Shelly stammered.

"I know what you meant. It's all right." Lucy sighed. "I'm just so frustrated. We've been trying for three years, Shelly. What's wrong with me?"

"Did you ever stop to think that maybe *you* aren't the problem?"

"What do you mean?"

"Oh, come on, Lucy! Maybe your plumbing is fine. Maybe it's Tom who's holding up the production line." Shelly could not get over how naïve her sister could be.

"Don't be crazy. Tom is a strong, vital man. It has to be me."

"Fine. Don't even ponder the chance that Tom is sterile. Ask your doctor about it," Shelly said, exasperated.

"Tom thinks we should just keep trying without involving other people. He said, 'If it's in God's plan for us to have a child, then we will.'" The theory had worn very thin with her over the past year or two.

"Tom thinks? What about what you think? God, Lou, you used to have a mind of your own!" Lucy heard a knocking in the background, most likely Francisco coming back for an encore. "Look, I have to go now. But do me a favor, okay?"

"What?"

"Remember that one plus one still makes two. You and Tom are not a single entity, Lou. God forbid, if he died tomorrow, who would you be?"

"Why should my cigarettes pay for loans to help schools that didn't even know how to budget their money in the first place, especially when I don't even have a kid in school?" Tom griped to his friends.

They had just finished a beautiful roast dinner and retired to Percy's den for cigars and local politics. Tom envied this haven of masculinity with its redwood bookshelves and dark leather sofa. It would be a good many years before he would be able to convince Lucy to convert their spare room into such a luxury.

"It's only a penny, Tom, for God's sake, and the children are the future of America. They will run this country when you are old, so you'd better invest in them, regardless if you're currently putting one through school or not," Percy countered over single malt scotch. "The Tribune endorses the tax, so I'm voting for it."

"By 'The Tribune,' you mean Dan Cobbledick. Who'd a thought old Gobbles Dick would have become the editor of the Tribune? I had him pegged for a military man myself," retorted Dean, puffing on his cigar thoughtfully.

"Gobbles Dick. I had forgotten about that. Speaking of the paper, did you notice our Chagrin Tigers are working on their 19th straight victory?" Tom asked with pride.

"Hell, yes! Go Tigers!"

The three men launched into a spirited sing-a-long of their alma mater's fight song as the women were finishing their coffee in the dining room. Percy's wife Suzy rolled her eyes dramatically as she signaled to her maid for refills.

"I hear the Tiger's celebration commencing in the den," she laughed.

"Those boys. You'd think they had won those games themselves," Loretta said as she accepted more coffee with a nod. Lucy declined, having barely touched her first cup, and the maid took her leave to the kitchen.

The three women discussed the upcoming play at Chagrin Valley Little Theater and agreed that obtaining Lance Bouregard for set design was quite a coo. They were all on the theater's committee and had been working diligently to raise the quality of productions to the level of downtown Cleveland's Playhouse Square. Chagrin Falls was on its way to becoming a beacon of culture in the East Cleveland suburbs.

"Did either of you see the engagement announcement in the paper for Sandy Ross's son Roy? He brought her home last weekend to make the announcement. Lovely girl he met at Ohio State, Beth Kingsley is her name I believe, and they are set to wed next fall," Loretta said wistfully, " I personally prefer spring weddings, but to each his own. Lucy dear, you look flushed. Are you all right?"

Loretta and Suzy looked at her quizzically.

A vision of Roy's hands entwined in struggling blond curls belonging to someone other than his fiancé engulfed her. But before she was pushed to make up a fabricated response, an earsplitting crash from the kitchen startled the women, saving her from embarrassment and sending half a cup of coffee into her lap.

"OH! That damned Mini!" Suzy exclaimed before rushing off to the kitchen.

Lucy excused herself and made her way down the hall towards the bathroom to try to clean her skirt. She could hear Suzy reprimanding the maid and saying something about "it's coming out of your paycheck!"

As she neared the den, she saw Suzy's three-year-old son Edward crying at the door. His brown curls were matted, and he clutched a yellow blankie that was damp with snot and tears.

"Wonderful, just wonderful. The dumb nigger woke him up," Percy complained loudly. The door to the den opened and a disgruntled Percy popped his head out just as Lucy scooped the little boy up in her arms.

"I'll put him back to bed, Percy. Come, sweetheart, shush now," Lucy soothed as she stroked the toddler's back and made for the stairs.

"Thanks, Lucy," he muttered before disappearing behind the door again.

The little boy sniffled and sucked his thumb as Lucy paced slowly back and forth in his room, humming softly and rocking him in her arms. Edward's room was covered in bright yellow and orange cowboys, so busy in design and detail it gave Lucy a headache looking at it even in the soft glow of his night light.

She lowered herself into a rocking chair and closed her eyes, rocking rhythmically as she stroked his hair. After emitting a defeated sigh, he finally fell limp in Lucy's arms and she tucked him into bed. Lucy studied his small face, praying for his sake that he would eventually grow into that unfortunate nose he had inherited from his father.

She walked back down stairs, savoring the baby smell that lingered on her clothes, and was nearly knocked over by the maid, Mini, who had her coat on and was rushing for the front door.

"Excuse me, ma'am," she said with her eyes lowered to the floor.

"Oh, that's all right."

"Sorry 'bout your skirt."

Lucy looked down at the stain and laughed. She had all but forgotten about the spill.

"Don't worry. That was just an accident," but instead of a response, she received a cold blast of air as Mini closed the front door behind her and darted out into the night.

"I would have fired her if I were Percy. Damn decent of him to let her keep her job," Tom proclaimed for the second time that evening as he readied himself for bed.

"It was an accident, for goodness sakes."

"You're too nice, Lou," he said, walking up behind her and wrapping his arms around her waist as she brushed out her hair. "And beautiful. I married an overly generous, beautiful woman."

Was it really overly generous to let a woman keep her income even though she dared to drop a saucer? An unfamiliar voice whispered deep in Lucy's mind. She dismissed it uneasily and continued with her hair, examining her face in the mirror while Tom kissed her shoulders.

"You still think I'm beautiful?"

He set her brush down on the counter and turned her toward him. Yes, she was just as beautiful as the day he laid eyes on her, many years ago. An innocent freshman in high school with doe eyes and the ability to fill out a sweater like no other.

"Absolutely," he said, kissing her cheek.

"Do you think we'll have beautiful children, Tom? Suzy's little boy is adorable, but I don't think he'll remain so as he gets older, poor thing."

"Well, why don't we give it another go and find out?" he said seductively as he lifted her up into his arms and carried her to bed. She squealed in mock protest before he discarded her gown. All uneasy thoughts of misplaced generosity and the corrupt morals of today's youth temporarily banished as she prayed, once again, that tonight would be *the* night.

"Hola, mija!" Shelly stood with arms out stretched on Lucy's porch next to a suitcase. Dark circles rimmed her eyes.

"Shelly!" Lucy exclaimed, dropping her laundry in the foyer and jumping into her sister's arms. "Oh how wonderful! What are you doing here?"

"A little vacation. Hope you don't mind I didn't call, but I wanted to surprise you." She also knew if she had given an advanced notice of her arrival, Tom would have magically yanked a last-minute vacation or must-attend out-of-town event out of his hat, forcing Lucy to say no.

"It's so good to see you." Lucy noticed a dilapidated car on the street that looked like it was on its' last leg. "Is that your car? My goodness, did you drive here?"

"Yep. Old Lola got me here in three days. Her back seat doubles as a Howard Johnson's."

"Oh, Shelly, you drove cross-country by yourself? And slept in the car? You're lucky you didn't get robbed," Lucy scolded. She helped lug the large orange suitcase covered with radical slogan bumper stickers into the spare bedroom then went into the kitchen to make a pot of coffee while Shelly changed into clean clothes.

Shelly's heart ached for Lucy as she examined the spare bedroom's sadly hopeful décor': checkered drapes in light pastels, matte walls painted a warm yellow, soft plush carpeting and a fuzzy throw blanket knitted with love that waited to swaddle and soothe the unborn child she knew her sister longed for.

After washing her face and brushing the tangles out of her hair, she joined Lucy in the living room for coffee and a tray of finger sandwiches she had whipped up.

"Eat. You're skin and bones," she insisted, passing her a small plate and gesturing to a food-laden silver platter on the coffee table.

Shelly didn't need to be told twice. She was on a tight budget where smokes and coffee were the staples and food a secondary consideration.

"So what brings you out here? How long can you stay?" Lucy queried.

"About a week. I'm writing an article on the protests at Kent State. Trying my hand at a little freelance work," Shelly said with her mouth full of tuna on rye.

"How exciting! What are they protesting?"

Shelly shook her head in wonder. Only her little sister could live a couple of hours from one of the biggest hotbeds of political activism in the country and not even know about it.

"Jeez, Lou, don't you listen to the news? Ever heard of the civil rights movement?"

"Well, I've just been so busy lately helping out with the Women's Auxiliary bake sale and what not. I'm also on the committee at the Chagrin Valley Little Theater. Between that and keeping up with the house and our social commitments, I haven't been able to keep up with much else," she stammered. She could hardly blame Shelly for the mildly patronizing look on her face. It sounded frivolous even to her own ears.

"It's not that I don't care Shell, I just…"

"Then why don't you come with me tomorrow down to Kent. See for yourself what is going on outside of Chagrin."

"Oh, I don't know. I'll have to talk to Tom about it," Lucy replied hesitantly.

"Why? Last time I checked he wasn't your father. Don't tell me you have to actually ask for his permission."

"Of course not! It's just… look we'll see, okay?"

Shelly could see that Lucy was embarrassed and didn't want to isolate her sister five minutes after her unannounced arrival.

"All right. So when does Tom get home from work? You going to call him and tell him I'm here?" Shelly yawned and stretched out on the couch.

"He probably just left work and is on his way to Harry's for a poker game. No need to disturb him there." *No need indeed. He'll be mad enough when he gets home.*

"You look exhausted. Why don't you take a nap, and I'll pop out to the store and pick up a few things." Lucy gave Shelly's hand a quick squeeze. "It's so good to see you, Shell. I've missed you."

"I've missed you too, Lou," Shelly replied, although she doubted that Tom would share Lucy's sentiments.

Tom gave a false smile to the young boy skipping through the crosswalk and suppressed the urge to tap the gas pedal and thump the little bastard. *Stupid ass kid.*

Tom didn't hate children but could see no rational explanation for canceling a poker game to go watch one in some crappy school play. Honestly, a bunch of snot-nosed kids in Woolworth costumes braying like a band of donkeys in ode to Halloween instead of good cigars, single-malt scotch and cards with the boys? Harry needed to get his priorities straight, and Tom told him as much when Harry called him at work to cancel the evening's game.

"You'll understand when you and Lucy have kids," was his response, one that Tom had heard on several occasions.

But that day would most likely never come, and he was fine with that. He had had plenty of time to get accustomed to the idea since his doctor first discussed the probability of sterility with him after a severe case of the measles when he was a young man.

He slyly let the fertility burden lie falsely with Lucy to publicly save face with his manhood. The first time she uttered her fears of being barren, he hopped on that train of thought like a gambler catching the last red-eye to Reno, offering reassuring words of comfort to Lucy while breathing an internal sigh of relief.

The child in the crosswalk finally passed, and Tom proceeded toward home, ruminating on his lousy day. *That bitch secretary, Debra. Who the hell did she think she was anyway? The boss's personal whore, that's who!*

The presumptuous little tramp mistook his generous offer to go out to lunch as a come-on. She was obviously too lowbrow to recognize an attempt to spread office goodwill. Sure, he had been wearing his favorite blue shirt, the one that Lucy said brought out his eyes, and had used an extra helping of his best cologne, but he was the assistant to the vice president now, and he had to look the part didn't he?

After a "No, thank you sir, I have plans," uttered while simultaneously trying to refrain from giggling, he went to the park alone to at least enjoy the remnants of the unusually warm weather and chewed unenthusiastically on Lucy's brown-bagged pastrami on rye while reading the sports page. On his way back to the office, he spotted Debra with the female clerk from Medic sitting in the window of the corner diner, laughing like hens and none too discreetly pointing his way.

I'm sure if I were the president of the company she wouldn't just eat with me, but swallow too... the stupid slut.

He turned onto his street and noticed a rusted out jalopy parked in front of his house. *Who the hell is that bringing down the real estate value of my property?*

He entered the house and found Shelly, asleep and sprawled out on the couch. The top buttons on her blouse were undone, exposing the tanned flesh of her breast. Her black skirt was hitched up her thighs and her athletic legs were splayed slightly apart. Tom could barely make out a small piece of her bright white panties and felt the beginnings of an erection when a car door slammed loudly in front, startling her awake and catching him in his voyeuristic excitement.

Their eyes met and a knowing "I caught you, you perv" grin spread across her face. Embarrassment stained his cheeks a deep red, but before he could open his mouth, Lucy came bounding in the door.

"Honey! I didn't know you'd be home so soon. I thought you were playing poker at Harry's house," she said breathlessly as she breezed past him and into the kitchen with two armloads of groceries, oblivious to what had just transpired.

He ran into the kitchen after her, thankful to have an excuse to flee from Shelly's accusatory stare. "What the hell is *she* doing here?" he hissed.

"I didn't know she was coming, or else I would have told you. She showed up this afternoon for a surprise visit."

"Just like her to intrude on people without so much as a courtesy call." Tom watched Lucy put away the groceries -- refried beans, expensive name-brand ice cream, frozen waffles.

"What is all this crap? Is this for her? How long does she think she is staying here?" he demanded.

"Shh! Keep your voice down. She's only here for a week."

"A week! Now, wait just one minute…" he started, but Lucy cut him off.

"Tom, she is my sister, the only family I have left," she said imploringly.

"WE are a family, Lucy. I'm your family," he stated matter-of-factly, as if this settled the matter.

"So is she, and if she wants to visit, then I expect her to be welcomed in this home." Lucy gave him a disappointed look and resumed putting the low fat milk in the refrigerator.

"That's just great. So I get to see her every morning messing up my couch."

"She'll stay in the spare bedroom. It's not like we're putting it to any use," Lucy replied with a less-than-subtle trace of bitterness.

"Hello, Tom. Long time no see." Shelly stood in the doorway, skirt adjusted and buttons fastened.

"Oh, um, hello, Shelly. And what brought you back to Ohio? I thought you hated it here," he stuttered, knowing she had been listening the whole time. He turned to the sink and washed his hands to try and avoid looking at her.

"I'm not fond of the state," she said, walking up to Lucy and hugging her closely, "but I am fond of my sister. Wanted to see a few of my old friends, too. Hope you don't mind the imposition." She knew damn well that he did and dared him to say so to her face in front of Lucy.

"Not at all. If you'll excuse me, I'm going to take a shower," he mumbled and skulked out of the kitchen.

While envisioning Debra the secretary and Shelly in submissive compromising positions involving gags and a horsewhip, he masturbated angrily in the shower.

After an awkward dinner, punctuated by Lucy's attempts at idle chatter to break the icy silence between her husband and her sister, everyone retired early. Tom turned his backside to her and shut off the light before she had even settled into bed.

The next morning she arose extra early and made Tom's favorite breakfast, sausage and eggs sunny side up. This seemed to ease his mood, and he eagerly discussed his new responsibilities at work with her while she sat with him at the table hanging on his every word. She kissed him good-bye, and he had almost forgotten that Shelly was there until he was walking out the door.

"Bye, Tom!" Shelly called from the hallway. "Have a good day at work. And thanks again for the hospitality. The spare bed is wonderful!" she said with cheer that could barely mask her antagonism.

"No problem," he said stiffly before closing the door with a tad more force than was required.

"Was that necessary?" Lucy asked tiredly as she went back into the kitchen.

"What? I was being nice!"

"Uh huh."

Shelly plopped down on a kitchen chair and watched her sister clean the morning dishes. Washing a dish five minutes after you were done with it was a completely foreign concept to her. She was usually on her way out the door to meet a deadline or go to a rally, constantly on the move to broaden her mind or arrive at some final destination, trying to complete a goal or on her way toward a new and more challenging one. Who the hell had time to do dishes?

It struck her then, so sharply that she had to tear her eyes away, that the plate Lucy was holding in her hand *was* her deadline, the laundry she would surely wash this afternoon *was* her destination and whatever goals she had today would be the same exact ones she would have completed yesterday and work toward yet again tomorrow. More disturbing than the thought that her sister deserved better than this was the possibility that this was all she wanted.

"Have you done any new artwork lately?" Shelly asked hopefully.

"Nothing recently," Lucy sighed. She put the last dish in the cupboard and sat down across from Shelly. "I did do a sketch a few months ago. Mr. Peterson next door had fallen asleep on his porch swing, and I drew him."

"Really? Interesting choice of subject. Let me see it."

"Oh, it's nothing," Lucy demurred.

"I'll be the judge of that. Come on, cough it up."

Lucy rolled her eyes and retrieved the picture from her bedroom closet. Shelly studied it closely. The charcoal sketch was rich in detail, from the deep lines that etched the man's age worn face to the late summer's afternoon shadows stretching across the porch, barely grazing the print on the folded newspaper that was just about to topple off of his lap. From looking at the sketch, you did not see an old man sawing logs on a swing, but instead had the impression of a man who had lived a long life and was taking a well deserved and much enjoyed rest.

"You don't know how talented you are, Lou. It makes me so angry."

"Angry?"

"You see so much more than most people do. I just..." Shelly bit her tongue. She knew better than to say what she really thought.

"Never mind. What do you want to do today?" she asked, changing the subject. "I thought we could head down to Kent a couple of hours early and stroll the campus."

"I don't know if I'm going, Shelly."

"Lou! Come on!" Shelly slapped the white kitchen table in frustration, making the mini glass salt and pepper shakers jump.

Before Shelly could launch her attack, the phone rang, saving Lucy from having to go on the defensive. Shelly threw her hands up in exasperation and headed off to take a shower as Lucy answered.

"Hello?"

"Lucy? It's me. I forgot to tell you last night, what with your sister causing a ruckus and all. Mr. Dickerson's nigger maid skipped town, and Ethel is all in a panic over some dinner they are supposed to be hosting tonight. I told him you would be happy to go over and help her cook. You need to be there by four."

Not only am I his maid, now he is lending me out to his boss?

"Lucy? Are you there?" Tom asked in an irritated tone.

"I'm sorry, but I can't."

"What do you mean you can't? Where else do you have to be?" he asked mockingly.

"I have plans."

"What plans... oh let me guess. It's HER, isn't it?" he hissed, trying to keep his voice down so as not to draw attention from his fellow staff.

"If by her you are referring to my sister, then no, it's not her. It's me. I have plans today, and I don't appreciate you telling him I would do it without asking me first."

"This is important, Lucy! This is my boss!"

"No Tom. I have to go now. Good-bye," she said calmly.

"Don't you hang..." he started to yell before she hung up the receiver.

Lucy walked down the hall and knocked on the bathroom door.

"Yeah?" Shelly called from the shower.

"Save me some water and hurry up. I need to stop off at the store before we head down to Kent."

"Woo hoooooo!" Shelly shouted with joy and turned the water off immediately.

Lucy, feeling a little nervous and a lot excited, searched through her closet for something "protest" appropriate.

"Are you sure this car is safe?" Lucy asked skeptically. She had flatly refused to drive her own car knowing that Tom would hit the roof if he found out where she was driving. He would be angry enough with her when he got home and found a frozen dinner with his name on it in the freezer.

"Lola? Absolutely. She might not be much to look at, but she'll get you where you want to go," Shelly said while patting the dashboard affectionately. "By the way, we'll be meeting my friend Donald when we get there. I met him at a rally at Berkley over the summer. Nice guy."

"Is this another one of your boyfriends?"

"I don't have a 'boyfriend' Lou, although I have been seeing a mechanic lately named Ronnie. He's the one who sold me Lola. And if you're asking me if I've slept with Donald, the answer is no."

Moments later, they arrived in Kent, a small college town southeast of Cleveland. Shelly parked next to one of a half-dozen bars and restaurants that sat perched on the slender river that ran down the middle of town.

"We're meeting Donald here for lunch, and then we can walk up to the campus. It's a mile or so up the road heading away from the river."

They found a table inside and were soon joined by Donald and his friend Martin. Shelly leapt out of her chair and embraced them both.

"Martin! I didn't know you were going to be here!" she exclaimed happily.

"Neither did I. Last-minute plans. Some friends of mine were on their way to New York from Berkley and I caught a ride with them," he replied, eyeing Lucy approvingly. "And who is this?"

"Martin, Donald, this is my little sister Lucy."

"Nice to meet you both," Lucy replied with a reserved tone, more than a little uncomfortable with the obvious visual inventory that Martin was taking of her.

Donald shook her hand quickly and excused himself to find a restroom. Martin took her hand into both of his and lingered longer than was socially acceptable. Shelly smacked his arm good-naturedly.

"Easy there. She's married."

"Well that *is* a shame," he said with mock dismay.

Donald returned and the four sat down to lunch. The three old friends laughed and relived their adventures in California while Lucy sat in silence, questioning her decision to come. She caught more than one disapproving look from the other patrons and could only imagine what a spectacle their table was through their eyes -- two black men and two white women eating together. They probably thought they were couples!

Thank goodness she knew no one in Kent. She nearly grew faint with the thought of the scandal this would cause.

"So how many people do you think will show today, Donald?" Shelly asked in between bites of her hamburger.

"Hard to say. Anywhere from twenty-five to fifty. But that's more than enough people to block the stairs into the administration building. We'll disrupt their day, and they'll be forced to see us no matter how hard they try to walk around us." Donald looked at Lucy as if realizing she was there for the first time. "Shelly spoke of you, Lucy, when I knew her in California. Thanks for coming today."

"You're welcome."

"Well, we should get going. It's a nice day, so I thought we could walk up to the campus and leave our cars here," Shelly said while tossing money on the table for the waitress.

The two men walked ahead while Shelly lingered behind with Lucy, taking deep breaths and closing her eyes serenely.

"Fall is the one thing I miss most about Ohio. The crisp air, the leaves blazing in yellow and red. The only leaves that blaze in L. A. are the pot leaves," she laughed.

"Shhh! Keep your voice down! People will think YOU smoke drugs," Lucy hissed.

"Yeah, and pot smoking at a college campus would be unheard of! Ha ha ha."

"Have you? I mean, have you smoked pot?"

"A few times, sure. I could really take it or leave it. Oh, don't look at me like that, Lou. It's not like I do every day. Besides, it's not the evil killer that you think it is. Look there! There's the campus," Shelly said, pointing ahead.

The gently sloping campus consisted of red brick buildings of no particular architectural interest. Lucy imagined that if it weren't for the bright splashes of color from the turning leaves, the campus would be rather bland.

They followed Donald and Martin, who were in the middle of a spirited debate about the true level of power a president wields versus the business interest groups that back him, up a green hill to the front of the administration building. A small group of people were already assembled, no more than a dozen, and they greeted the newcomers vigorously. A tall lanky woman with a megaphone, who appeared to be the leader, thanked them for coming and directed them to the front steps while more students started to arrive.

"Thank you all for coming! Please, stand in a line on the steps. You there, could you step up? Yes, there you go. Thanks. If you could join arms together, yes, like that, and form a chain. Perfect!"

Lucy found herself linked in between Donald and Shelly, part of a human shield meant to block the entrance into the administration building, when she dully realized that she didn't even know what they were protesting! She considered asking Shelly, but was too embarrassed to chance having anyone around her alerted to her ignorance.

Two campus security guards stood off to the side watching and chatting amongst themselves, but did not intervene. A few students not associated with the protest walked toward the building, but thought better of trying to cross the barrier and rambled back the same way they came. When everyone was in place, maybe thirty or so people in all, the lanky redhead with the megaphone began.

"Students of Kent State! Are you aware of the inequity of your fine school?! The social injustice that lives in this institution of higher learning?" she yelled passionately.

Two young men walked up the steps and tried to pass through the line in between Martin and a large black girl, but they would not yield.

"I'm sorry, brother, but I can't let you pass right now," Martin said smiling.

"You ain't my brother, you Alabama porch monkey. Now get the hell out of my way!" spat the larger of the two.

His friend snickered and pushed Martin roughly. Martin, with his unfaltering smile, answered in turn with a biting upper cut to his slack jaw, and all hell cut lose. The police jumped on Martin, wrestling him to the ground in a chokehold, and Shelly flung herself onto one of their wide backs, beating her fists wildly and shouting, "Police brutality!"

People were screaming and scattering like ants while Lucy stood dazed. Someone grabbed her hand abruptly as Martin and her sister were being hauled off in handcuffs and dragged her away from the melee. She followed blindly, not realizing who it was until they were a block away and Donald stopped to catch his breath.

"Unbelievable. One racial slur and he's throwing fists. Idiot," he said with disgust.

Lucy was still too stunned to speak. Donald looked at her with concern and touched her shoulder gently.

"Hey, are you okay?"

Lucy shook her head slowly.

"Oh, it will be fine," he soothed, "Just fine. Come on, I'll get you a pop."

He bought her a soda and led her to a bench overlooking the river. She drank it slowly and watched the fall leaves float lazily down the river while he ran to make a phone call. A few minutes later he returned and sat quietly next to her until she was ready to talk. He felt mild amusement and pity for this sheltered girl whom he assumed had most likely never seen violence in her entire life.

"What's going to happen to my sister?" she finally managed. "What are they going to do with her? Oh, how am I going to get home?"

"She'll be fine. It's not the first time Shelly's been arrested," he chuckled.

From the shocked look on Lucy's face, he deduced that there was much that she didn't know about her sister.

"I mean from protests. Don't worry. They'll hold her for a while then let her go. As for you, I'll drive you back home if you'd like."

"Thank you, Donald. That's very kind of you."

He showed her to his car, and she got in apprehensively. She was not accustomed to driving with strange men, especially black ones. Lucy sat uncomfortably in the front seat wedged as close to the door as humanly possible.

Any further over and she would be climbing through the window, Donald mused to himself. Shelly had told him all about her little sister so he felt no insult from Lucy's unease.

"I take it that was your first time at a protest," he said in an attempt to break the silence.

"Yes, it was," she answered with embarrassment. "I guess it was fairly obvious."

"Everyone has a first time. We aren't born with a megaphones or picket signs in our hands."

Lucy took sideway glances at Donald as he signaled and merged onto the highway. She took note of his strong hands guiding the steering wheel.

"I live in Chagrin Falls, although I'm not quite sure how to get there from here."

"It's all right. I know how to get to Chagrin. I grew up there." He caught the startled look on Lucy's face and laughed good-naturedly. "I grew up in the park. My family has lived in the allotment for years."

Chagrin Falls Park, also known as the "allotment," was a notch of land less than a mile south of down town Chagrin that was all black. Lucy had heard wild stories of the development, that was scarcely more than a shantytown to hear tell of it, and steered a wide berth past its entrance at all cost. *You wouldn't want to be driving alone and have your car break down in front of the park. They'd steal your car with you still in it!*

When the estate was still technically considered part of Chagrin Falls, the exclusively white townspeople had voted early on to have the county lines rerouted to include the park into Bainbridge Township, forcing the children of the park to be bussed miles away to attend school.

"You don't live there now?" she asked.

"No. When I graduated from Kenston I got a full ride on a track scholarship. I share a place off campus at Kent State with my friend, Leo."

"Your family must be very proud. I bet you're glad to be out of there."

"I'm not running from there," Donald said defensively, "I'm getting an education, so I can come back and help make a difference."

"I didn't mean to offend you. I just thought that if you had a chance to get away from that life, to better yourself..." Lucy's voice trailed off in mid explanation and she sank lower into her seat.

Donald mentally chastised himself. How could he judge Martin for reacting to blatant racial hate when he himself was getting worked up and defensive over this young woman who was just trying to make small talk?

"Let me ask you something," he started in a gentler tone, "Have you ever had black friends, or even been in a black person's home, or car?"

"No," she admitted sheepishly.

"Why did you come today?"

"I... I don't know. I wanted to see what was going on outside of my world. I'm sure that sounds frivolous to you. I know there is more going on than dinner parties and historical society meetings. It's not that I don't care, I just don't know. I wanted to learn."

Donald grinned.

"You want an education? Do you really want to see something outside of your world?" he asked as if challenging her in a game of truth or dare.

She pondered for a moment. She supposed in order to find some truth she'd have to take the dare. "Yes. I do," she responded firmly.

"Well then, I will show you another world right behind your own fence. Right now if you want me to."

"I'd like that."

Darkness was beginning to fall as they turned into the park thirty minutes later. Donald made a quick left down a narrow street and pulled to a stop.

"Here's the house where I grew up. Home."

Calling it a house was being kind. It was more aptly described as a patchwork shack, a junkyard jigsaw puzzle of varying building materials ranging from cement blocks to warped plywood. The yard was a virtual swamp from last week's rain and the makeshift walkway to the front door consisted of large flat stones spaced two feet apart that Lucy had to hop across with Donald's assistance. When he knocked sharply on the bright red door, Lucy was surprised the whole structure didn't fall in on itself like a deck of playing cards a child had stacked one too many cards high.

She could hear people laughing and singing within. Donald smiled at her and knocked again, louder this time. A moment later the door swung open and little girl with short braids stood grinning broadly.

"Uncle Donald!" she squealed with delight before jumping into his arms.

"Hey, girl! You all got room for two more in there?"

"Two more?" she asked quizzically before spotting Lucy behind him. "Who she?"

"That's a friend of mine. Lucy."

"Hello," Lucy said timidly.

She wobbled on the unsteady stone and prayed she didn't fall over into the thick mud. The little girl simply stared. Not rudely, but in a manner that made Lucy feel like a small interesting bug discovered on the underside of a freshly picked flower.

"Mary, where are your manners?" Donald chastised gently.

"Hello ma'am. I'm Mary."

"It's nice to meet you, Mary. I'm Lucy."

Having sized Lucy up to be a non-threatening bug, the girl turned her full attention back to her uncle.

"What did you bring me, Uncle Donald?" she asked while reaching into his coat pocket. Donald laughed and pulled out a red lollipop from his pants pocket and entered the house with Mary in his arms, happily licking the sucker.

"Girl, what you doin out there?" a booming voice called from within. "You lettin' all the cold air in! What... wait! Is that? Lord, have mercy! Mae, get in here! It's Donald!"

Lucy stood behind Donald in the doorway, blocked from view as he greeted what seemed like a dozen people. He finally had to set his niece down to prevent her from being crushed by the onslaught of friends and relatives jockeying to shake his hand or grab him in a bear hug. A large woman that Lucy took to be his mother had Donald's face in her meaty hands saying, "My boy is home, Lord, my boy is home!"

Little Mary tugged on the woman's smock insistently, demanding her attention.

"What, child? What do you want?" she asked exasperatedly.

"Gram Mae, look! Uncle Donald brought home a white lady!" Mary said, pointing to Lucy.

The room fell silent. Mae pushed Donald to the side and saw Lucy, cowering in the doorway, wishing she had opted to topple off the stone and sink into the deep mud and tall grass.

"Momma, this is my friend Lucy."

Lucy smiled and forced herself to meet the multiple glares boring through her in the room. She counted eight people including Mae, Mary and someone who looked oddly familiar.

"You two staying for dinner?" Mae inquired gruffly.

"If you'll have us, Momma."

"If I'll have'em. Do you all hear this boy? Miss, you can go wash up in the kitchen. Donald, come with me," and she led him out of the small room to the back of the house.

The rest stared for a moment longer and then dismissed her and resumed their chatter. Mary alone stood facing her, crunching the remains of her sucker. Lucy followed her nose to the left and went to the kitchen to wash her hands. A large wash basin stood next to the stove which was humming with boiling pots. She rinsed her hands and was searching for something to dry them with when a woman entered the small space and handed her a towel.

"Oh, thank you," Lucy said, then realized with a start where she knew this woman from.

"You replace your skirt yet?" Mini asked.

"Replace? Uh, no."

"You going to?"

"I have enough skirts. I told you, Mini. It was really no big deal. My fault for being clumsy. Why do you ask?" Lucy was starting to feel flushed from more than just the boiling pots beside her.

"I lost half a week's pay for it. For that and the cup I broke," she responded caustically.

"Half of your pay? Oh my, well, that's outrageous! I certainly didn't ask Suzy to do that!" Lucy gasped.

"Mini!" a voice called from the other room, "Get back in here, girl! It's your turn!"

"I'm coming!" she hollered, then turned back to Lucy with a sly smirk. "Your people know you're here?" she asked before exiting the kitchen.

Lucy was about to leave when Mae came in, her large mass blocking the doorway. "I wasn't expecting more for dinner," she said before handing Lucy a potato peeler. "Why don't we leave Donald to catch up with the family, and you can give me a hand? We'll need a few more potatoes and carrots. Stool's right there if you want to sit."

Lucy was at a loss for words. She silently set to work on the vegetables while Mae stirred the pots, adding a pinch of salt here and a dash of pepper there.

"Donald tells me you live in Chagrin," Mae asked without raising her head from the stove.

"Yes, I do. Just down the road," Lucy stuttered.

"Your family been here long?"

"My grandparents lived in Cleveland. My parents moved to Chagrin when I was a child." She was terrified of this mammoth woman, terrified that if she gave the wrong answer... well, she wasn't sure what would happen, but she didn't think it would be anything good.

"Well, now, there is something we have in common," Mae laughed. She wiped the sweat off her brow and pulled up another rickety stool. Lucy was amazed at its ability to withstand her weight.

"Pardon me?"

"Our family migration. My parents moved here when I was a child, too. Hand me that knife there and the carrots you peeled." Mae started to chop the carrots on a crude cutting board and continued to speak. "My momma and daddy came to Cleveland with Harold when he was four or five. I wasn't even born yet. They come up from MacDonald, Georgia, on the train and stayed with my auntie and her family, just north of the old Woodland Market. The boll weevil done destroyed the cotton crops down south and a bunch of our kin had come up north to Cleveland to find work. I was born after they moved."

Mae signaled for more carrots without a pause. "We shared a house with three other families, each family had to share one room. Momma got to missin' her garden, missin' home, and daddy wanted a piece a land of his own, so Daddy started workin' double shifts at the factory and squirrelin' away every penny he could.

"One of his friends had told him 'bout a place out east, a place where you could buy a little plot of land and build your own house. Momma and Daddy came out here to take a look and bought the land the same day. We stayed another year down in Cleveland and on the weekends Daddy would come out and work on building the house. He couldn't afford all the materials, so he would buy them piece by piece and haul them out here in my uncle's truck. Everyone pitched in. We would come with him in warm weather and have picnics with the other families trying to build. I was little at the time, but I remember everyone working together. We finally got the house built and moved in."

Lucy was so engrossed in the peeling and with listening to Mae's family history that she didn't notice Donald in the doorway, a look of pride and devotion softening his chiseled features.

"Sure, we missed having indoor plumbing and electricity, but we got by. Lord, yes, I remember using the outhouse when it was ten degrees outside! Many years later Momma and Daddy passed away, and me and Harold got the house. When Donald's daddy was still alive, God rest his soul, he and Harold added more rooms, ran in electricity and plumbing. We've come a long way with the Lord's help."

"And will go a lot further. Isn't that right, Momma?" Donald asked, kissing his mother on the forehead. Mae smiled and patted him lovingly on the arm.

"That's enough vegetables, Lucy. Donald, go show your guest how your uncle cheats at cards."

The rest of the family, which consisted of cousin Larry and his wife Mini, their children, little Mary and not so little Eugene, and Uncle Harold and Auntie Mavis, were all polite yet uneasy with Lucy initially. By the time dinner was served and Harold had announced himself Chagrin Park's card champion, much to the cat-calling and protest of the others given his tendency to have cards fall out of his sleeves, most had warmed up to Lucy, with the exception of Auntie Mavis who kept a cool distance and a watchful eye upon her.

Given the limited space, they served themselves buffet style from the kitchen and brought out extra folding chairs to surround the circular dining table and collapsible card table that had been pushed together. Lucy was placed in between Donald and Mary and when Mae cleared her throat, everyone bowed their heads.

"Lord, we give thanks to you for your glorious blessings. Please bless this food we are 'bout to eat and keep safe watch over our family and friends. Amen."

The food was wonderful and the conversation lively. Lucy had never been around a group of people so animated in discussion, which revolved around topics ranging from the new pastor at the Baptist church, gossip about the disbursement of funds for the community recreations center and plans for the upcoming holidays. Lucy noted with palpable relief that Donald did not bring up the day's earlier events in Kent.

After every last scrap of food was eaten and the dishes cleared, Donald announced that it was time for them to go. It took another thirty minutes of good-byes and promises for Donald to return at Thanksgiving before they were able to depart.

"Mae, thank you very much for dinner. It was wonderful and I really enjoyed it," Lucy said, shaking the woman's large warm hand.

"Any time. Glad you enjoyed yourself."

They navigated the muddy stones without incident and were driving toward Lucy's house when it dawned on her. *What am I going to tell Tom?* With all of the day's commotion she hadn't given him a second thought.

"Lucy? You look ill. I thought you had a good time?" Donald said a bit wounded.

"I did! Very much so, Donald, and I can't thank you enough for taking me. You were right, it was a learning experience. I just..." her voice trailed off. She couldn't bring herself to say *I'm not sure how I'm going to explain to my husband about my going to Kent, watching my sister get carted off to jail, then going to dinner with a strange black man to the allotment.*

"It's just my husband, and he didn't know, I mean I didn't tell him," she mumbled.

"Oh, I see." He pondered her dilemma for a moment. "Why don't I drop you off down the street from your house if you are worried?"

"That's a good idea. Turn right here. You can stop at the next block." While she was grateful for his gracious understanding, she still felt ashamed of her own embarrassment, for her need to cover up.

"Here you are," he said, pulling to a stop. "Thanks again for coming to Kent. And I'm glad you came for dinner. I'm assuming that my family wasn't what you expected."

"They were great. As I said, it was a wonderful... experience. Maybe our paths with cross again, at another protest maybe. Although if you decide to punch someone, I won't guarantee that I'll jump on a cop's back for you."

They both laughed at that visual and Lucy was pleased with her own wit.

"Thanks for driving me home. Good night, Donald."

"Good night, Lucy. And good luck," he added, casting a look down the street at her house.

He drove away and she walked the rest of the way home slowly, formulating a plausible story for Tom. She prayed that Shelly was okay but also hoped that she didn't call the house looking for bail money and alert Tom to what had happened. He would keel over from a heart attack if he knew what she had done today. She was already in for it for not going to his boss's house tonight.

"I'll make it up to him," she thought. "I'll make him dessert and give him a back massage and apologize for this morning. Then tomorrow I'll get up early and make his favorite breakfast. And when Shelly calls, I'll tell her it would be best if she didn't stay with us, and I'll give her money for a hotel. He'll be mad for a day or two and then he'll be fine."

When she entered the house Tom was watching the evening news.

"Hello, sweetheart," she chimed, trying to sound casual instead of guilty as hell.

"Oh *now* I'm sweetheart, after you've been gallivanting around all day with your floozy sister. But this morning? No, no 'sweetheart' then. Then I was just a thorn in your ass looking for you to do your duty and help your husband get ahead at work."

He was slurring his words slightly, and his eyes were bloodshot. Lucy caught the stench of scotch and burned TV dinner as she sat down on the couch. He had spilled gravy on the carpet, knocked over a drink on the coffee table and flicked ashes on the couch, retribution for her daring to say no to him, daring to not be his indentured maid for one day.

She felt a foreign stirring within her, overpowering the guilt and shame that was making her nauseous only moments earlier.

"Where is the floozy anyway?" he inquired.

"We went to see Lawrence of Arabia -- she hadn't seen it before -- and ran into some friends of hers. She drove me home and will be staying with them for a bit. And really, I can't say that I blame her, what with the reception you gave her yesterday," she replied matter-of-factly.

Lucy stunned herself. Not only with her ability to lie fluidly on short notice, but to then turn the lie around on Tom and his poor behavior the day before. Given the state of his jaw, which was dropped down to his chest in disbelief, she guessed she stunned him with her boldness, too.

"Now, if you will excuse me, I'm going to take a shower and get ready for bed."

And with that, Lucy marched down the hall and left Tom to stew in his own scotch-soaked juices.

The next afternoon Shelly stopped by to pick up her suitcase while Tom was at work. She had been bailed out of jail by her editor in California but would have to come back to Ohio to face charges on assaulting a police officer. Her editor was salivating to get her story of racial hatred supported by the local police in print and wanted her back in L. A. pronto. She was giving Martin, also bailed out by her editor, a ride back to California, and he waved to Lucy from the car as Shelly bade her hasty farewell.

"God, Lou, I'm so sorry about what happened. I mean, dragging you down to Kent and then leaving you on your own like that," she apologized while pulling her suitcase out on to the porch. "Was Tom furious? What did you tell him?"

Lucy wasn't sure what frame of mind her husband was currently in. He had slept in the spare bedroom then left the house before she woke up.

"Don't worry about Tom. I'm just glad to see you're all right, Shell. Besides, I wasn't alone. Donald was with me."

Shelly stopped, momentarily caught off guard by an undercurrent in her sister's tone she couldn't quite identify. Before she could question Lucy further, Martin honked the horn impatiently and signaled to his watch.

"Even though the circumstances sucked, I'm still glad I got to see you." She hugged Lucy quickly before lugging her suitcase down the walkway. "I'll call you when I get home and give you all the details!"

"I can't wait to hear. Safe trip back!" she called out as Shelly's car roared into life and disappeared down the street.

Lucy went about her daily routine of cleaning and ironing. When Tom came home from work, sullen and hung over, they ate pot roast and corn on the cob and watched the evening news in silence before retiring to bed together.

The next morning, Lucy made toast and eggs over easy before wishing her husband a good day at work and received a reluctant kiss on the cheek. She ironed the laundry, spoke with Loretta about an upcoming committee meeting, did the grocery shopping at Heinen's and listened to Tom during their meatloaf and mashed potato supper as he relayed, in painstaking detail, the day's work scenario with him cast as the managerial superhero who saved the day.

After placating him sexually and sending him off to a deep and peaceful slumber, she pulled out her sketchbook, curled up on the couch and drew a pair of hands, a pair of strong, dark hands smoothly guiding a steering wheel.

The following week, Lucy received a phone call from Shelly. The article she produced brought raves from her editor, and she was ecstatic. The assignments were starting to pour in, and she was on her way out the door to San Francisco.

"By the way, before I go, I spoke to Donald about you the other day."

Lucy's palms became slick with sweat.

"Did you? About what?" she queried casually.

"He's in charge of developing a logo for a new club at school. He has the ideas, but not the artistic ability to finish the job. I told him what an amazing artist you are, and he asked me to ask you if you would consider lending him a hand."

"Um…" Lucy hesitated, torn between wanting desperately to be involved with something creative and… what? What was there to be torn between? She wasn't sure.

"Come on, Lou. What can it hurt? It's a crime that your talents are being wasted!" Lucy could see another sisterly rant heading her way and told herself later that was why she acquiesced so quickly.

"You're right. Tell him I'd love to."

Shelly was stunned into silence. She had been prepared to wage a battle over the topic and found herself at a loss for words. Lucy never gave into anything easily that would take her out of her comfort zone and routine.

"Are you there?"

"Yeah, I'm here. That's great, Lou. You can tell him yourself, though. I've gotta run. Here's his number."

Throughout the morning, Lucy picked up the phone and set it back down seven times before dialing Donald's number. When she finally managed to press the numbers and he didn't answer after the sixth ring, she hung up and was flooded with relief and disappointment. She tried five more times that afternoon before Tom came home from work.

The next day she called twelve times, letting the phone ring and ring before hanging up in frustration. That evening, Tom, annoyed at her obvious preoccupation and persistent glances towards the phone, asked her who the hell she was expecting to call. She muttered something about Loretta and a committee meeting, but Tom didn't buy it and he remained irritable and aloof the rest of the evening.

On the third day, during her fourth attempt, while writing out her grocery list, Donald answered, startling the hell out of her and sending her pencil flying across the kitchen.

"Hello?"

She froze, momentarily considering the option of setting down the phone quietly and just walking away from it.

"*Helloooo?*"

"Is this Donald?" she asked quickly.

"Speaking. Who is this?"

"This is Shelly's sister Lucy."

"Oh, Lucy, hi! I'm glad you called. To be honest, I wasn't sure if you would. I mean, I wasn't sure if you would be able to lend a hand with the project, that is." The genuine happiness in his tone put her at ease and made her feel ever so warm inside.

"Shelly said you needed help creating a logo. What is this new club?"

"Entrepreneur's Club. We're trying to advocate for minorities starting their own businesses."

"That's wonderful! What ideas do you have for the logo?" She picked up her pencil from the floor and wrote the word 'entrepreneur' in large block letters.

"Just sketches really. I'm not very artistically inclined. I appreciate art, but I also appreciate the fact that I'm horrible at it," he said sheepishly.

"I'm sure you aren't that bad."

"I am, and worse."

Again, for the millionth time since they had met, she thought of his hands, strong and fluid in their movement. She laughed to herself for assuming that he was artistic because of them.

"Well, what would you like me to do?"

"Maybe you could come up with some ideas. Something that conveys independence… leadership… ethnic diversity. Let's do this: you and I will both sketch some ideas on our own and then compare them. We can go from there."

"That's fine." She had filled in the large block letters and was doodling as they spoke.

"Can we get together this weekend?"

Lucy paused. A few stolen hours during the week was easy enough to keep from Tom since he was at work, but during the weekend? That would be much more difficult. "Actually, during the week works better for me if you don't mind."

"All right. How is Monday?" he asked.

"Monday's great. Morning work for you?"

"Sure. We can look at our sketches over breakfast. Same restaurant as before, say, ten-ish?"

"Ah, you're an *ish* person are you?" she teased.

"I admit it," he laughed, "Between work, clubs, track and school, I am unfortunately forced to run on the ish time clock and rely on the tolerance of those waiting on me."

"I'll keep that in mind."

"Thanks for the help, Lucy. I'll see you Monday."

"You're welcome. See you then."

Stolen time. Why was time taken to do something that she wanted to do something that had to be *stolen,* and whom was she stealing it from?

She looked down at the paper. Next to "entrepreneur" was a large dark hand holding out an hourglass that was just beginning to trickle grains of sand, as if in offering. Or was it to show that the clock was ticking?

Saturday brunch with Tom's boss and his snobbish wife, Ethel, had her feeling like a bored child ordered to church, forced to wear her itchy Sunday best and listen to the gospel of the rich and boring. She began to loathe the sound of Tom's loud, false laughter at Mr. Dickerson's outdated jokes and refused to emit even the smallest obligatory chuckle when Tom cast piercing glares her way.

After the two men retired to the study to discuss office politics, instead of accompanying Ethel to the living room for tea, Lucy excused herself and took a long walk around their Pepper Pike neighborhood, studying the carefully trimmed lawns and newly washed cars in the driveways. She tried to imagine what was going on inside the large white colonial on the corner and the one-story brick house next to it.

When she returned, Tom was fuming. He retrieved their coats, thanked the Dickerson's for a wonderful time and ushered her to the car.

"What the hell is wrong with you?" he demanded as soon as they had waved their good-byes and pulled out into the street.

"Don't yell at me, Tom."

"I'm not yelling. What the hell is wrong with you? Have you lost all of your manners? First you sit there during brunch like a little kid squirming in her seat, and then you disappear without a word? Where in God's name did you go?"

"I went for a walk. I didn't realize that was considered a crime in the state of Ohio," she replied in a bored tone.

"While it's not a crime, Lucy, it is considered a pretty fucking rude thing to do when you are a guest in the middle of a brunch!"

"If I had to hear that woman utter the word 'marvelous' one more time, I was going to impale my eardrums with an ice pick. You'd think with that much money, they could afford to buy her a vocabulary with a range of more than ten words."

"How could you be so rude to her?!" Tom asked with incredulous disbelief.

"How would you know if I were rude or not? You had your nose planted so far up her husband's ass, I'm surprised you would notice if I were alive or dead, more or less being rude to someone," she countered.

Tom slammed on the brakes and brought the car to a screeching halt in the middle of the road, attracting the curious stares of a couple taking their poodle out for a leisurely stroll.

"What the fuck is wrong with you, Lucy? Since when do you talk to me or anyone else like that? I swear you have been acting more and more like *your sister* ever since she came for her little impromptu visit!" Tom spat 'your sister' out of his mouth with such force and distaste, he looked like he was choking on battery acid.

The driver behind them honked in agitation, but Tom continued to stare at her, refusing to budge, waiting to hear an explanation that she couldn't give. The annoyed driver laid on his horn again, more insistently.

"They're waiting, Tom," she said and resumed staring out the window.

He punched the accelerator and sped home in silence

The rest of the weekend passed in dog's years, hours of white noise that she phased Tom's voice into when she would internally brainstorm her ideas for Donald, punctuated with moments alone to flesh them out on paper.

When Tom awoke Monday morning, he found Lucy already showered and his breakfast waiting for him on the table. Mistaking her actions for guilt ridden compensation for her outrageous behavior on Saturday, he ate heartily, kissed her good-bye and left for work in high spirits, pleased with the prospect of getting to work a few minutes early to impress his boss.

The minute his car was out of sight, Lucy spread out the map she had taken from his glove box while he was still asleep. It was a fairly straight shot down into Kent. She couldn't believe she had felt so lost before on the ride home.

After fixing her hair and makeup, she gathered her drawings and drove south, passing the allotment on her way down. She clocked the distance from her own front door at barely over a mile. What other hidden worlds laid within a one-mile radius of her home?

She thought about the places she had been over the past year and mapped them out in her mind, appalled at the realization that her existence encompassed less than a five-mile area. *I live in a bubble, and a very small one at that.* With every passing mile she drove, she envisioned that bubble growing, its transparent gossamer wall expanding across the map that lay next to her in the car.

She arrived at the restaurant thirty minutes early and ordered a coffee. After reading the menu twice, even though she wasn't remotely hungry, and checking her watch a dozen times, she pulled out a blank piece of paper and started to draw the interior of the restaurant. She loved the contrast of the ornate woodwork with the modern light fixtures and appliances, enjoying the challenge of conveying the varying textures on paper. Her pencil broke and when she reached for her purse to find another, she felt someone staring at her.

She looked up and saw Donald standing motionless a few tables away, a curious smile on his face as he observed her thoughtfully.

"I'm sorry. I was just watching you work," he said apologetically, taking note of her deep blush as he took a seat across from her. "You were just so... intense looking. I didn't want to disturb you."

"Oh, I was just doodling," she said, flustered.

Donald took the picture and admired it. Not only had she captured the minutest detail of the wood molding on the ceiling, she even managed to show the reflective shine on newly polished silverware.

"If this is what you consider doodling, I can't wait to see what you consider a serious sketch," he said with open admiration.

"Thank you."

"But before we get down to work," he picked up a menu and scanned it, "have you eaten yet?"

"No, but I'm not really hungry. You can go ahead and order, though."

"Well, I'm starving. And since I can't decide between an omelet or a stack of pancakes, you'll have to do me the favor of sharing since I'm going to order both and I don't want to look like a pig."

"I'll see what I can do," Lucy laughed, as Donald waved for the waitress.

As they waited for their food, they reviewed each other's work. Lucy discovered that Donald had not been exaggerating when he said he had no artistic ability. Although he lacked the skills to bring his ideas to life on paper, his creativity and vision were impressive. After much discussion, they finally decided on one of Lucy's initial sketches with a few minor changes based on Donald's suggestions.

"We make a great team, if I do say so myself," Donald said enthusiastically as the food arrived.

"I agree. It feels good to be part of a team, to do something productive," Lucy mused.

"You're probably more productive than you think, Lucy," he replied somewhat solemnly. "Now, if you want to continue to be a team player, help me eat this food."

They ate heartily. Lucy surprised herself with a newfound appetite and spent the rest of the morning engrossed in conversation ranging from a controversial art exhibit by a local artist that Lucy had read about in the paper, to the rapid increase of the African American population in Cleveland and how their interests were sorely lacking representation in government. By the time their plates were cleared and they were working on their third round of coffee, the conversation gravitated to the night they met.

"I've been curious to know... what did your family think of my little surprise visit?"

"Hmm, let's just say I've heard mixed reviews," Donald answered with slow deliberation.

"Yeah, I bet you have. Let me guess that one of the less favorable reviews came from your aunt."

"You would be guessing right. You have to try to understand it from her perspective, even though I know it's a narrow one. Mini is her daughter, and she heard all about that dinner party you were at. Now keep in mind, Mini didn't have anything negative to say about you, but you're still a part of that world that treats her and her daughter like second-class citizens. My aunt views all whites the same based on her life experiences, which haven't been favorable ones. I'm trying to expand my family's horizons, but it's going to take some time. I guess I was hoping to show not only you a different perspective that night, but her, too."

"So I was supposed to be the shining example of a 'nice' white person?" Lucy laughed. "I'm flattered you had assessed me as being so, after knowing me for such a short time."

"You have an inherent goodness about you that is apparent to anyone who is around you for more than two minutes, Lucy," Donald said softly.

And instead of avoiding his sincere eyes or blushing modestly, she met his gaze steadily.

"So do you."

Weekly trips to Kent, under the guise of putting the final touches on Donald's logo, finally gave way to no-pretense biweekly visits as the red and yellow foliage of October faded into the leafless chill of November. Lucy and Donald shared countless picnics of cold cuts and steaming coffee beside the river while engaging in amiable debates over politics, comparing childhood milestones and lamenting over exotic countries they would love to visit but would probably never see.

With Donald's encouragement, Lucy started drawing daily, saving each sketch in a folder carefully hidden between the mattress and box spring in the spare bedroom to present for his appraisal at their next rendezvous. She now lived to bask in his praise and viewed her daily life in Chagrin as a due to be paid, a sentence to be served until her biweekly parole to freedom. She would have gone to Kent even more often if she could cover the cost of gas without skimping more on the groceries.

As it was, Tom was growing exceedingly agitated not only with the decline in the quality of his meals, but also with the decline in his wife's attention, in and out of the bedroom.

Feigning interest in his monotonous anecdotes about his petty trials and tribulations at the office was becoming more and more of a mental challenge for her. With each passing week, she became increasingly repulsed not only by his narrow-minded view of the world, which completely revolved around him, but also by his sexual advances.

When her flimsy excuses to avoid sex started to wear thin one Sunday night, she indulged in half a bottle of Merlot and begrudgingly acquiesced, consoling herself with the fact that it would be over in less than a minute. When his share of the wine kicked in, inhibiting his ability to achieve an erection, she wholeheartedly told him not to fret about it and went to sleep, thankful to have escaped any forced intimacy with him.

The next morning, as she nursed a mild hangover, the phone rang.

"Hello?"

"Lou! How's my favorite sister?" Shelly yelled into the phone, or so it seemed to Lucy's throbbing head.

"Mmm, I'm fine. How are you?" she replied in a hushed tone.

"You don't sound fine. In fact, you sound like crap. Are you sick?"

"No. I had a little too much wine last night. Bit of a headache."

"The hell say you? My little sister boozing it up? Did you and Tom have a wild night last night?" Shelly teased.

"Hardly."

"Ah, was this an anger-driven drinking binge?"

"No, Shelly. I just had too much to drink on an empty stomach, okay?" Lucy snapped impatiently.

"Jeez, all right. No need to get snippy."

Lucy sighed tiredly.

"I'm sorry, Shell. How are you doing? How is work?" she inquired, hoping to steer the topic away from last night.

"It's fantastic! My story received rave reviews. The pigs down in Kent got wind of it and dropped all charges against me and Martin. They didn't want any more bad press coverage."

"That's good news. I'm glad to hear it."

"So, did you ever call Donald and help him with that logo?" Shelly inquired, fully ready to launch into another sermon on Lucy's need to get the hell out of that house at least once in a blue moon.

"Yes," she replied, her tone brightening, "We've been working together on it, and it looks great. The other club members loved it, too. And you'll be pleased to hear that I have done quite a bit more artwork besides that."

Shelly was stunned. "Oh, Lou that's wonderful! What else have you drawn?"

"A few sketches of the Kent campus, a profile or two of Donald, although he is a reluctant model, some other pictures out in the garden. I must say that my best to date is one of Donald's profile with the river in the background. I think I really captured his personality, his demeanor..."

Shelly again caught the now not-so-subtle undercurrent in Lucy's voice.

"Hmm. Sounds like you and Donald have been spending a lot of time together, Lou."

"Oh, well, we meet now and again."

"Uh huh, and I'm assuming that Tom is unaware of these meetings."

"What are you implying, Shelly? You're the one who encouraged me to help Donald in the first place. We're just... friends. And when I say friends I don't mean YOUR definition of friends. I mean we enjoy each other's company. And further more ..."

"Whoa, whoa! Easy, Lou! I'm glad you are getting out more. No need to attack me."

"Well if you are insinuating that anything inappropriate is going on, I don't appreciate it."

"I'm not, Lucy. But this is ME you're speaking to, and I'm not so dimwitted that I don't hear the change in your tone and mood when you speak of him. Don't start acting all pious virtue with me when we both know you have a little crush on him, regardless of your visits' being innocent or not."

Lucy was startled into silence. She wanted to tell Shelly that the notion was absurd, but she knew she wasn't that good of a liar, even with all the practice she'd had with verbal fabrication lately.

"Hello? You still there?"

"Yes," she answered meekly.

"Ah, Lou, there is nothing wrong with your enjoying someone else's company, especially given what a winner your husband is and…"

"I have to go, Shelly. Someone's at the door," she lied hastily and hung up.

Donald's friends had also taken note of his new companion and openly balked at him for referring to a married white woman as his "friend."

"You're going to get strung up in a tree, boy. A white girl is bad enough, but a married one? You crazy," his roommate Leo chastised one afternoon as they were finishing up at track practice.

"We're just friends," Donald insisted indignantly. The defensiveness in his own voice made him uneasy. He put himself in check mentally as he wiped the sweat off his brow and took a long drink of water.

"I know the idea of having a relationship with a female that is purely platonic is beyond you," he countered in a somewhat forced jovial mood, "but it can happen."

"Yeah, you tell her husband and his buddies that when they're putting the noose around you're dumb-ass black neck."

"Oh, for God's sake, Leo," Donald quipped.

"All I'm saying is, if you want a 'platonic' relationship, you could have a safer one with a nice black single coed. I'm just worried about you, man, that's all. I mean, I know this woman is fine and all, but we got some fine-ass sisters here at Kent, too," Leo countered before cracking Donald on the ass with a towel and heading off to the showers.

Yes, indeed, some fine-ass black women who had given him death glares as they strolled past Lucy and Donald on their last picnic. He had heard the whispers along with the much louder blatant comments, "Black man gets educated then all of a sudden a black woman isn't good enough anymore?"

But if he was going to preach racial equality and integration, he rationalized, then he would have to take the heat over his friendship with Lucy. Besides, he wasn't doing anything wrong. It's not like they were having an affair!

As Lucy carried her grocery bags toward the store's exit, replaying in her mind the morning's conversation with her sister, her friend Loretta walked in slowly, looking pale and wide-eyed.

"Loretta? Are you okay? My goodness, you're white as a ghost!" Lucy exclaimed.

"On the radio! It's happening! It's really happening! I thought Dean was off his rocker when he said it would happen, but it's happening!" Loretta muttered to herself.

"What is? You're not making any sense. What's happening?" Loretta was always so poised. It unnerved Lucy to see her friend so discombobulated.

"The Russians! They're invading America, Lucy, and they've just shot the president down in Dallas!"

"No... no. It must be a mistake," Lucy said incredulously.

"It's true," an old man interjected as he made his way past them and into the store, "I heard it, too. Serves that commie bastard right... getting shot by his new buddies. I'm going to get me some ammo and be waiting for those Reds when they get to Cleveland, you better believe it. I won't be learning any damn Russian."

The cashier pulled his radio out from behind the counter and tuned into the local station. A half-dozen customers, frozen in place with random purchases in hand, huddled to listen with jaws dropped in despair. Mrs. Burge wept into her handkerchief. Mr. Smith shook his head in perpetual slow motion, back and forth. The young clerk from the hardware store said he heard it was a plot by the Texans to overthrow the government.

Loretta clung to Lucy's arm, which was starting to ache from clutching her bags. "The boys were right. Kennedy had to become chummy with the commies, and now look what..." but Lucy didn't hear the rest of Loretta's commentary. She tore her arm away from her friend and fled to her car.

In the parking lot, people sat in disbelief in their cars, yelling out to pedestrians, "Did you hear? Did you hear?"

Two cars blocked the driveway as the drivers were leaning out their windows to each other exclaiming, "I think he's dead!" Lucy had to blast her horn repeatedly to get them to move.

She sped south, and halfway to Kent it dawned on her. The first person she thought of when faced with insanity, the only voice of reason in her life that she respected, the one compass she would turn to when lost in the storm, was virtually a stranger, a feared taboo.

Shelly was wrong. She didn't have a crush on Donald. She was in love with him.

By the time Lucy reached Donald's apartment, the newscaster had confirmed that America was not being invaded by the Russians, or any other communists for that matter, but President Kennedy was dead. The President had been murdered.

She ran up the stairs, blinded by tears and frightened of her compulsive need to see him, and pounded on his door, not expecting anyone to be home, but not knowing where else to go. A moment later, Donald opened the door. He stood in the doorway, grim-faced and hunched over, like a long balloon that had been partially deflated.

Lucy heard the radio blaring from within, a grief-stricken voice proclaiming over and over again that the president had been shot... he was dead.

She started to cry and Donald took her in his arms. "It's madness," she sobbed.

"I know it is. The world's gone crazy."

He took her inside, and they sat on his couch. As time passed, neither one took notice of the news announcer. Lucy, held tightly in his embrace with her head on his chest, instead listened to his steady heart beat, and Donald heard nothing but her softening sobs as they gradually evolved into peaceful sighs.

"I called you. Leo went to a study group after practice, and I came home. I made a sandwich and flipped on the radio and... and the world turned upside down. And the first thing I did was call you." He stroked her hair softly and laid his cheek on her head. "It wasn't until I hung up that I thought, what if your husband had picked up the phone?"

He stopped stroking her hair and lifted her chin up towards his face. "What are we doing, Lucy?"

She couldn't bare the pained look in his eyes, couldn't stand the thought that for one minute she could be the cause of any suffering or confusion in his life. He was so wonderful, honest and pure. She wanted nothing more than to make him happy and to bring the goodness into his life that he, more than anyone else she knew, deserved.

"I'm so sorry, Donald. I... I should go," she said in a feeble attempt to extract herself from his athletic arms. He held her steadily.

"Lucy, I think... no, I know. I love you. I'm probably going to hell for it, but I love you nonetheless."

He caressed her face. She closed her eyes as she stood on the precipice. A life of longing and discontent, quietly rotting from within while living the socially acceptable status quo, lay like a barren wasteland behind her. In front of her, a cliff made of dark volcanic rock and razor sharp edges, making for a treacherous descent into a lush valley of indescribable vibrancy and beauty below.

She opened her eyes and took one last deep breath before she leapt, arms open wide, into the chasm. "If you're going to hell, then I'll be holding your hand on the descent. I love you, too."

Without further discussion, they made love on his tattered couch. The phone rang, the radio continued to blare, and an irate motorist outside honked his horn as Donald and Lucy devoured and discovered each other, oblivious to everything but the melding of their bodies.

Hours later, drenched from head to toe by their intermingled sweat, in awe of her first mind-numbing orgasm, Lucy dozed peacefully, unknowingly glowing from within with the tiny gift that Donald had given her.

If she broke every speed limit from Kent to Chagrin, she would arrive an hour after Tom got home from work.

I was down at the metro park alone. Yes. I was so grief-stricken over the President's assassination that I went to the park and walked the paths in solitude. It was plausible. She had seen many people on the streets of Kent wandering aimlessly: small groups of students consoling fellow strangers, solo individuals lost in deep thought as they stared into the distance.

Having to spend the mental energy on formulating an excuse for Tom irritated her, removed her further from the safe cocoon of Donald's couch. She closed her eyes and inhaled. Even after a hasty shower, she could still smell him. His musky scent permeated her hair, her clothing, and she was drunk with it.

She hated having to leave, to be thrust back to reality without him. When they had parted, it was without a word, neither of them wanting to break the spell. To do so would be to acknowledge the deal with the devil they had just willingly signed together.

When she arrived home, Tom's car was not there. She tentatively entered the house and called out his name. No answer. She then checked all the rooms, one by one and had to resist the urge to open closet doors and peer around corners. *This is ridiculous. I'm being ridiculous.*

After finally convincing herself that he was indeed not home waiting to pounce on her, she didn't know whether to be relieved or worried. A few moments later the phone rang making her yelp like a frightened puppy. *Jesus, woman, get a hold of your self!*

"Hello?"

"Lucy, it's Suzy. How are you, dear? Loretta said she saw you at the market when you both heard the news. Where'd you run off to?"

"Oh, I'm fine. Tried to do some errands then just went walking down in the metro parks to clear my head. How are you doing?"

"I know… it's so upsetting. We're holding up, though. Tom wanted me to let you know he's here. He and Dean came straight over after work. The men are in the study right now listening to the news over drinks. Why don't you come over? Loretta and I are baking sugar cookies."

"Thank you, Suzy, but I think I'm going to pass. I have a terrible headache, and I think I'm going to lie down for a bit."

"I'll let Tom know. Please come over if you feel better."

After hanging up and breathing a shaky sigh of relief, she realized that while Donald's first response was to phone her, Tom's first response was to run and have drinks with his friends with not so much as a courtesy call to his wife. If she had not just committed adultery, she would have been wounded. As it was, she counted herself lucky for the brief reprieve.

Thankful for the extra time alone, she finished her neglected chores and went to bed early, burying herself under the covers in a vain attempt to close her eyes and recapture in her mind the deliciousness of the afternoon. When Tom staggered home and climbed into bed hours later, reeking of scotch and cigars, she was sleeping deeply.

The next morning as Tom was in the shower, she forced herself out of bed to make breakfast. Even with a solid night's sleep, she felt sluggish and drained. As she stood in front of the stove, mindlessly frying an egg, she looked out the open window and let her mind's eye float through it.

She envisioned soaring above the house, escaping like a kept bird that had discovered a broken latch to its cage, waiting for the moment when its owner's back was turned. She circled once, twice, taking in the manicured lawns with their strategically placed bales of hay, fat orange pumpkins and craft-work scarecrows that elicited a contrived country feel, and then changed her flight path to the highway, following its paved lanes. She flew above the allotment, spotting Donald's childhood home amongst the makeshift buildings. The acrid aroma of pine filled her senses as she skimmed the treetops, intermixed with log fires and a hint of Donald's sweat.

"Lucy, what the hell is that smell?" Tom hollered from a distance.

Oh my God, he can smell him! He can smell him on my wings! The thought filled her with terror as she plummeted down into the allotment below.

Rough hands pushed her aside as she snapped back to her kitchen. Tom, still wet and wearing a towel wrapped around his waist, grabbed the smoking skillet and tossed it under the running faucet in the sink. Water hissed and Tom cursed as the smoke turned to steam, scalding his hand.

"Damn it, Lucy, what the hell is wrong with you? Are you trying to burn the house down?!" he shouted.

She stared at him blankly, too stunned to speak.

"Answer me! What the fuck is wrong with you?!" he demanded.

"I... I don't know. I'm sorry," she stammered, and began to sob.

"I mean, Jesus, the egg was smoking right in front of you, and you just stood there staring out the window," he said in exasperation, torn between wanting to berate her further for her stupidity and being flat-out scared by her bizarre behavior. He had heard of wives losing their marbles and feared the scandal of Lucy needing a "vacation" at a locked retreat that specialized in Valium and one-on-ones with a shrink.

She dried her tears and searched her mind for an explanation he would swallow. "I was cooking... and I started thinking about... poor President Kennedy. I guess I'm still in shock."

He had to physically restrain himself from rolling his eyes. Damned hysterical women!

"Well, I know it's upsetting Lou, but it's not like you knew him personally. I mean, it's not like this will have any effect on you."

She watched him as he shut off the water and grabbed the toast she managed to not send up in flames. He poured himself a cup of coffee and smirked, shaking his head slowly.

"Were you upset when you heard, Tom?"

"Of course I was! I mean the implications... how it will affect our country, the political landscape of the future..."

"So it will affect this entire country's future, but it won't affect me?"

"Oh, damn it, Lucy, you know what I mean. Look, I have to get ready for work. I don't have time for this nonsense."

He tossed the remainder of his toast in the sink and headed toward the hall, but Lucy blocked his exit, refusing to budge. The glare from her that was boring a hole into his head unnerved him.

"What?"

"I'm a nonhuman being to you. I don't even count as a citizen of this country to you, Tom," she stated matter-of-factly.

"I told you, I don't have time for this nonsense," he said dismissively and pushed past her.

The guilt she had felt moments earlier over fantasizing about fleeing back to her lover drained from her. She went to the living room and surveyed the knickknacks and pictures they had accumulated over the years. She remembered spending half an afternoon agonizing over whether or not the vase they had bought while vacationing in Charleston two years ago would look better on the coffee table or the bookshelf, and had to laugh out loud.

She sank into the couch and examined their silver-framed wedding photo, marveling at their smiling faces and loving embrace. Was that really only a few short years ago?

Lucy and Donald carried out their affair over the next few weeks like starved animals, snapping testily at those around them, much to the dismay and irritation of their friends and families, then devouring each other's bodies and souls when they could, never fully satisfying their rabid hunger.

"You own me. You do know that, don't you?" she said, basking in the afterglow of one of their late morning lovemaking marathons.

"I what?"

"You own this body, completely," she purred.

His body, warm and yielding, turned tense. He pushed her off gently and sat up, looking sternly in her eyes.

"People aren't to be owned, Lucy, like pieces of property."

"Why are you getting upset?" she asked, bewildered by his sudden turn of mood and taken aback by his obvious misunderstanding of what she meant.

"My ancestors were 'owned.' I never want to own anyone, or be owned."

"Donald, I didn't mean it like that." The pleading look in her eyes softened him once more, and he took her back in his arms.

"I'm sorry. I know you didn't," he consoled, kissing her on the forehead. "It's just that words matter, Lucy. Carelessly used words help to perpetuate the stereotype and prejudice I've tried to stand against all my life."

They cuddled in silence, each feeling slightly awkward, not wanting to ruin one of the few precious moments they were able to steal together. While they typically flowed harmoniously on the same wavelength, there were times they talked two completely different languages. They both felt the pain of not having the luxury of time to explore these differences, but were unable to bring themselves to articulate the loss.

"Well, then, let me rephrase," Lucy said, climbing up to straddle his lap and putting a light finger on his lips before he could interject. "No one has ever made my body feel the way that you do. Nor has my body responded to another's touch the way it responds to yours."

"Well, thank you," he said half-heartedly as he gently removed her from his lap.

She watched him get out of bed and walk in his naked splendor to the kitchen to pour a glass of water, finding herself once again enamored with the contour and masculine definition of his muscles.

He came back to bed and she reached into her bag to pull out her pad and charcoal. Being in the presence of his glorious body never failed to inspire her, sexually and artistically, so she set to work on yet another sketch.

Donald watched her brow knit in concentration as she worked away. She would occasionally stop and peer at him with close scrutiny before returning to her paper. She scratched her nose and left a charcoal smudge at the slightly upturned tip.

He loved her passion for art and enjoyed observing her during her creative process. Seeing her sitting Indian style on the end of his bed, naked and intense with that small smudge of gray on her adorable nose melted his heart. It was beyond him how any man could take her for granted.

"Hey, what's on your mind?" Lucy asked. She had set her pad and pencil down and was gazing at him inquisitively. "You look miles away."

"I was wondering, have you… I mean, do you and Tom still…?" he began.

"NO! No, we don't!" she exclaimed. "I know I'm an adulteress, but I'm not a whore. I can only make love to one man at a time, Donald, the man I'm in love with. And that's you. *Only* you."

She crawled up the bed and laid her head on his chest.

"Doesn't he wonder?"

"I'm sure he does. He kept trying for a while, but quite frankly, I think he has finally given up."

She rested her chin on her hand and traced his face with her fingers. "To tell you the truth, it never was something I looked forward to with him. That three minutes once a week was simply my wifely duty after I gave up on ever getting pregnant."

"Three minutes?"

"Yep."

"How in the world any man could have daily access to you and only touch you once a week, for three minutes, is beyond my comprehension," he said with a sly smile.

She giggled as he pulled her on top of him again for the third time that morning.

Lucy hated getting her annual check up. She knew it was silly, but she never could get accustomed to seeing a stranger's head between her legs, poking and prodding, even if he was a doctor. So when her physician's receptionist phoned and told Lucy that Dr. Smith wanted to see her for a follow-up visit, she was less than thrilled.

"But I just saw him last week," she complained.

"I know, Lucy, and he would like to see you for a brief visit today."

"Is anything wrong?"

"No, don't be alarmed. We'll see you at one."

She tapped her foot nervously as she sat in the bright waiting room and tried in vain to focus on an old edition of Reader's Digest from the magazine rack. She finally gave up and closed her eyes, wishing she could be down in Kent with Donald instead.

Unfortunately, she had to wait two more days before she could see her lover again. Tom was becoming more vocal about his displeasure with stretched-out leftovers, questioning what she was doing with the grocery money after having reheated a meatloaf for the third time in the span of a week. She knew she had been pushing her luck driving down to see Donald as much as she had, and they made a promise to force themselves to limit their visits.

The receptionist finally called Lucy's name, and she met with Dr. Smith, a kindly older gentlemen whom she had been seeing for years. A joyous expression lit up his worn face.

"I have wonderful news, Lucy."

"Really? What's that?" she asked, bewildered.

"You're pregnant! You and Tom are expecting your first child," he exclaimed, patting her on the shoulder. "I know you have been trying for a long time now, and I'm so very happy for you both."

He chuckled at her awestruck expression.

"Are... are you sure?"

"Very. I thought you might be when I was conducting your exam, but I didn't want to get your hopes up until I got your test results back. I'm sorry to call you down here like this, but I really wanted to give you the good news in person. Congratulations," he said, walking her back to the receptionist's desk. "Make an appointment with Ethel for your first prenatal check up."

"Oh, I will. Thank you," she said, unable to fully digest what had just happened.

"Lucy? Did I hear prenatal visit?" squealed Marilyn Dodds, the wife of one of Tom's poker buddies.

Lucy turned around to find Marilyn, and her young boy Benjamin bleary-eyed and clinging to a nappy teddy bear, standing behind her.

"Oh my goodness, congratulations, dear! I've been praying for you both, and now God has blessed you and Tom with a baby," she said, clapping her hands together, clearly taken with her own misguided influence with the man upstairs.

"Thank you, Marilyn," Lucy stammered, "but… could you do me a favor and keep this to yourself? I want to wait until the time is right to surprise Tom with the news."

"You aren't going to tell him now?" she asked quizzically. "My goodness, I would be bursting at the seams!"

Just then, the receptionist told Marilyn she could take her son back into the examination room, saving Lucy from having to fabricate any further explanations.

"Please, Marilyn. Keep this to yourself for now. I want to tell people on my own," she pleaded.

"Of course, dear. Take care, and congratulations!"

Donald was finishing up a paper for his economics class when he heard frantic knocking at his front door. He found Lucy outside with a mixed expression of excitement and panic on her flushed face.

"Hey, you! I wasn't expecting to see you again until later this week," he said as she rushed into his arms. "Is something wrong, Lucy? I'm not complaining that I get to see you or anything, but you seem…"

"Pregnant. I seem pregnant," she said in a rush.

Donald extracted himself from her and looked her in the eyes.

"Come again?"

"I just found out from my doctor. I'm pregnant, Donald, four or five weeks along with your child," she said nervously as she walked over and sat on his couch, the same plaid couch where their child was conceived.

"I thought you couldn't get pregnant," he said slowly as he took a seat beside her, taking her hands in his.

"I thought so, too."

They sat together on his couch, dumbstruck and wondering what the other was thinking.

"Is there any chance that it's his, Tom's?" Donald asked apprehensively.

"I told you," she began in a wounded tone, "that once I made love to you, Tom and I didn't sleep together again."

"Oh, sweetheart, that's not what I mean! I don't know how they count the weeks, or, I mean, I don't know about this stuff. What if you conceived right before we… you know?"

"I haven't had sex with Tom in two and a half months. I had my last period right before I met you. There is no possible way it's his," she concluded stiffly.

"Then it's really mine. I'm going to be a father… wow," he said with unchecked awe.

"What am I going to do?" she asked softly.

"What are *you* going to do? Don't you mean what are *we* going to do?" He took her face in his hands. "Lucy, this is our baby. I love you," he said tenderly, kissing her cheeks. "I want you *and* our baby."

She smiled gratefully, shedding tears of joy.

"But what are we, I mean how are we going to…" she started to stammer before he put a quieting finger on her lips and shushed her gently.

"I only have one semester left. You're going to leave Tom and stay with me. I'll be graduated in June, and then we can move where ever we want to."

"Are you sure?"

"Never been more sure of anything in my entire life."

She collapsed back into his embrace as relief and joy flooded her. He loved her and wanted their baby, the baby she had always wanted. And now she would have a wonderful father to share her child's life with. *If Marilyn Dodds only knew how her prayers were misinterpreted during translation.*

"Let's wait until after the holidays, Donald, until things are a bit quieter for the both of us."

"I agree. I'll have a few weeks off from school in between semesters. That will give us time to do what we need to do to get you down here."

"What about your roommate?" she asked, fully knowing that Leo was none to fond of her seeing Donald.

"He'll deal with it or he'll find somewhere else to live. The lease is in my name." He tilted her face up to his. "I know you're scared, but we can do this. We love each other, and that's all that matters."

In between school finals and holiday preparations, they spent every spare minute they had discussing their baby and their future together as a family. While neither one of them thought it well-advised to stay in Chagrin Falls after Donald finished school, they both agreed to move to a neighboring suburb, so that Donald could remain close to his family and start the advocacy work and political activism he planned for the residents of the allotment.

When they touched ever so lightly on the topic of Lucy's leaving Tom, it was only in a logistical sense, careful to steer a wide berth around his possible reaction. So swept away in love and youth's blind optimism, they scarcely allowed themselves to acknowledge the possible perils that lay ahead and assumed that everyone around them who might scoff at first would come around eventually when faced with their deep feelings for each other.

One late afternoon, Donald took a nervous Lucy to a get-together at a friend's house for his Entrepreneur Club. After previously encountering Leo's disapproving looks one morning when he came home early from class and found them together, they were careful to curb their displays of affection in front of his other friends. And while they hated to curtail their expressions of love for each other, they deemed it prudent to limit any physical intimacy whatsoever to the seclusion of Donald's bedroom until they were ready to tell the world.

Everyone was immediately warm and welcoming to Lucy, instantly abating her anxiety, and they thanked her profusely for her work on their logo. She eagerly joined in their discussions, enjoying the mental stimulation and comradeship. After a potluck dinner and a round of drinks, they all huddled together in the front yard for a group photo and encouraged Lucy to come back again.

"Did you enjoy yourself?" he queried as he drove back to his apartment.

"You know I did. Your friends are wonderful."

"Well, I could tell they thought you were pretty wonderful, too." He kissed the top of her head as she nuzzled against his shoulder. "So what's on your agenda for the rest of this week?"

"Ugh," she groaned, "Christmas shopping for Tom's family. Absolutely the last thing I want to be doing. I'm just glad this year Christmas Eve dinner will be at his mom's house. At least I won't have to cook for twelve hours. What are you doing for Christmas?"

"Besides seeing my family Christmas morning, I was hoping to share some holiday cheer with you."

Lucy tapped her chin thoughtfully.

"I've got it! I'll tell Tom that Shelly is in town visiting a friend and I want to go see her. He'll agree to anything to avoid seeing her."

Lucy beamed up at Donald, pleased with her creativity, and was puzzled by his saddened face.

"Hey, what's wrong?"

"I hate these lies. I just want to tell the world, 'The woman I love is carrying my baby!' I just want to get our lives started," he said.

"Soon, sweetheart. I'm just as eager as you are." She snuggled in closer to him, patting her stomach lovingly.

The roads were treacherous, making Lucy's progress slow. She had heard on the radio of an earlier car accident due to the icy roads on the same route she was driving, but nothing, not even Mother Nature, would keep her from seeing Donald this Christmas Day.

Christmas Eve had been torture, listening to Tom drone pompously about his advancement at work while his mother fussed and fawned over him like he had just won the Nobel Peace Prize. Lucy wore a pleasant smile all evening and responded politely when spoken to. *I can be as nice as pie to you people, because after tonight, I never have to see you again.*

She was so cheered by this thought that when his mother commented that her deviled eggs were a bit dry and sparse on the paprika, Lucy responded with a sincere , "You're right Mary, but then again, no one's deviled eggs are as good as yours."

The next morning, Tom had presented her with her two presents: a new skillet to replace the one she had burned and a horrid perfume that smelled like his mother, a scent similar to molding roses. Lucy had managed half-hearted enthusiasm before giving him his presents -- a cheap work shirt she had bought on fire sale and an equally awful tie to match.

"Uh, thanks, Lou," he mumbled before retiring to the living room to watch television.

Making her way to the highway, she smiled remembering the classic look of disgust as he examined the tie when he thought she wasn't looking. And that perfume! What kind of sick bastard wants his wife to smell like his mother? She laughed out loud, but was then startled as she came to a curve in the road and started to skid slightly. Her adrenaline rushed, making her sick to her stomach.

She slowed the car and managed the curve, then noticed a tree on the right shoulder that had been smashed into splinters, most likely by an automobile. A cold shudder wracked her body and she clenched the wheel.

Her nerves finally eased and she breathed a sigh of relief as she pulled into the parking lot of Donald's apartment complex, which was more crowded than usual. *Probably a holiday party*.

But the mood of the dozen or so people congregated on the steps and second floor landing was far from festive. Women were crying, their faces distorted with grief, as they hugged and clung to each other while the men shook their bowed heads. Lucy stood at the bottom of the stairs, reluctant to intrude, searching for Donald's face in the crowd. She spotted his roommate Leo and tentatively waved. He nodded solemnly and an overwhelming dread engulfed her as he made his way through the small crowd.

"Leo, what's going on?" she asked apprehensively.

His eyes were bloodshot, and Lucy could smell alcohol on his breath. He shuffled his feet in the snow and would not make eye contact.

"Leo, where's Donald?" she pleaded more than asked.

"He was in a car accident earlier today," he began slowly. "He was driving back from visiting his family. They think he hit some black ice and lost control of the car."

The vision of that splintered tree hit her like a brick. *Oh, god. Oh no, no, no....*

"He's dead, Lucy."

Her legs went out from under her and she sat with a thud on the cold wet step. *No, no, no, no, no, no...*

"The police got his address off of his license and came here," he said gruffly, struggling to maintain his composure. "They found this in his car. He had a present for you."

She looked up at the tiny red foil box and the card Leo removed from his coat pocket and took it shakily from his extended hand.

"I'm sorry," he mumbled, patting her on the shoulder awkwardly. He disappeared back into the crowd, leaving her alone at the bottom of the stairs.

She stared at the box, dumbfounded, unable to move for minutes... hours? She didn't know. Time was as frozen as her face and trembling hands from the numbing cold.

People eventually started to make their way down the stairs, bumping past her, some giving her hard sideways glances before shuffling off in the snow. She forced herself to walk back to her car and turned the heat on.

She opened the box and in its velvet-lined interior found a delicate gold ring. The sides were beveled and it had a heart-shaped green gemstone. It slipped smoothly onto her slender pinky.

She stared at the bright green gem, a shade she had never seen on a ring before, then opened the card. It showed a picture of a cheerful family of snowmen beside a Christmas tree: a father smoking a pipe and a mother wearing a pink scarf holding a little snow baby sucking on a blue pacifier. Tears ran down her cheeks when she saw Donald's fluid handwriting.

Lucy,

Next Christmas, my love, this will be us, together with our gift from God. Although the year ahead will bring trying times and many challenges, we will prevail together. Our child will be living proof that love knows no boundaries, a beautiful symbol of unity.

This green gem will be our August baby's birthstone. I hope you like it.

Merry Christmas, my angel.
Donald

Tears dropped on his signature, making the ink bleed, along with her heart.

Lucy had no idea how she made it home that night, crawling along the highway at a snail's pace, headlights blurred through tears and angry motorists blaring their horns behind her. When she arrived home, she curled up in the fetal position in the front seat of the car, and rocked back and forth rhythmically as she sobbed.

After seeing the bedroom light go out and waiting another thirty minutes until Tom was most likely asleep, she crept into the house and went to the spare bedroom.

She put the card to her nose, inhaling deeply, desperately searching for any trace of his scent, but there was none. She then pulled out her sketches -- Donald's hands on a steering wheel, his sleeping naked body, his profile as he laughed. Her body ached with the thought of never kissing his lips, feeling his strong hands on her body, or hearing his deep voice or contagious laugh again. She caressed her stomach and wept.

How will you ever know what a wonderful man your father was? Oh, God, how am I going to raise you? She heard the faint rumbling of Tom's snores from the other room. *I can't raise you here... with him!*

She started to hyperventilate with anxiety over the thought. *No, not now, not tonight. Deep breaths. I will figure this out. I will go to bed and make a plan tomorrow.*

She put the sketches away and dragged herself into the bed, mindful to hide her ring in her coat pocket. After hours of weeping, merciful exhaustion conquered grief and she slept.

"Whoever you are, waking me up at six in the morning, you better be near death or I'm going to kill you," Shelly snarled.

"It's Lucy. I need to talk to you," Lucy said in a business like tone.

Shelly sat up in her bed. It wasn't like Lucy to skip the required phone pleasantries.

"Hey, sis. What's wrong?"

"Promise me you won't interrupt until I'm done. No commentary, nothing, until I'm done."

"Um, okay. You're making me kinda nervous here, Lou."

Lucy told her everything, from the day of Kennedy's assassination to the surreal drive back from Kent the night before. She spoke with an uncharacteristic even calm, with little inflection and even less emotion. When she had finished, Shelly was speechless.

"Oh, Lou," she managed softly. "I don't know what to say."

"Say you'll help me."

"You know I'll help you! Just tell me what you want me to do."

"I'm leaving Tom, and I need a place to stay, Shell."

"Of course you can stay here, Lucy, as long as you want."

"I'm a little over a month along. I shouldn't start to show for another month or two. That should give me enough time to save some money, and then I'm coming out to California."

The thought of traveling cross-country alone terrified her, but the thought of staying in Ohio and having to face Tom, of having her child born into an intolerant community, chilled her more deeply to the bone.

"Are you going to tell Tom?"

"Yes... when I'm safely on the other side of the country. I'll tell him everything he wants to know."

"So... you're going to sneak away? What if he finds out? What if he catches you?"

"What's he going to do? Lock me up in a closet so I can't go? Besides, he won't find out. As long as I keep ironing his shirts and cooking his food, he won't think anything is wrong," she said dryly.

"Oh, Lou, I'm so sorry, for you and for Donald. He was a good man."

A lone tear made its way down Lucy's cheek and she quickly swiped it away. No time for mourning, no time for self-indulgent tears anymore.

"I can't feel sorry for myself. I have to focus on taking care of my child. She's the only thing that matters now."

December passed into January as Lucy bided her time. A nasty flu that lingered for weeks had been going around, giving her the perfect alibi for her blunted mood and lethargy. When she suggested she keep a safe distance away from Tom and slept in the spare room under the pretense of not wanting him to get sick, he agreed whole heartedly. He hated to be sick and had found his wife's companionship to be sorely lacking in the past few months anyway.

Her attentions had been limited to cooking and cleaning, and with him participating in a little extracurricular activity after work with the petite brunette from the dry cleaners, that suited him just fine. No more whining about wanting children, no more distraction from his sports. A clean house, cooked meals waiting for him and solitary peaceful evenings of football on the television after a hard day at work and a more rigorous hour at the local motel with Debbie was all he could ask for. Life was good.

One evening while Lucy was soaking in the bath, he snuck out to pick up a bouquet for his mistress, under the guise of running to the store for more beer. He stashed the flowers in the trunk for the next evening's liaison and patted himself on the back for being so thoughtful. He had driven almost all the way home before slapping himself on the forehead for forgetting the beer. He made a quick U-turn and headed back to the market.

He was lost in pleasurable thought, imagining Debbie's gratitude for the flowers and how she would shower him with her appreciation, as he walked down the produce isle toward the back of the store when he nearly ran smack into Marilyn Dodds, the high-strung wife of his friend Harry. Marilyn had never been a fan of Tom, or any of Harry's poker buddies for that matter, and typically treated him with measured politeness.

"Oh, sorry, Marilyn," he said with a nod before trying to pass.

"Tom, how have you been?" Marilyn grasped his arm and greeted him with uncharacteristic enthusiasm.

"Just fine, Marilyn. And you?"

"I can't complain. So tell me, how is Lucy feeling?" she asked, excitedly.

"Uh, fine."

"Oh, I'm just so happy for the both of you," she gushed. Marilyn noted the confused look on Tom's face. "For the baby? I know poor Lucy has desperately wanted a child for so long now. And it can't be easy, being just about the only couple left in Chagrin without children."

"I'm sorry, but I have no idea what you are talking about," he said, unable to mask his mounting irritation.

"Oh. Oh my," she stammered nervously, fingering the delicate strand of pearls around her pale throat. "Well, I don't think I could be mistaken. I was there, taking little Benjamin in to have his ears looked at... I just thought she would have told you by now."

Tom's face flushed with heat. He clenched his fists in his pockets with the dawning realization that his wife was pregnant and, if this gossiping hen already knew, then he was most likely the last one in town to know. His wife was pregnant, and unless it was an immaculate conception...

"Oh my. I... I shouldn't have said anything. I've ruined the surprise. But it was weeks ago and I just assumed she would have," Marilyn stuttered in her own defense.

"You must be mistaken," he said briskly. "Give my regards to Harry. Now, if you will excuse me."

Tom stalked out of the store, leaving Marilyn to stand in the produce isle with her mouth agape, twisting her pearls till they left red marks on the delicate flesh of her neck.

He tore out of the parking lot, skidding on the icy road and nearly slammed into an embankment.

Lucy pulled her pruned self out of the tub and examined her naked body. She touched her flat stomach and tried to imagine what she would look like in six months, what it would be like to press her hand to her huge belly and feel the baby kick. She sighed, wrapped herself up in her soft robe and was walking down the hall toward the kitchen for a cup of tea just as Tom burst through the front door. He glared at her, nostrils flaring, and her pulse began to race. *Oh no.*

"Guess who I ran into at the store, Lucy," he hissed.

She stood silently, too afraid to speak.

"Can't think of a guess? I'll save you the effort then... Marilyn Dodds. And imagine my surprise when she *congratulates* me. Can you guess what she congratulated me on? No? Cat got your tongue? She tells me I'm going to be a father! Well, fancy that, I think to myself! My own wife failed to mention it!"

He advanced toward her threateningly, head down, fists clenched by his sides. He looked like an enraged bull about to charge and she was the dangling red cape.

"I'm sorry. I didn't want you to find out that way. I just hadn't found the right time," she stammered.

He towered over her menacingly.

"Yeah, I bet. When *is* the right time to find out your wife is a fucking whore? Yes, that's right. I KNOW it's not mine, because aside from the fact that I haven't even been allowed to fuck my own wife much lately, I was told long ago that I would most likely be sterile," he said with a malicious grin.

"You're sterile?" she said softly. "You knew you were sterile and... and you let me think it was me all along?"

The years of praying, of thinking she was defective, less than a woman, with him standing by all the while knowing the truth, letting her suffer to protect his own pride...

"How could you? How could you do that?" she said in disgust. She wanted to hurt him, to lash out at him and cause him pain... even a fraction of the pain she had felt reading every one of their friends' birth announcements or the loathing she felt month after month toward her own body when her period came.

Their entire marriage had been a lie, and any residual guilt she'd had about her affair vanished.

"Oh, that's rich coming from the slut who's been cheating on her husband! What were you going to do? Try to pass it off as mine?" he laughed sarcastically.

Lucy stuck her chin out and met his glare with one of her own.

"Well, that would be hard to do since the baby will be *black*," she spat at him, letting the last word linger, and then roll off her tongue. It hung in the air between them, and she reveled in watching it pierce his racist heart to the core. His face contorted with the effort to digest it. When true realization shone in his eyes, she smirked in triumph.

He then struck her defiant chin square on, sending her flying into the wall. "YOU. WILL. NOT. HUMILIATE. ME!" he bellowed, punctuating each word with a blow to her head.

The hall was spinning in a haze of fists and blood as he broke her nose with a vicious right hook. She stumbled into the living room and collapsed on the floor in the fetal position, trying to protect her stomach and shield her mutilated face. He charged in behind her, further enraged at her attempt to protect her bastard child. He kicked her over and over again, fracturing her rib and breaking his own toe.

The pain in his foot quickly overcame his desire to inflict further damage upon her and he stood above her panting. Sweat dripped from his flushed face and fell in salty droplets, mixing with the blood that was slowly staining the powder blue carpet. He spat on her quivering body before limping to the front door and throwing it open.

"Get your shit and get out, you nigger-loving whore! Go live down in the allotment where you belong!" Tom screamed.

Oh, God, this can't be happening. This can't be happening.

Lucy moaned. He spat on her again for good measure before lurching down the hall to their bedroom. She heard a distant crash as he yanked out her drawers onto the floor and grabbed fistfuls of clothing. Moments later he reappeared, arms full of her lingerie, then disappeared out the front door. Her vision grew hazy, then dark, as she was granted a brief reprieve and fainted into blissful oblivion.

The sound of shattering glass roused her and her eyelids tried to flutter open in vain. Her left eye was swollen shut, and the right was reduced to a puffy slit.

"Get up, you stupid whore! Get your shit and get out!" Tom screamed at her before disappearing down the hall.

She struggled to her feet, dazed and nauseous, and staggered out onto the porch. The freezing wind tore through her robe and ripped the veil of blurry surrealism from her minds eye, bringing the moment back into focus with blinding clarity. Tom had tossed half of her belongings out of the house. White panties dangled from the blinking Christmas lights that lined the snow-covered bushes like cotton icicles. Her clothes were in wet piles on the lawn along with shoes, photo albums and her art supplies.

Their front yard looked as if a mad man had decided to host a mid-winter yard sale.

She felt something crunch beneath her. Her porcelain jewelry box was shattered and its contents strewn helter-skelter. A green sparkle caught her eye, and she spotted the ring Donald gave her lodged in a clump of snow near the steps. She knelt down and slipped it on, letting the frozen gold numb her finger to the bone, and wept. Crouched on the step, wracked with grief, she shivered as the wind whipped her wet hair around her pummeled face.

She didn't hear Tom come up behind her. She didn't know he watched her put the ring on, a ring he knew he had not bought for her. She also did not know that as the neighbors started to peer out their windows and burn up the phone lines between houses with speculation, one anonymous soul passed on the gossip mongering and phoned the police instead.

Tom let out an inhuman snarl before kicking her from behind with such force that she went flying off the porch. She sailed through the air and landed on the frozen cement, face first. The last thing she heard before blacking out was the sound of her front tooth cracking cleanly in half.

Lucy took half of her tuna sandwich and offered it to Shelly.

"Oh, God, no. I'll puke if that gets anywhere near my mouth."

Lucy smirked and took a large bite, thankful that she never experienced the dreaded nausea that most women do. She dug her toes into the sand and tilted her head toward the sun. She wouldn't be surprised if the baby was born covered in sand after all the long summer days spent lounging on the beach with Shelly and her sketch pad.

"So, I've been thinking... since you're set on naming my niece Kennedy, wouldn't it be cute if I named my girl Jackie? People would think we were calling for the First Lady when we yell at the kids. Jackie! Kennedy! Time for lunch!"

"You think you're having a girl?"

"Absolutely. The universe wouldn't dare entrust me to raise a male. No, we are both going to have girls," Shelly declared as she patted her flat stomach. She was only two months along and not starting to show yet whereas Lucy was overdue, three days past due to be exact. She felt like a fat ticking time bomb waiting to explode, waiting to bring life into the world with a bang.

"And does Ronnie think it's a girl, too?" Lucy asked.

"How the hell would he know? He's not with child. I am. And besides, Ronnie doesn't care. He's just so thrilled to become a father. I'm only two months along, and he's already nesting enough for both of us."

Lucy laughed in agreement.

"That's true." She looked at Shelly thoughtfully. "He really does love you, Shell."

"I know he does. I don't know if he's happier about becoming a father or that he found a way to settle me down."

Shelly held up her hand and admired her gold wedding band. She had made an exotic-looking bride last month standing on the beach at sunset, barefoot and wearing a pastel wraparound dress from a local street vendor, as an artist friend, who was an ordained minister, conducted the brief yet poetic ceremony.

It was bittersweet joy as she danced with her new husband in the drum circle, kicking up sand next to the bonfire, while Lucy stared at them with a confused smile and faraway look in her eyes. She knew Lucy was happy for her, but the irony that Shelly was the one heading full steam ahead into family life while little Lucy sat alone and hugely pregnant on a beach blanket was not lost upon her.

"I must admit, I never thought anyone would ever be able to tame you," Lucy mused.

"Who said anything about tame? Settled with a more long-term address, yes. Tame, never," she replied dramatically with a flip of her hair. She leaned over Lucy's lap and placed her cheek on her stomach.

"Hello in there! Aren't you ready to come meet your Aunt Shelly? I'm even making a little girl cousin for you to play with!" She lifted her head and looked at Lucy. "A house with two little girls. Wow, we're really in for it, aren't we?"

"Yep. Two smart, independent strong girls," Lucy said.

"That's right. We will raise warrior queens!" Shelly exclaimed enthusiastically.

"Well, we already know that this one is a warrior, a survivor," Lucy said with pride while caressing her huge stomach.

Shelly put an arm around Lucy's shoulders and squeezed her tight. She studied her sister's once delicately beautiful face, now marred by a crooked nose and red angry scar that arced above her eye. She missed Lucy's sweet innocence and the soft vulnerability in her features. Her quick smile was now slower to grace one with its presence. And where her eyes used to sparkle and invite you openly through the windows to her soul, there was now steady reserve, an edge that hardened her gaze.

It had soothed Shelly's vengeful soul when they had received the news three months earlier that Tom had met his maker in an unexplained house fire. Lucy had been unnervingly stoic as she read the forwarded letter from the insurance company and then confirmed the report with a call to the Bainbridge fire department. After she had hung up the phone, she simply said, 'It's true. He's dead,' then had gone back to mixing her watercolors.

The subsequent insurance settlement had enabled both of them, along with Shelly's husband, Ronnie, to move from their cramped apartment in the valley to a comfortable bungalow in Venice Beach. Since that phone call, Shelly had secretly envisioned Tom's fiery death in painstaking detail every time she heard Lucy crying late at night.

"I'm going to head back and start on that stew for dinner tonight. I don't know if I'm ever going to get the hang of this cooking crap." Shelly stood up and extended a hand to Lucy. "You coming?"

"No, not yet. Maybe I'll jog a few laps up and down the beach to try and coax this kid out." Shelly eyed her skeptically. "Shell, I'll be fine. I won't be long behind you. I promise."

"If you're not back in thirty minutes, I'm sending in the troops," she warned before trotting up the sand to the boardwalk.

Lucy finished the rest of her sandwich and then picked up her sketchpad and charcoal pencil. She drew a quick sketch of a particularly large sea gull that was perched on the lifeguard tower, waiting for the haggard mother below to turn her back for five seconds on the picnic she had just unpacked on her blanket.

Lucy flipped to the next page and let her mind and her hand wander. Short curly hair, broad nose, a firm chin. Before she knew it, she had drawn yet another picture of Donald to add to her collection -- Donald lounging on a boulder next to the creek, Donald raising his fist in triumph, Donald sitting with his uncle at the park laughing raucously. She had only one real photograph of him, and she wanted to capture him in as many pictures as her mind would remember, before the images grew fuzzy with time.

It was the memories that she *wanted* to forget she was sure would remain etched in her mind forever -- like the look of fear and pity on the faces hovering above her when she had awoken in Donald's childhood home.

Uncle Harold had found her limp body underneath the welcome sign leading into Chagrin Falls Park, dumped there by an unscrupulous friend of Tom's on the police force who had been briefed by Lucy's neighbors about the scandalous nigger-loving whore she had turned out to be. Uncle Harold had brought her to the house, much to the objections of his wife and friends. When Mae opened the door and saw Lucy in his arms, she shooed everyone but family away and had Harold lay her on their dilapidated couch. When Lucy came to hours later, a heated debate about what to do with her was raging.

"Not another word!" Mae had shouted above the grumblings. "She'll stay 'til she's better. Then we'll send her to her kin."

Lucy convalesced on the couch for a week, Mae fussing over her and administering her own brand of grassroots medicine around the clock, before catching a bus to California. Uncle Harold had taken a collection from everyone in the park to purchase her ticket, conning, cajoling and calling in a few favors to raise the needed cash. One neighbor even donated a coat and change of clothing.

Uncle Harold drove Lucy and Mae in his truck down to the bus station, ignoring the pointing and curious stares from passing pedestrians. When he had left them to go purchase her ticket, Mae turned to Lucy.

"Now, I know you carrying my grandbaby. Yeah, dat's right, I knew. Donald told me bout it day 'fore he died."

Mae reached inside her heavy coat and pulled out a small yellow quilt. It was frayed around the edges and thread bare.

"This was Donald's baby blanket. You give it to my grandbaby."

"I will." Lucy's eyes filled with tears.

"You listen to me now. You make sure dat baby know who his daddy was. And you make sure he goes to school, to college like his daddy."

Lucy could only nod in response as Mae looked at her appraisingly.

"You got a hard row to hoe ahead of you. You know dat, dontcha girl?"

"Yes, I know."

Mae handed her a bag filled with sandwiches and dried fruit for the trip and hugged her gently. Uncle Harold, man of few words that he was, handed her the ticket and bade farewell with a sincere, "Luck to ya. Lord's speed on ya trip," before taking Mae's arm and leading her back to the truck.

When Lucy arrived on Shelly's doorstep three days later, exhausted and out of food, she didn't have the strength to tell her what had happened. She didn't need to; the state of her face told it all. Shelly fed her, put her to bed and let her sleep for twelve hours before taking her to a doctor.

After the doctor examined Lucy and checked the baby's heartbeat, he exclaimed, "Well, there's not much we can do for your nose, but you're very lucky, Mrs. Dawson, that this baby is still alive after the beating you took! What did you say happened again?"

After they returned home, Shelly started the interrogation. When Lucy finished over an hour later, Shelly was foaming at the mouth like a rabid dog.

"That son of a bitch! That fucking son of a bitch! He can't get away with it! We have to call the police. File a report… something!"

"The police know, Shelly. Remember? They're the ones who were kind enough to leave me for dead outside the allotment."

"I'm going to kill him. I'm going to drive out to Ohio with a baseball bat and…" she ranted before Lucy sternly cut her off.

"No, you are not. It's over. I am never going back there again and I never want to speak about it again."

"But…"

"I mean it, Shelly!" Lucy yelled. "Never again. That part of my life is over. It's dead to me now."

Shelly had never seen her sister so adamant, so forceful. She let the subject drop until the next day. When she tentatively tried to bring it up again over breakfast, Lucy shot her an ice-cold glare that froze her mouth shut for good on the topic.

The seagull found his opportunity and swooped down on the unattended picnic. The haggard mother threw a beach ball at him and sent the seaside vulture flying up the beach with two sandwiches secured in his greedy mouth. Lucy chuckled to herself before gathering up her things in her knapsack and waddling down to the water's edge.

She let the water cool her feet as she scanned the beach. A small group of young men, black and white, sat together in the sand strumming their guitars softly, the deeply tanned lifeguard leaned over his tower and flirted with a minion of bikini-clad girls, a Hispanic man played catch with a young boy, and a dozen or so college coeds walked up the boardwalk with homemade banners calling for the end of the war and singing folk songs. The vision of community, of all walks of life sharing the beach in peaceful co-existence, moved her and made her feel safe.

This is the world I want for you. This is the beauty I want to share with you, little girl. Don't you want to come out and see it?

As if in direct response to the question, Lucy was brought to her knees with her first contraction. The Hispanic man dropped his ball, and the guitarists stopped strumming. All rushed to her side and guiding hands were upon her, black, white and brown alike to assist her. One of the bikini-clad girls ran to a pay phone to call Shelly, while the lifeguard pulled his convertible up to drive Lucy to the hospital.

As the first contraction subsided, a serene smile swept across her face. This baby, a product of love and unity that broke all boundaries, would be nurtured and welcomed into the world.

Epilogue

Mazzy parked her Neon and surveyed the campground. January's weather proved equally as gloomy as December's and the place was again deserted with the exception of one lone Hummer dominating the parking lot. Of course, not many people had her flexible work schedule, allowing her to visit mid-week while the rest of Los Angeles were in their nine-to-five grinds.

She didn't know why she felt compelled to come back and finish the hike.

After being treated in the emergency room to another uterine scraping to remove the excess placenta that was causing her to hemorrhage, Mazzy had convalesced at Abby's for two days before Abby would even consider letting her go back home. Even then she had to promise to call twice a day to check in. If she dared miss a call Abby was on her door step pounding loud enough to evoke cries of anger from Mazzy's otherwise easy going neighbors.

After one day of twiddling her thumbs she headed back to work, not wanting too much free time to pace her apartment and dodge Alan's calls. She was forever indebted to him for saving her life, but still did not know what to say to him or what their future might hold, if anything.

A week later Gramma Lucy's letter had arrived, shaking her world to its foundation all over again. The urge to return to Cold Water Lake had called to her ever since.

The letter, with its honesty and revelations, was bitter sweet joy. Mazzy vacillated between basking in the fact that her mother had wanted her and mourning her loss all over again. No, not all over again. *For the first time.* In the past, she had grieved for the lack of a mother; this time she was actually grieving for *her* mother, Kennedy Dawson, a real person who had loved her.

Mazzy had called Gramma the next day to meet for lunch. Lucy allowed Mazzy to question her for hours on end. *Where did my mother go to college? What is Kelly Judd really like? How long did my mom use heroin?* Though it was painfully difficult for her, Gramma Lucy had answered each and every question. She even agreed on a trip to Chagrin Falls during the summer to show Mazzy where her grandfather had lived, perhaps even to meet his family.

After utilizing the graffitied port-a-potty at the camp ground, Mazzy double-checked her light backpack and headed off past the ashy fire pits to Cold Water Lake trail. The trail head near the campsite was one of three that lead to the lake. It snaked upward hitting the lake from the south. Another entered from the west from a small mountain community and the third came downhill from the north. Mazzy wasn't sure where that trail led and considered continuing on past the lake to find out, depending on her stamina.

She took her time hiking, relishing the clean air but dismayed by the random trash thrown along the trail -- an empty six-pack of Bud, candy bar wrappers, cigarette butts and garbage bags. People could be so careless and ungrateful. What was once beautiful and natural was starting to look like downtown Los Angels, minus the traffic. According to Gramma Lucy, Chagrin Falls was lush and green, and the townsfolk would never dream of littering their community. *What makes one town cherish their surroundings while another treat theirs like a trash can?*

Mazzy neared the lake and was greeted by the piercing shrieks of children. *Great. So much for a peaceful hike.*

As she rounded the last littered bend in the trail she saw two redheaded boys, no older than eleven or twelve, standing on the weather worn dock at the edge of the lake. The slightly smaller boy, sporting the same pointy nose as his older brother, was laughing and pointing as big brother was throwing something into the bitterly cold water.

When Mazzy got closer to the scene she realized that that something was a dog. And not just any dog. *That's Scrappy Doo!* As she ran towards them, she could see the poor mutt struggling to the shore line.

"Get away from him you little assholes!" Mazzy screamed.

The boys turned, momentarily startled out of their game of canine torment.

"What if we don't?" the older one countered after he regained his composure. "What are you gonna do about it?"

Mazzy marched right up to the boy's face, expecting him to shrink away and run, but he defiantly stood his ground, unfazed. She towered his spindly preteen frame by a good six inches and tried to utilize her height to full advantage to glower down into his beady eyes, but he still would not budge. His obvious disregard for authority, as meager an authority figure that she posed, unnerved her.

"Yeah, that's what I thought. Nothing," he spat.

"Yeah, that's right! Nothing!" squeaked Little Red with his small fists on his hips.

Big Red smiled, pleased with his own moxie. As he turned to walk away, Mazzy grabbed him by the back of his sweatshirt and shoved him into the lake. She watched him flail and sputter as the air was ripped from his chest by the bone chilling water. *Shit. I hope the brat can swim.*

He finally caught his breath and made his way up to the dock's ladder.

"You want to go for a dip too?" she asked Little Red as the laughter died on his lips.

"I'm gonna tell!" he whined as he turned tail and sprinted up the northern path.

Big Red dragged him self out of the lake crying and looking very much like a drowned rat.

"How'd that feel? Not so nice, was it?" Mazzy asked.

"You… you're gonna get it, you bitch! My… my dad's a cop!" he blubbered in between sobs.

"Go ahead you little shit, and I'll tell him and your momma how you were abusing this dog. I'll have him file an arrest for you, too, for animal abuse. We can share a cell together," Mazzy said as she advanced on him.

But this time, instead of holding his ground, he ran off after his brother, screaming like a little girl.

Mazzy searched the area for Scrappy Doo and spotted him ten yards away whimpering behind a bush. He was shaking uncontrollably, soaked to the bone. The sight of him, scared and unloved, pulled on unfamiliar heart strings, striking a protective chord within her.

"Come here buddy, I won't hurt you," she coaxed as she jumped off the dock and slowly walked towards him. The closer she advanced, the farther he retreated. She stopped mid-way between him and the dock.

"I can understand if you're gun shy."

She took out her granola bar, unwrapped it and left it on the ground before returning to the dock. She sat down and nonchalantly took out her sandwich. Not wanting to be thrown in the lake again, the dog struggled between hunger and self preservation as he remained shivering behind the bush.

Gramma Lucy had told Mazzy that where she grew up, people would get together at an ice cream shop that over looked a waterfall before strolling the lazy river that ran through the middle of town to toss bread to the ducks. They even had road signs posted for duck crossings! *The people here would probably lay on the gas peddle for sport if they saw a live animal trying to cross a road.*

Was she truly this jaded towards her home town, she wondered, or were the last few weeks taking its toll on her? Either way, she needed to escape from L. A. for a while and couldn't wait for the upcoming summer.

She finished her tuna sandwich and noted the sacrificial granola bar untouched.

"I'm leaving now, so you can come get your food. I better make myself scarce before Daddy Cop shows up," she called out as she gathered her backpack and started down the path to the campsite.

The hike back to her car was not enjoyable. She was even more perturbed by the trash along the trail as she lamented on the scene she had just observed. *If the children are our future, then we are fucked.*

She envisioned being old and bed ridden in a nursing home, wallowing in her own excrement as Big Red laughed in her doorway heading out for his next hour long smoke break. Mazzy was so wrapped up in her own dejected thoughts, she didn't hear the sound of something following her in the underbrush.

Tired and parched, she arrived at the parking lot and rummaged through her trunk for a spare water bottle. She closed the trunk, unsuccessful in her search, and heard a whimpering yelp. *It couldn't be.*

There he was, Scrappy Doo, cowering a few yards away next to the port-a-potty. She knelt down on one knee and studied him as he decided for himself if she were friend or foe. He was rakishly thin and no discernable breed that she could recognize. His fur was multi colored; brown with patches of dingy white, black and red, blended together in a gnarled mess.

Mazzy tried to envision him as a puppy -- squishy and soft instead of sinewy and lean, bouncy and playful instead of fearful and skittish, eyes full of trust and happiness instead of loneliness and apprehension. *He should have been loved.* The thought saddened her so deeply she closed her eyes and softly cried.

The dog tentatively edged his way towards her, inch by apprehensive inch, unbeknownst to her, until he rested his head on her foot. She looked down and, with careful tenderness, stroked his dirty head.

"And yet, once again, you come to console me," she sniffled. "After everything you have probably been through, you still hold out hope for love. You're my freaking hero, Scrappy Doo."

He licked her hand and she grinned, repressing the desire to grab him up in her arms for fear of giving him a doggy heart attack.

She eased into a standing position, and he scurried backwards a few feet. After a moment's deliberation she walked to her car, unlocked the passenger door and swung it wide open.

"You coming?" she asked as he watched her every move.

She tossed her backpack onto the floor and climbed into the driver's seat. The dog advanced a few paces and stopped.

"Come on," she coaxed. "You don't really want to stay here, do you?"

197

She waited, not sure if he would take the invitation, not sure what she would do if he didn't. After a few more minutes of uncertainty, Scrappy Doo did a belly crawl to the car door, allowing himself one brief tail wag before jumping into the passenger seat.

With that settled, Mazzy closed the door and drove home, contemplating how her new companion would handle a cross country trip to Ohio.

Please email any questions or comments to the author at TeresaCSmith@aol.com.

Printed in the United States
129168LV00002B/289-345/P